PENGUIN BOOKS

A SHORT HISTORY OF TRACTORS
IN UKRAINIAN

'An entertain ... of
unlikely charac ... ith
conventional E ... he
prose is lyr ... *New Statesman*

'Most entertaining' *Evening Standard*

'Engaging . . . hilariously and affectingly records the fall-out
when an elderly Ukrainian widower long resident in Britain
falls for a flamboyantly busty Russian gold-digger in search
of a passport to prosperity' Peter Kemp, *Sunday Times*

'Very welcome – fully deserved the attention it got'
Susan Hill, *Spectator*

'A book that put and kept a smile on my face all year. The
culture clash between eastern and western Europe so ripe
for comic treatment is captured in this delicious story of
sibling rivalry' *Glasgow Herald*

A Short History of Tractors in Ukrainian

MARINA LEWYCKA

PENGUIN BOOKS

PENGUIN BOOKS

Published by the Penguin Group
Penguin Books Ltd, 80 Strand, London WC2R ORL, England
Penguin Group (USA) Inc., 375 Hudson Street, New York, New York 10014, USA
Penguin Group (Canada), 90 Eglinton Avenue East, Suite 700, Toronto, Ontario, Canada M4P 2Y3
(a division of Pearson Penguin Canada Inc.)
Penguin Ireland, 25 St Stephen's Green, Dublin 2, Ireland
(a division of Penguin Books Ltd)
Penguin Group (Australia), 250 Camberwell Road, Camberwell, Victoria 3124, Australia
(a division of Pearson Australia Group Pty Ltd)
Penguin Books India Pvt Ltd, 11 Community Centre, Panchsheel Park, New Delhi – 110 017, India
Penguin Group (NZ), cnr Airborne and Rosedale Roads, Albany, Auckland 1310, New Zealand
(a division of Pearson New Zealand Ltd)
Penguin Books (South Africa) (Pty) Ltd, 24 Sturdee Avenue, Rosebank, Johannesburg 2196, South Africa

Penguin Books Ltd, Registered Offices: 80 Strand, London WC2R ORL, England

www.penguin.com

First published by Viking 2005
Published in Penguin Books 2006

11

Copyright © Marina Lewycka, 2005
All rights reserved

The moral right of the author has been asserted

This is a work of fiction. Names, characters and incidents
are the product of the author's imagination, and any resemblance
to actual persons, living or dead, is entirely coincidental

Set in Monotype Dante
Printed in England by Clays Ltd, St Ives plc

ISBN-13: 978-0-141-02576-6
ISBN-10: 0-141-02576-X

For Dave and Sonia

Acknowledgements

Many people have contributed to the making of this book. I would like to thank, first of all, my family and friends, for their patience, encouragement and good suggestions. Thanks, especially, to Sarah White, Tessa Perkins and Lesley Glaister, to Chris and Alison Tyldesley for help with history and grammar, and without whom my cat would have died of neglect, and to Eveline and Patrick Lessware, in whose lovely house in Totnes the last four chapters were written. I am very grateful to Bill Hamilton for his kindness and sound advice, and to Livi Michael, Jane Rogers, Juliet Annan and Scott Moyers for their many helpful comments on the text. Thanks, also, to all at Viking, Penguin and A. M. Heath for being such a delight to work with. Finally, thanks are due to many writers, often anonymous, whose postings on the internet on the subject of tractor history and aeronautics provided me with inspiration. A list of those to whom I am particularly indebted is included at the back.

I

Two phone calls and a funeral

Two years after my mother died, my father fell in love with a glamorous blonde Ukrainian divorcée. He was eighty-four and she was thirty-six. She exploded into our lives like a fluffy pink grenade, churning up the murky water, bringing to the surface a sludge of sloughed-off memories, giving the family ghosts a kick up the backside.

It all started with a phone call.

My father's voice, quavery with excitement, crackles down the line. 'Good news, Nadezhda. I'm getting married!'

I remember the rush of blood to my head. Please let it be a joke! Oh, he's gone bonkers! Oh, you foolish old man! But I don't say any of those things. 'Oh, that's nice, Pappa,' I say.

'Yes, yes. She is coming with her son from Ukraina. Ternopil in Ukraina.'

Ukraina: he sighs, breathing in the remembered scent of mown hay and cherry blossom. But I catch the distinct synthetic whiff of New Russia.

Her name is Valentina, he tells me. But she is more like Venus. 'Botticelli's Venus rising from waves. Golden hair. Charming eyes. Superior breasts. When you see her you will understand.'

I

The grown-up me is indulgent. How sweet – this last late flowering of love. The daughter me is outraged. The traitor! The randy old beast! And our mother barely two years dead. I am angry and curious. I can't wait to see her – this woman who is usurping my mother.

'She sounds *gorgeous*. When can I meet her?'

'After marriage you can meet.'

'I think it might be better if we could meet her first, don't you?'

'Why you want to meet? You not marrying her.' (He knows something's not quite right, but he thinks he can get away with it.)

'But Pappa, have you really thought this through? It seems very sudden. I mean, she must be a lot younger than you.'

I modulate my voice carefully, to conceal any signs of disapproval, like a worldly-wise adult dealing with a love-struck adolescent.

'Thirty-six. She's thirty-six and I'm eighty-four. So what?' (He pronounces it 'vat'.)

There is a snap in his voice. He has anticipated this question.

'Well, it's quite an age difference . . .'

'Nadezhda, I never thought you would be so bourgeois.' (He puts the emphasis on the last syllable – wah!)

'No, no.' He has me on the defensive. 'It's just that . . . there could be problems.'

There will be no problems, says Pappa. He has anticipated all problems. He has known her for three months. She has an uncle in Selby, and has come to visit him on a tourist visa. She wants to make a new life for herself and her son in the West, a good life, with good job, good money, nice car – absolutely

2

no Lada no Skoda – good education for son – must be Oxford Cambridge, nothing less. She is an educated woman, by the way. Has a diploma in pharmacy. She will easily find well-paid work here, once she learns English. In the meantime, he is helping her with her English, and she is cleaning the house and looking after him. She sits on his lap and allows him to fondle her breasts. They are happy together.

Did I hear that right? She sits on my father's lap and he fondles her superior Botticellian breasts?

'Oh, well . . .' I keep my voice steady, but rage burns in my heart, '. . . life's just full of surprises. I hope it works out for you. But, look, Pappa' (time to be blunt) 'I can see why you want to marry her. But have you asked yourself why she wants to marry *you*?'

'*Tak tak*. Yes, yes, I know. Passport. Visa. Work permit. So vat?' Cross, croaky voice.

He has it all worked out. She will care for him as he grows older and frailer. He will put a roof over her head, share his tiny pension with her until she finds that well-paid job. Her son – who, by the way, is an extraordinarily gifted boy – genius – plays piano – will get an English education. They will discuss art, literature, philosophy together in the evenings. She is a cultured woman, not a chatterbox peasant woman. He has already elicited her views on Nietzsche and Schopenhauer, by the way, and she agrees with him in all respects. She, like him, admires Constructivist art and abhors neo-classicism. They have much in common. A sound foundation for marriage.

'But, Pappa, don't you think it might be better for her if she married someone nearer her own age –? The authorities will realise it's a marriage of convenience. They're not stupid.'

'Hmm.'
'She could still be sent back.'
'Hmm.'

He hasn't thought of this. It slows him down, but it doesn't stop him in his tracks. You see, he explains, he is her last hope, her only chance to escape persecution, destitution, prostitution. Life in Ukraine is too hard for such a delicate spirit as hers. He has been reading the newspapers, and the news is grim. There is no bread, no toilet paper, no sugar, no sewerage, no probity in public life, and electricity only sporadically. How can he condemn a lovely woman to this? How can he walk by on the other side of the road?

'You must understand, Nadezhda, only I can save her!'

It's true. He has tried. He has done his best. Before he hit on the plan of marrying her himself, he searched all around for suitable husbands. He has already approached the Stepanenkos, an elderly Ukrainian couple who have a single son still living at home. He has approached Mr Greenway, a widower living in the village whose unmarried son visits him from time to time. (A sensible type, by the way. An engineer. Not a common type. Would be very good match for Valentina.) They have both refused: they are too narrow-minded. He told them so, in no uncertain terms. Now neither the Stepanenkos nor Mr Greenway will speak to him any more.

The Ukrainian community in Peterborough has disowned her. They, too, are narrow-minded. They are not impressed with her views on Nietzsche and Schopenhauer. They are bound up in the past, Ukrainian nationalism, Banderivtsi. She is a modern, liberated woman. They put out vile rumours

4

about her. They say she sold her mother's goat and cow to buy grease to put on her face to attract Western men. They speak rubbish. Her mother had chickens and pigs – she never had a goat or a cow. This just goes to show how foolish these gossipy types can be.

He coughs and splutters on the other end of the telephone. He has fallen out with all his friends over this. If needs be he will disown his daughters. He will stand alone against the world – alone apart from the beautiful woman by his side. His words can barely keep up with the excitement of his Big Idea.

'But Pappa . . .'

'And one thing more, Nadia. Don't tell Vera.'

Not much chance of that. I haven't spoken to my sister for two years, since our row after Mother's funeral.

'But Pappa . . .'

'Nadezhda, you have to understand that in some respects the man is governed by different impulses to the woman.'

'Pappa, please, spare me the biological determinism.'

Oh, what the hell? Let him learn the hard way.

*   *   *

Perhaps it started before the phone call. Perhaps it started two years ago, in this same room where he is sitting now, where my mother lay dying while he paced about the house in an ecstasy of grief.

The windows were open, and the breeze that fluttered through half-drawn linen curtains carried the scent of lavender from the front garden. There was birdsong, voices of people passing on the street, the neighbour's daughter flirting with her boy-friend by the gate. Inside the pale, clean room, my mother gasped for breath hour after hour while her life slid away, and I fed her morphine from a spoon.

Here are the rubbery accoutrements of death – the nurse's latex gloves, the waterproof sheet on the bed, spongy-soled slippers, a pack of glycerine suppositories gleaming like golden bullets, the commode with its functional cover and rubber-tipped legs, now full of a lumpy greenish liquid.

'Do you remember . . . ?' I recite the stories of her and our childhood over and over again.

Her eyes flicker darkly. In a lucid moment, her hand in mine, she says, 'Look after poor Kolya.'

He was with her when she died in the night. I remember the roar of his pain. 'Me too! Me too! Take me too!' His voice thick, strangled; his limbs rigid, as though gripped by a convulsion.

In the morning, after they had taken her body away, he sat in the back room with a haunted look on his face. After a while he said,

'Did you know, Nadezhda, that apart from the mathe-matical proof of Pythagoras there is also a geometric proof? Look how beautiful it is.'

On a sheet of paper, he drew lines and angles, connected with small symbols, and murmured over them as he unfolded the equation.

He's completely off his trolley, I thought. Poor Kolya.

*   *   *

In the weeks before she died, Mother worried as she lay propped up on the pillows of a hospital bed. Linked with wires to a monitor that recorded the pitiful pulsing of her heart, she grumbled about the mixed ward with only the privacy of a cursorily drawn curtain, and the intrusive noises of the wheezing, coughing, snoring old men. She flinched under the impersonal, stubby fingers of the young male nurse who came to tape the wires above shrunken breasts, carelessly revealed under the hospital gown. She was nothing but a sick old woman. Who cared what she thought?

Quitting life is harder than you think, she said. There are so many things to be taken care of before you can depart in peace. Kolya – who would take care of him? Not her two daughters – clever girls, but so quarrelsome. What would happen to them? Would they find happiness? Would they be provided for by those charming but good-for-nothing men they had ended up with? And the three granddaughters – so pretty and no husbands yet. Still so much to sort out, and her strength was failing.

Mother wrote her will out in hospital, while my sister Vera and I both stood over her, because neither of us trusted the other. She wrote it out in her quavering longhand, and two of the nurses witnessed it. She was weak now, who for so many years had been strong. She was old and sick, but her legacy, her life savings, throbbed full of life in the Co-op bank.

One thing she was definite about – it shouldn't go to Pappa.

'Poor Nikolai, he's got no sense. He's too full of crazy schemes. Better you two will have half and half.'

She talked in her own DIY language – Ukrainian sprinkled

with words like handheldblendera, suspenderbeltu, green-fingerdski.

When it was clear that there was nothing more they could do in hospital, they discharged her to die at home in her own time. My sister spent most of the last month up there. I visited at weekends. It was some time during that last month, when I wasn't there, that my sister wrote out the codicil dividing the money equally among the three granddaughters, my Anna, and her Alice and Alexandra, instead of between my sister and myself. My mother signed it, and two neighbours witnessed it.

'Don't worry,' I said to Mother before she died, 'everything will be all right. We'll be sad, and we'll miss you, but we'll be all right.'

But we weren't all right.

*   *   *

They buried her in the churchyard in the village, in a new plot that bordered on to open country. Her grave was the last in a row of new neat graves.

The three granddaughters, Alice, Alexandra and Anna, tall and blonde, threw roses into the grave, then handfuls of earth. Nikolai, bent with arthritis, grey-skinned, vacant-eyed, clung to my husband's arm in tearless grief. The daughters, Vera and Nadezhda, Faith and Hope, my sister and I, prepared to do battle over our mother's will.

When the funeral guests come back to the house, to pick at cold refreshments and get tipsy on Ukrainian samohonka, my sister and I confront each other in the kitchen. She is wearing a black knitted silk two-piece from some discreet little second-hand dress agency in Kensington. There are small gold buckles on her shoes and she carries a Gucci handbag with a little gold clasp, and a fine gold chain hangs around her neck. I am wearing an assortment of black garments I found in Oxfam. Vera looks me up and down critically.

'Yes, the peasant look. I see.'

I am forty-seven years old and a university lecturer, but my sister's voice reduces me instantly to a bogey-nosed four-year-old.

'Nothing wrong with peasants. Mother was a peasant,' four-year-old retorts.

'Quite,' says Big Sister. She lights a cigarette. The smoke curls upwards in elegant spirals.

She bends forward to replace the lighter in her Gucci bag, and I see that on the gold chain round her neck hangs a little locket, tucked away inside the lapels of her suit. It looks old-fashioned and quaint against Vera's stylish outfit, as though it doesn't belong. I stare. Tears are in my eyes.

'You're wearing Mother's locket.'

It is Mother's only treasure from Ukraine, small enough to hide in the hem of a dress. It was a gift from her father to her mother on their wedding day. Inside the locket, their two photographs smile fadedly at each other.

Vera returns my gaze.

'She gave it to me.' (I cannot believe this. Mother knew I loved the locket, coveted it more than anything. Vera must have stolen it. There is no other explanation.) 'Now, what exactly do you want to say about the will?'

9

'I just want things to be fair,' I whine. 'What's wrong with that?'

'Nadezhda, it's enough that you get your clothes from Oxfam. Must you get your ideas there also?'

'You took the locket. You pressured her into signing the codicil. Split the money equally among the three granddaughters, instead of between the two daughters. That way, you and yours get twice as much. Greedy.'

'Really, Nadezhda. I'm shocked that you could think this way.' Big Sister's groomed eyebrows quiver.

'Not nearly as shocked as I was when I found out,' Bogey-nose bleats.

'You weren't there, were you, my little sister? You were off doing your wonderful thing. Saving the world. Pursuing your career. Leaving all the responsibility to me. As you always do.'

'You tormented her last days with stories of your divorce, of your husband's cruelty. You chain-smoked at her bedside while she lay dying.'

Big Sister flicks the ash from her cigarette and sighs theatrically.

'You see, the trouble with your generation, Nadezhda, is that you've just skated over the surface of life. Peace. Love. Workers' Control. It's all idealistic nonsense. You can afford the luxury of irresponsibility, because you've never seen the dark underside of life.'

Why does my sister's upper-class drawl infuriate me so much? Because I know it's fake. I know about the single bed we shared and the toilet across the yard and the squares of torn newspaper to wipe your bum. She can't fool me. But I have my ways of needling her, too.

'Oh, it's the dark underside that's bothering you? Why don't you go and get some counselling?' I suggest slyly in my best professional let's-be-sensible voice, my look-how-grown-up-I-am voice, the voice I use with Pappa.

'Please don't talk to me in that social-worker voice, Nadezhda.'

'Get some psychotherapy. Get to grips with that dark underside, flush it out into the open, before it eats you away.' (I know this will infuriate her.)

'Counselling. Therapy. Let's all talk about our problems. Let's all hug each other and feel better. Let's help the underprivileged. Let's give all our money to the starving babies.'

She bites fiercely into a canapé. An olive hurtles to the floor.

'Vera, you're going through bereavement and divorce. No wonder you're feeling under stress. You need some help.'

'It's all self-delusion. Underneath, people are hard and mean and out for themselves. You can't imagine how I despise social workers.'

'I can imagine. And Vera, I'm not a social worker.'

My father is in a rage, too. He blames the doctors, my sister, the Zadchuks, the man who cut the long grass behind the house, for causing her death. Sometimes he blames himself. He slopes around muttering, if this hadn't happened, if that hadn't happened, my Millochka would still be alive. Our little exile family, long held together by our mother's love and beetroot soup, has started to fall apart.

Alone in the empty house, my father lives out of tins and eats off folded newspapers, as if by punishing himself he will bring her back. He will not come and stay with us.

Sometimes I go and visit. I like to sit in the churchyard where my mother is buried. The tombstone reads:

Ludmilla Mayevska
Born in 1912 in the Ukraine
Beloved wife of Nikolai
Mother of Vera and Nadezhda
Grandmother of Alice, Alexandra and Anna

The stonemason had trouble getting all the words on. There is a flowering cherry tree and beneath it a wooden bench facing the neat square of grass half-turned to recent graves, and a hawthorn hedge dividing it from a wheat field which rolls on into other wheat fields, potato fields, oilseed rape fields, on and on to the horizon. My mother came from the steppes, and she felt at ease with these open horizons. The Ukrainian flag is two oblongs of colour, blue over yellow – yellow for the cornfields, blue for the sky. This vast, flat, featureless fenland landscape reminded her of home. Only the sky is seldom as blue.

I miss my mother, but I am beginning to come to terms with my grief. I have a husband and a daughter and a life elsewhere.

My father prowls around the house where they lived together. It is a small, ugly, modern house, pebble-dashed with a concrete slab garage at the side. Around the house on three sides is the garden, where my mother grew roses, lavender, lilacs, columbines, poppies, pansies, clematis (Jackmanii and Ville de Lyon), snapdragons, potentilla, wallflowers, catmint, forget-me-nots, peonies, aubretia, montbretia, campanula, rock roses, rosemary, irises, lilies and a purple trailing wisteria, pinched as a cutting from a botanical garden.

There are two apple trees, two pear trees, three plum trees, a cherry and a quince, whose yellow fragrant fruits have won prizes at the village show for the last twenty years. At the back, beyond the flower garden and the lawn, are three vegetable patches where my mother grew potatoes, onions, runner beans, broad beans, peas, sweet corn, marrows, carrots, garlic, asparagus, lettuce, spinach, cabbages and Brussels sprouts. In between the vegetables, dill and parsley grow wild, self-seeded. To one side, a soft-fruit patch of raspberries, strawberries, loganberries, red and black currants and a cherry tree is enclosed in netting on frames that my father has made to keep off the fat, greedy birds. But some of the strawberries and raspberries have escaped the net, and run off to propagate in the flower borders.

There is a greenhouse where a purple grape-vine luxuriates above fruitful beds of tomatoes and capsicums. Behind the greenhouse are a water butt, two potting sheds, a compost heap and a dung pile that is the envy of the village. It is rich, crumbly, well-rotted cow-manure, a gift from another Ukrainian gardener. 'Black chocolate,' my mother called it. 'Come on, my little darlings,' she would whisper to the marrows, 'have some black chocolate.' They gobbled it up, and grew and grew.

Each time my father goes out into the garden he sees my mother's shape, bent down among the marrows, reaching to tie the runner beans, a blur through the glass of the greenhouse. Sometimes her voice calls him from room to room of the empty house. And each time he remembers she is not there after all, the wound bursts open again.

*   *   *

The second phone call came a few days after the first.

'Tell me, Nadezhda, do you think it would be possible for a man of eighty-four to father a child?'

See how he always gets straight to the point? No small talk. No 'How are you? How are Mike and Anna?' No chit-chat about the weather. Nothing frivolous will hold him up when he is in the grip of a Big Idea.

'Well, I'm not sure . . .'

Why is he asking me? How would I know? I don't *want* to know. I don't want this kick of emotion that drags me back to the bogey-nose days, to the time when my Daddy was still my hero and I was still vulnerable to his disapproval.

'And if it is, Nadezhda,' he rattles on before I can marshal my defences, 'what do you think are the chances it would be mentally defective?'

'Well now, Pappa,' (pause for breath, keep the voice cheery and sensible) 'it is quite well established that the older a woman is, the greater her chance of having a baby with Down's Syndrome. It's a kind of learning disability – it used to be called mongolism.'

'Hmm.' (He doesn't like the sound of that.) 'Hmm. But maybe it's a chance we should take. You see, I am thinking that if she is mother to the British citizen, as well as wife of British citizen, they surely would not be able to deport her . . .'

'Pappa, I don't think you should rush into . . .'

'Because British justice is best in world. It is both a historical destiny and burden, which one might say . . .'

He always speaks to me in English, eccentrically accented and articled, but functional. Engineer's English. My mother spoke to me in Ukrainian, with its infinite gradations of tender diminutives. Mother tongue.

'Pappa, just stop and think for a minute. Is this really what you want?'

'Hmm. What I want?' (he pronounces it 'vat I vant'). 'Of course to father such a child would be not straightforward. Technically it may be possible . . .'

The thought of my father having sex with this woman makes my stomach turn.

'. . . Snag is, hydraulic lift no longer fully functioning. But maybe with Valentina . . .'

He is lingering over this procreation scenario too much for my taste. Looking at it from different angles. Trying it for size, as it were. '. . . what do you think?'

'Pappa, I don't know what to think.'

I just want him to shut up.

'Yes, with Valentina it may be possibility . . .'

His voice goes dreamy. He is thinking of how he will father this child – a boy, it will be. He will teach him how to prove Pythagoras from first principles and how to appreciate Constructivist art. He will discuss tractors with him. It is my father's great regret that both his children were daughters. Inferior intellectually, yet not flirtatious and feminine, as women should be, but strident, self-willed, disrespectful creatures. What a misfortune for a man. He has never tried to conceal his disappointment.

'I think, Pappa, that before you rush into anything, you should get some legal advice. It may not turn out the way you think. Would you like me to talk to a solicitor?'

'*Tak tak.*' (Yes yes.) 'Better you talk to a solicitor in Cambridge. They have all types of foreign there. They must know something about immigration.'

He has a taxonomic approach to people. He has no concept of racism.

'OK, Pappa. I'll try to find a solicitor who specialises in immigration. Don't do anything till I get back to you.'

*   *   *

The solicitor is a young man from an inner city practice who knows his stuff. He writes:

If your father was to marry, then he would need to make an application to the Home Office for his wife to stay. For this to be granted, she would have to show the following:

1. That the main purpose of the marriage was not to secure her entry or stay in the UK.
2. That they have met.
3. That they intend to live permanently together as husband and wife.
4. That they can support and accommodate themselves without claiming Public Funds.

The main problem is that the Home Office (or an Embassy if she applies after leaving the United Kingdom) is likely to believe that, because of the age difference, and because the marriage took place shortly before she had to leave the UK, the main purpose of the marriage is simply for immigration.

I forward the letter to my father.

The solicitor also tells me that the chances of success would be measurably improved should the marriage last for five years, or should there be a child of the marriage. I do not tell my father this.

2

Mother's little legacy

My mother had a pantry under the stairs stocked from floor to ceiling with tins of fish, meat, tomatoes, fruit, vegetables and puddings, packets of sugar (granulated, caster, icing and Demerara), flour (plain, self-raising and wholemeal), rice (pudding and long-grain), pasta (macaroni, twirls and vermicelli), lentils, buckwheat, split peas, oatmeal, bottles of oil (vegetable, sunflower and olive), pickles (tomato, cucumber, beetroot), boxes of cereals (mainly Shredded Wheat), packets of biscuits (mainly chocolate digestives) and slabs of chocolate. On the floor, in bottles and demi-johns, were gallons of a thick, mauve liquor made from plums, brown sugar and cloves, a glass of which was guaranteed to render even the most hardened alcoholic (and there were plenty of those in the Ukrainian community) comatose for up to three hours.

Upstairs under the beds in sliding boxes were kept preserves (mainly plum) and jars of home-made jam (plum, strawberry, raspberry, blackcurrant and quince in all combinations). In the potting-sheds and garage, cardboard fruit-boxes were stacked with the latest crop of apples, Bramleys, Beauty of Bath and Grieves, all separately wrapped in newspaper, exuding their fruity perfume. By next spring, their skins would be waxy, and the fruit inside shrivelled, but they were still good for Apfelstrudel and Blini. (The windfalls and damaged fruit had been picked out, cut up, and stewed as they fell.) Nets of carrots and potatoes, still preserved in their coat of clayey soil, bundles of onions and garlic, hung in the cool dark of the outhouse.

When my parents bought a freezer, in 1979, the peas, beans, asparagus and soft fruits soon piled up in plastic ice-cream tubs, each one labelled, dated and rotated. Even dill and parsley were rolled in little plastic bundles and stored away for use, so that there was no longer any season of the year when there was scarcity.

When I teased her about these supplies, enough to feed an army, she would wag her finger at me and say,

'It's in case your Tony Benn ever comes to power.'

My mother had known ideology, and she had known hunger. When she was twenty-one, Stalin had discovered he could use famine as a political weapon against the Ukrainian kulaks. She knew – and this knowledge never left her throughout her fifty years of life in England, and then seeped from her into the hearts of her children – she knew for certain that behind the piled-high shelves and abundantly stocked counters of Tesco and the Co-op, hunger still prowls with his skeletal frame and gaping eyes, waiting to grab you the moment you are off your guard. Waiting to grab you and shove you on a train, or on to a cart, or into that crowd of running fleeing people, and send you off on another journey where the destination is always death.

The only way to outwit hunger is to save and accumulate, so that there is always something tucked away, a little something to buy him off with. My mother acquired an extraordinary passion and skill of thrift. She would walk half a mile down the High Street to save a penny off a bag of sugar. She never bought what she could make herself. My sister and I suffered humiliation in home-made dresses stitched up from market remnants. We were forced to endure traditional recipes and home-baking when we craved junk food and white sliced bread. What she couldn't make had to be bought second-hand. Shoes, coats, household things – someone else had always had them first, had chosen them, used them, then discarded them. If you had to get it new, it had to be the cheapest money could buy, preferably reduced or a bargain. Fruit that was on the turn, tins that were dented, patterns that were out of date, last year's style. It didn't matter – we weren't proud, we weren't some foolish types who waste money for the sake of appearances, Mother said, when every cultured person knows that what really matters is what's inside.

My father lived in a different world. He went to work every day as a draughtsman, in a tractor factory in Doncaster. He earned his wage, bought the things the other men at work bought – new clothes (what's wrong with that shirt? I could have mended it), a camera (who needs camera?), a record player and vinyl discs (such extravagance!), books (and so many good books in public library), DIY tools (for making crazy things in house), furniture (could get same cheaper in the Co-op), a new motor-bike (drives like a madman). Every week, he gave my mother a fixed, not ungenerous amount for housekeeping, and spent the rest.

So it was that after fifty years of saving, preserving, baking, and making, my mother had accumulated a small nest-egg of several thousand pounds from the money my father gave her every week. This was her poke in the eye to hunger, her comfy safe feeling in the night, her gift of safety to her children in case hunger ever came for us. But what should have been a gift became a curse, for, to our shame, my sister and I squabbled about how her little legacy should be divided.

After our stand-off at the funeral, my sister and I bombarded each other with hate-filled letters and teemed venom down telephone wires. Once it started, there was no stopping it.

*   *   *

She phoned me late one evening, when Anna was in bed, and Mike was out. She wanted me to countersign to release some money for one of her daughters who was buying a flat. I let the phone ring nine times before I picked it up, because I knew it was her. Leave it! Leave it! said a sensible voice in my head. But in the end I picked it up, and all the hurtful things we had never said before came tumbling out. And once they were said, they couldn't be unsaid.

'You bullied and tricked her into signing that codicil, Vera. You stole her locket.' (Is this really me, saying such horrible things to my sister?) 'Mother loved us both equally. She wanted us to share what she left behind.'

'Now you're being ridiculous.' Her voice snaps like ice. 'She could only give the locket to one of us. She gave it to me. Because I was there when she needed me. I was always there when she needed me. And you – the favoured one, the little darling – you let her down in the end.' (Ouch! How can she say this to me, her baby sister?) 'As I knew you would.'

We both subscribe to the best-defence-is-attack school of diplomacy.

'Mother loved me. She was terrified of you, Vera. Yes, we were all terrified of you – your sarcasm, your temper. You bossed me around for years. But you can't boss me any more.'

Saying it should make me feel grown up, but it doesn't. It makes me feel four years old again.

'You just disappeared off the scene, as you've done all your life, Nadezhda. Playing at politics, playing your pathetic little games, being so clever and putting the world to rights, while other people get on with the real hard work. You just sat back and left it all to me.'

'You just barged in and took over.'

'Someone had to take charge, and it obviously wasn't going to be you. You didn't have time for Mother. Oh no, you were too busy with your fabulous career.'

(Bif! She has hit a sore point. I am consumed with guilt that I didn't drop everything and rush to Mother's bedside. Now she has me on the defensive, but I go straight back in for attack.)

'Oh, listen to you, who never did a day's work in your life! Lived off hubby's money.' (Baf! I aim a low punch.) '*I've* always had to work for my living. I have responsibilities, commitments. *Mother* understood. *She* knew about hard work.'

'That was proper work – not this namby-pamby mollycoddly waste-of-time do-gooding nonsense. It would have been more useful to grow vegetables.'

'You don't understand work, do you, Vera? You always had Big Dick with his expense account, his share options, his annual bonuses, his clever little deals and ways of avoiding tax. Then when it all went wrong, you tried to fleece him for every penny he had. Mother always said she could understand why he divorced you. You were so nasty to him.' (Ha! I scored there.) 'Your own mother said that, Vera!'

'She didn't know what I had to put up with.'

'She knew what *he* had to put up with.'

The telephone spits and crackles with our rage.

'The trouble with you, Nadezhda, is that your head is so full of nonsense that you don't know the real world.'

'I'm forty-seven, for God's sake, Vera. I know the world. I just see it in a different way.'

'Forty-seven doesn't make any difference. You're still a baby. You always will be. You've always taken everything for granted.'

'I gave back, too. I worked. I tried to make things better for people. More than you ever did,' the whining four-year-old pipes up again.

'Oh, my goodness! Tried to make things better for people! How noble you are!'

'Well look at you, Vera – you just went out to feather your own nest, and sod everybody else.'

'I had to learn to fight for myself. For myself and my girls. It's easy to be superior when you don't know what hardship is. When you're in a trap, you have to fight your way out.'

(Oh, please! She's still going on about all that old wartime stuff! Why can't she let it go?)

'What trap? What hardship? That was fifty years ago! And just look at yourself now! All bitter and twisted like a snake with jaundice.' (Now I put on the social-worker voice.) 'You need to learn to let go of the past.'

'Don't give me this new age hippy nonsense. Let's just talk about the practicalities.'

'I'd rather give the money to Oxfam, Vera, than let you win by extortion.'

'Oxfam. How pathetic!'

So Mother's little legacy stayed in the bank, and after that my sister and I didn't talk to each other for two years, until a common enemy brought us together.

3
A fat brown envelope

'So did you get the letter from the solicitor, Pappa?'

'Hmm. Yes. Yes.'

He's obviously not feeling chatty.

'So what did you think?'

'Aha, well . . .' He coughs. His voice sounds strained. He doesn't like talking on the telephone. 'Well, I have shown it to Valentina.'

'And what did she say?'

'What she says? Well . . .' More coughing. 'She says it is impossible that the law will separate a man from his wife.'

'But didn't you read the solicitor's letter?'

'Yes. No. But still, this is what she says. This is what she believes.'

'But what she believes is wrong, Pappa. Wrong.'

'Hmm.'

'And what about you? What do you say?' I struggle to control my tone.

'Well, what can I say?' There is a little helpless shrug in his voice, as though he has surrendered to forces beyond his control.

'Well, you could say you don't think it's such a good idea to get married after all. Couldn't you?'

My stomach contracts with dread. I realise he really is going to go ahead with this marriage, and that I am going to have to live with it.

'Aha. Yes. No.'

'What do you mean, yes, no?' Irritation grates in my throat. I am trying my best to keep my voice sweet.

'I cannot say this. I cannot say anything.'

'Pappa, for goodness' sake . . .'

'Look, Nadezhda, we are going to get married and that is that. There is no more point to talk about it.'

I have a feeling that something terrible is going on, but I can see that my father is alive and excited for the first time since my mother died.

This isn't the first time he has harboured fantasies of rescuing destitute Ukrainians. There was once a plan to track down members of the family whom he had not seen for half a century, and bring them all over to Peterborough. He wrote letters to town halls and village post offices all over Ukraine. Dozens of replies came pouring in from dodgy-sounding 'relatives' who wanted to take him up on his offer. Mother put her foot down.

Now I see his energy is all redirected towards this woman and her son – they will become his substitute family. He can speak with them in his own language. Such a beautiful language that anyone can be a poet. Such a landscape – it would make anyone an artist. Blue-painted wooden houses, golden wheat fields, forests of silver birch, slow wide sliding rivers. Instead of going home to Ukraina, Ukraina will come home to him.

I have visited Ukraine. I have seen the concrete housing blocks and the fish dead in the rivers.

'Pappa, Ukraina isn't like you remember it. It's different now. The people are different. They don't sing any more – only vodka songs. All they're interested in is shopping. Western goods. Fashion. Electronics. American brand names.'

'Hmm. So you say. Maybe it is so. But if I can save one lovely human being . . .'

He's off again.

There is a problem, however. Her tourist visa expires in three weeks, my father explains.

'And she still must get divorce papers from husband.'

'You mean she's married to someone else?'

'Her husband is in Ukraina. Very intelligent type, by the way. Polytechnic director. I have been in correspondence with him – even spoken to him on telephone. He told me that Valentina will make excellent wife.' There is a smug lilt in his voice. The soon-to-be-ex-husband will fax divorce papers to the Ukrainian Embassy in London. In the meantime, my father will make arrangements for the wedding.

'But if her visa expires in three weeks it sounds as though you've left it rather late.' (I hope.)

'Well, if she has to go back, then we will be married when she returns. On this we are absolutely decided.'

I notice that 'I' has become 'we'. I realise that this plan has been developing over quite a long time, and that I have been permitted to know about it only in its very latest stages. If she has to go back to Ukraine, he will write her a letter and she will come back as his fiancée.

'But Pappa,' I say, 'you read the solicitor's letter. They may not allow her to come back. Isn't there someone else, someone a bit younger she could marry?'

Yes, this resourceful woman has an alternative marriage plan, my father says. Through a domestic care agency she has met a young man who is totally paralysed following a road accident. He, by the way (says Pappa), is a very decent young man from good family. Used to be teacher. She has been looking after him – bathing, spoon-feeding, taking to toilet. If she is rejected as my father's fiancée, she will arrange to be invited back as an '*au pair*' to look after this young man. This kind of work is still permitted under immigration regulations. During the year she is permitted to stay as an *au pair*, he will fall in love with her and she will marry him. Thus her future in this country will be secured. But this would be a life sentence of servitude for poor Valentina, for he is totally dependent on her, twenty-four hours a day, whereas my father's needs are small (says Pappa). My father knows this, because she has invited him to the house where she works, and has shown him the young man. 'You see what he's like?' she said to my father. 'How could I marry that?' (Only of course she said it in Ukrainian.) No, my father wishes to spare her that life of slavery. He will make the sacrifice and marry her himself.

I am riven with anxiety. I am consumed with curiosity. And so I put aside two years of bitterness and telephone my sister.

*   *   *

Vera is uncompromising where I am woolly-mindedly liberal. She is decisive where I am wavering.

'Oh my God, Nadezhda. Why didn't you tell me before? We've got to stop her.'

'But if she makes him happy . . .'

'Don't be so ridiculous. Of course she won't make him happy. We can see what she's after. Really, Nadezhda, why do you always take the side of the criminals . . .'

'But Vera . . .'

'You must meet her and warn her to back off.'

I telephone my father.

'Pappa, why don't I come over and meet Valentina?'

'No no. This is absolutely impossible.'

'Why impossible?'

He hesitates. He can't think of excuses fast enough.

'She doesn't speak English.'

'But I can speak Ukrainian.'

'She is very shy.'

'She doesn't sound shy to me. We could discuss Schopenhauer and Nietzsche.' (Ha ha.)

'She will be working.'

'Well, I could meet her afterwards. After she finishes work.'

'No, this is not the point. Nadezhda, it's better we don't talk about this. Goodbye.'

He puts the phone down. He's hiding something.

A few days later I ring him again. I try a different tack.

'Hi, Pappa. It's me, Nadezhda.' (He knows it's me, but I want to sound friendly.)

'Aha. Yes. Yes.'

'Pappa, Mike's got a couple of days off this weekend. Why don't we come over and see you.' My father adores my husband. He can talk to him about tractors and aeroplanes.

'Hmm. *Tak*. That will be very nice. When will you come?'

'On Sunday. We'll come for lunch on Sunday, about one o'clock.'

'OK. Good. I will tell Valentina.'

We arrive well before one o'clock, hoping to catch her, but she has already gone out. The house looks neglected, dispirited. When my mother was here there were always fresh flowers, a clean tablecloth, the smell of good cooking. Now there are no flowers, but used cups, piles of papers, books, things that have not been put away. The table is bare dark brown formica, spread with newspaper on which some chunks of stale bread and apple peelings are waiting to be thrown away. There is an odour of stale grease.

My father, however, is in great spirits. He has an intense, animated air. His hair, which is now quite silver and thin, has grown long and wispy at the back. His skin has colour and seems firmer, a bit freckled, as if he has been out in the garden. His eyes are bright. He offers us lunch – tinned fish, tinned tomatoes, brown bread, followed by Toshiba apples. This is his special recipe – apples gathered from the garden, peeled, chopped, packed into a pyrex dish and cooked in the microwave (a Toshiba) until they are sticky and solid. Proud of his invention, he offers us more and more and more, and some to take home with us.

I worry – is it healthy to be eating so much out of tins? Is he getting a balanced diet? I check the contents of his fridge and larder. There is milk, cheese, cereal, bread, plenty of tins. No fresh fruit or vegetables, apart from Toshiba apples and some very speckled bananas. But he looks well. I start to make a shopping list.

'You should eat more fresh fruit and vegetables, Pappa,' I say. He consents to cauliflower and carrots. He no longer eats frozen peas or beans – they make him cough.

'Does Valentina cook for you?' I ask.

'Sometimes she does.' He is evasive.

I grab a J-cloth and start to tackle the grime. All the surfaces are covered in dust, and brown sticky patches where things have been spilt. There are books everywhere: history, biography, cosmology, some he has bought himself, some from the public library. On the table in the front room I find several sheets of paper covered with his fine, crabby, spiky handwriting, with many additions and crossings-out. I have to struggle to read hand-written Ukrainian, but I can tell from the way the lines are set out that it is poetry. My father published his first poem at the age of fourteen. It was a eulogy to a new hydro-electric power station that was built on the River Dnieper in 1927. When he was training to be an engineer in Kiev, he belonged to a secret circle of Ukrainian poets, which had been outlawed as part of the drive to impose Russian as the lingua franca of the Soviet Union. I am pleased that he is still writing poetry. I am even a bit proud. I tidy the papers into a neat pile and wipe the table.

In the next room, Mike is slumped in the armchair with his eyes half open and a glass of plum wine in his hand, valiantly maintaining a listening expression on his face, while my father's voice drones on.

'It is a terrible tragedy what has happened in this beautiful country. The twin evils of fascism and communism have eaten her heart.'

On the wall above the fireplace he has hung a map of Europe. Russia and Germany are scored through with heavy lines, so violently that the paper has been torn. Crude drawings of a swastika, an imperial eagle, and a hammer and sickle are covered with angry scribbles. My father's voice is raised and trembling as he warms to his climax.

'If I can save just one human being – one human being – from this horror, do you not think this is the moral thing to do?'

Mike mumbles something diplomatic.

'You see, Mikhail,' his voice takes on a confiding, man-to-man tone, 'a child can have only one mother, but a man can have many lovers. This is perfectly normal. Don't you agree?'

I strain to hear Mike's reply, but can catch only a vague mumble.

'I can understand that Vera and Nadia are not happy. They have lost their mother. But they will come to accept when they see what a beautiful type is Valentina.' (Oh will we?) 'Of course my first wife Ludmilla was beautiful when I first knew her in youth. I rescued her also, you know. She was under attack from some boys that wanted to steal her skates, and I intervened on her behalf. From that time we became close friends. Yes, it is the natural instinct of man to be the protector of woman.' (Oh, *please!*) 'Now, with this Valentina, I am presented with another beautiful woman who appeals for my help. How could I pass by on other side of the road?'

He starts to catalogue the horrors he is saving her from. The talk in the Ukrainian community is of no food in the shops.

The only food is what people grow in their plots – just like the old days, they say. The hrivna has fallen through the floor, and keeps falling every day. There has been an outbreak of cholera in Kharkiv. Diphtheria is sweeping through the Donbass. In Zhitomir a woman was set upon in broad daylight and her fingers chopped off for her gold rings. In Chernigov, trees from the forests around Chernobyl have been felled and turned into radioactive domestic furniture which has been sold all around the country so people are irradiated in their own homes. Fourteen miners were killed in an underground explosion at Donetsk. A man was arrested at the railway station at Odessa and found to have a lump of uranium in his suitcase. In Lviv a young woman claiming to be the second coming of Christ has convinced everybody that the world will end in six months' time. Worse than the external collapse of law and order is the collapse of any rational or moral principles. Some people run to the old Church, but more run to the new fantasy Churches they are bringing in from the West, or to soothsayers, millenarians, out-for-a-quick-buck visionaries, self-flagellants. Nobody knows what to believe or whom to trust.

'If I can save just one human being . . .'

'Oh, for goodness' sake!' I fling the J-cloth at him. It lands wetly in his lap. 'Pappa, haven't you tied yourself up in some ideological knots here? Valentina and her husband were party members. They were prosperous and powerful. They did all right under communism. It isn't communism she is fleeing from but capitalism. You're in favour of capitalism, aren't you?'

'Hmm.' He picks up the J-cloth and absent-mindedly wipes his forehead with it. 'Hmm.'

I realise that this thing with Valentina isn't really about ideology.

'So when will we get a chance to meet her?'

'She should come here when her shift finishes, about five o'clock,' says my father. 'I have something to give her.' He reaches for a fat brown envelope on the sideboard which appears to be stuffed with papers.

'Well why don't I just pop out and get your shopping? Then we can all have tea together when she comes back.' Cheery, sensible voice. English voice. Distances me from all the pain and madness.

On the way back from the supermarket, I pull up outside the nursing home where Valentina works. It is the same nursing home where my mother came briefly before she died, so I know the lie of the land. I park outside on the road, and then, instead of going in through the front door, I go round the side and look in through the kitchen window. A fat middle-aged woman is stirring something on the stove. Is it her? Next to the kitchen is the dining-room, where some of the older residents are gathering for tea. A couple of bored teenagers in pinafore overalls are shoving them around in wheelchairs. There are other people with trays of food, but they are too far away to see. Now some people are coming out through the front door, and making their way to the bus stop. Are they staff, or visiting relatives? What am I looking for, anyway? I am looking for someone like my father's description – a beautiful blonde with an enormous bust. No one like that here.

When I get home, my father is in a state of distress. She has telephoned to say that she isn't coming. She is going straight home. Tomorrow she travels back to Ukraine. He must see her before she goes. He must give her his gift.

The envelope is not sealed, and from where I am sitting I can see that it contains several sheets of paper covered with the same crabbed handwriting, and some banknotes. I cannot see how many. I feel rage rise in me. Red blood swims before my eyes.

'Pappa, why are you giving her money? You have little enough from your pension to live on.'

'Nadezhda, this is absolutely none of you business. Why you so bothered what I am doing with my money? You thinking there will be none left for you, hah?'

'Can't you see she's conning you, Pappa? I think I should go to the police.'

He catches his breath. He is scared of the police, the local council, even the uniformed postman who comes to the front door every day. I have frightened him.

'Nadezhda, why you are so cruel? How I have raised such a hard-hearted monster? Leave my house. I never want' (vant) 'to see you again. You are not my daughter!' Suddenly he starts to cough. His pupils are dilated. There are flecks of saliva on his lips.

'Oh, stop being so melodramatic, Pappa. You said that to me before – do you remember? When I was a student and you thought I was too left-wing.'

'Even Lenin wrote that left-wing communism is infantile.' (Cough cough.) 'Infantile Disorder.'

'You said I was a Trotskyist. You said "Leave my house I never want to see you again!" But, look, I'm still here. Still putting up with your nonsense.'

35

'You *were* Trotskyist. All of you student revolutionaries with your foolish flags and banners. Do you know what Trotsky did? Do you know how many people he killed? And in what a manner? Do you? Trotsky was a monster, worse than Lenin. Worse than Vera.'

'Pappa, even if I was a Trotskyist, which by the way I was *not*, it was still an unkind thing to say to your daughter.'

That was more than thirty years ago and I can still remember the shock of hurt – I who had always believed until then that my parents' love was unconditional. But it wasn't really about politics; it was about will – his will against mine: his right to command me, as my father.

Mike intervenes.

'Now, Nikolai, I'm sure you didn't mean that. Now Nadezhda, there's no need to rake over past disputes. Sit down, both of you, and let's talk about it.'

He's good at that sort of thing.

My father sits down. He is shaking, and his jaw is clenched. I remember that look from childhood, and I want to punch him, or to run away.

'Nikolai, I think Nadezhda has a point. It's one thing to help her to come to England, but it's another thing if she's asking you for money.'

'It's for her tickets. If she is to come back, she needs money for tickets.'

'But if she really cares about you, she'll come and see you before she goes, won't she? She'll want to say goodbye,' says Mike.

I'm not saying anything. I'm keeping out of it. Let the old fool go to hell.

'Hmm. This may be so.'

My father looks upset. Good. Let him be upset.

'I mean, it's understandable that you should feel attracted to her, Nikolai,' says Mike. (What's this? Understandable? We'll talk about this later.) 'But I think it's a bit suspicious, that she won't meet any of your family, if she's really thinking of marrying you.'

'Hmm.' My father doesn't argue with Mike the way he does with me. Mike is a man and must be treated with respect.

'What about the money she's been earning with all her jobs? That should be enough for the tickets.'

'She has some debts to pay. If I don't give her money for tickets, maybe she will never come back.' There is a look of utter loss on his face. 'And some poems I have written for her. I want her to read.' I realise, and Mike realises in the same moment, that he is completely in love. The stupid fool.

'Well, where does she stay in Peterborough?' asks Mike. 'Maybe we could call round at her house.' He is as worried as I am now. And maybe intrigued.

We pile into the car, all three of us. Father has put his best jacket on, and tucked the brown envelope into the inside breast pocket, next to his heart. He directs us to a narrow street of terraced red-brick houses near the centre of the city. We pull up outside a house with a wicket gate and a crumbling tarmac path leading up to the door. My father is out of the car in a trice, and hurrying up the path, clutching the envelope in front of him.

I see him dispassionately for a moment, and I am struck by how old he is, how bent and shuffling his gait. But his eyes are aflame. He rings the bell. There is no reply. He rings again. And again. And again. Longer and longer. After a long while, there is a grating sound of a sash window being opened. My father looks up eagerly. He is holding out the envelope. His hands are shaking. We all hold our breath, expecting to see a beautiful blonde with an enormous bust, but instead, a man pokes his head out of the window. He is maybe forty, with a fuzz of brown hair and a white shirt, open at the neck.

'Piss off, will you? Just piss off!'

My father is speechless. He extends the envelope with his trembling hands.

The brown-haired man ignores it.

'Don't you think you've caused enough trouble already? First the letter from the solicitor, then pestering her at her work, now following her home. You've upset her. Now just piss off and leave her alone!' He slams the window shut.

My father seems to shrink and crumple on the spot where he stands. Mike puts an arm round his shoulder and leads him back to the car. When we get back to the house, he can barely speak.

Mike says, 'I think you had a lucky escape there, Nikolai. Why don't you put the money back in the bank tomorrow, and forget about her.'

My father nods dumbly.

'Do you think I am so very foolish?' he asks Mike.

'No, no,' says Mike. 'Any man can lose his head over a beautiful woman.' He catches my eye and gives me a little apologetic smile.

My father perks up a bit. His masculinity is intact.

'Well, I will have nothing more to do with her. You are quite right.'

It's getting late now. We say goodbye and prepare for the long drive back to Cambridge. As we are leaving the house, the phone rings, and we hear my father talking in Ukrainian. I can't hear what he's saying, but something in his tone makes me suspicious – a lingering, gentle note. I suppose I should stop, listen, intervene, but I'm tired, and I want to get home.

'Do you know how much money was in that envelope?' Mike asks.

We are driving through twilight, half-way home, and mulling over the events of the day.

'I saw there was quite a wad of notes. Maybe a hundred pounds, I'd say.'

'It's just that I noticed the top note was a fifty. When you go to the bank to draw money out, they don't usually give you fifties. They give you tens or twenties. Unless you're taking a lot of money out.' He frowns with concentration into the bending road. 'I think maybe we should find out.' He pulls to a halt abruptly outside a red telephone booth in a village. I see him fumbling for coins, dialling, talking, feeding the coin box, talking some more. Then he comes back to the car.

'Eighteen hundred pounds.'

'What?'

'In the envelope. Eighteen hundred pounds. Poor old man.'

'Poor old fool. It must be all his savings.'

'Apparently Valentina rang him and tried to get him to pay the money into her account.'

'She wasn't interested in reading his poetry then?' (Ha ha.)

'He says he'll put the money back in the bank tomorrow.'

We drive on. It is Sunday night, and there are few other cars on the road.

Dusk has fallen now, with strange streaks of light across the sky where the sun has gone down behind clouds. We have the windows down, and the scents of the country buffet our faces – hawthorn, cow parsley, silage.

It is about ten o'clock when we get home. Mike rings my father again. I listen on the extension.

'Just letting you know we got back safely, Nikolai. Are you sure you'll be able to get to the bank tomorrow? I don't like the thought of you having all that money in the house overnight. Can you put it somewhere safe?'

'Yes . . . no . . .' My father is agitated. 'What if I give it to her after all?'

'Nikolai, I don't think that's a good idea. I think you should put it in the bank, like you said you would.'

'But what if it's too late? What if I given it her already?'

'When did you give it to her?'

'Tomorrow.' He is confused, and the wrong words come tumbling. 'Tomorrow. Today. What it matters?'

'Hang on, Nikolai. Just hang on.'

Mike puts on his coat and picks up the car keys. He looks terribly tired. In the early hours of next morning, he returns with the envelope, and stows the £1,800 safely in the drawer under his socks, until he can get to the bank tomorrow. I don't know what happened to the poems.

4

A rabbit and a chicken

I'm not sure at what point Valentina sweet-talked my father into handing over the money, but she got it in the end.

I know I have to report this to Vera but something makes me hold back. Every time I phone my father or my sister, it is like crossing a bridge from the world where I am an adult with responsibilities and a measure of power, to the cryptic world of childhood where I am at the mercy of other people's purposes which I can neither control nor understand. Big Sister is the absolute monarch in that twilit world. She rules without demur or pity.

'My God, what an idiot he is!' she exclaims when I tell her about Valentina and the envelope of money. 'We've got to stop him.' Big Sister is always certain.

'But, Vera, I think he's really serious about it – about her. And if she makes him happy . . .'

'Really, Nadezhda, you are so gullible. We read about these people in the papers every day. Immigrants, asylum seekers, economic migrants. Call them what you will. It is always the most determined and ruthless people who make it over here, and then when they find it isn't so easy to get a good job, they will turn to crime. Can't you see what will happen if she comes and stays? We've simply got to stop her coming back from Ukraine.'

'But he's so determined. I'm not sure we *can* stop it . . .'

I'm transfixed between two certainties – his and hers. This is how it's been all my life.

My sister telephones the Home Office. They tell her to put it in writing. If my father finds out he will not forgive her, as he has never forgiven her for anything before, so she writes anonymously:

She came here on a tourist visa. This is her second tourist visa. She has been working illegally. Her son is enrolled in an English school. Three weeks before her visa was due to expire she came up with the idea of marriage. Her intention is to marry Mr Mayevskyj in order to obtain a visa and work permit.

Then she telephones the British Embassy in Kiev. A bored-sounding young man with a blue-chip accent tells her that Valentina's visa has been granted already. There was nothing in her application to indicate that she should be refused. But what about . . . ? Vera lists the points she made in her letter. The young man gives the telephonic equivalent of a shrug.

'So you see I'm relying on you, Nadezhda,' Big Sis says.

I raise the subject a couple of weeks later, while we are sitting having lunch at my father's house, Mike, my father and I. Tinned ham, boiled potatoes, boiled carrots. His daily diet. He has prepared it for us with pride.

'Have you heard from Valentina, Pappa?' (Voice chatty, conversational.)

'Yes, she has written. She is very well.'

'Where is she staying? Has she gone back to her husband?'

'Yes. She is staying there now. He is very educated type, by the way. Polytechnic director.'

'And what are her plans? Is she coming back to England?' Bright keeping-a-distance voice.

'Hmm. Maybe. I don't know.'

He does know, but he won't say.

'So who was the man with brown hair, the man in the window, who was so rude to you?'

'Aha. This is Bob Turner. A very decent type, by the way. A civil engineer.'

My father explains that Bob Turner is a friend of Valentina's uncle in Selby. He has a house in Selby where he lives with his wife, and the house in Peterborough, which was his mother's, where he had installed Valentina and Stanislav.

'And what do you think is his relationship with Valentina?' It seems obvious to me, but I am trying to lead him through a sort of Platonic dialogue to see the truth.

'Aha, yes. It was a relationship. There was even some possibility that he would marry her, but his wife will not give him divorce. Of course this relationship is finished now.'

'Of course it's not finished, Pappa. Can't you see that you're being taken for a ride?' I can hear my voice getting shrill. But he isn't listening. A faraway look has come into his eyes. He has turned into an eighty-four-year-old teenager, tuned in to his private music.

'He paid for my naturalisation, by the way,' he murmurs, 'so when I marry her, I will be British subject.'

When he marries her.

'But Pappa, ask yourself – why? Why did Bob Turner pay for you to be naturalised?'

'Why?' A little self-satisfied smile. 'Why not?'

My Platonic dialogue hasn't got me very far so I try another approach. I invoke the spirit of Big Sister.

'Pappa, have you talked to Vera about this business with Bob Turner? I think she would be *very* upset.'

'Why should I talk to her? It is abso*lu*tely none of her business.' His eyes refocus. His jaw twitches. He's scared.

'Vera's worried about you. We both promised Mother we would look after you.'

'She will look after me only to put me in my grave.'

He starts to cough violently. Particles of boiled carrot fly around the room and land on the walls. I fetch him a glass of water.

In the shadowy kingdom of childhood, where my sister was queen, my father was the exiled Pretender. A long time ago, they went to war against each other. It was so long ago that I don't know what they first clashed about, and they have probably forgotten too. My father made a tactical retreat into the domain of his garage, his constructions of aluminium, rubber and wood, his coughing and his Big Ideas. From time to time he would surge forth in angry blazing forays directed towards my sister and, after she had left home, towards me.

'Pappa, what is all this bad-mouthing of Vera? Why do you two always argue? Why do you . . . ?'

I hesitate to use the word 'hate'. It is too strong, too irrevocable. My father starts to cough again.

'You know this Vera . . . She is terrible in temper. You should see the way she was pestering Ludmilla – you must give all to the granddaughters, you must make a codicil. All the time, even as she was dying. She is too much interested in money. And now she wants me to make my will like that, divided in three for the grandchildren. But I have said No. What you think?'

'I think you should leave it half and half,' I say. I'm not going to be drawn into his game.

Ha! So Big Sister is still scheming for the inheritance – though there is only the house and his Pensioners Bond left to divide. I don't know whether to believe him. I don't know what to believe. I have a sense of something terrible that has happened in the past, which no one will tell me about because even though I am in my forties I am still the baby: too young to understand. I believe what he says about how she obtained the codicil. But now he is playing a different game, trying to enlist me on his side against my sister.

'What you think if I make in my will to leave everything to you and Michael when I shall die?' he says, suddenly lucid.

'I still think you should leave it half and half.'

'If you say so.' He sighs peevishly. I'm refusing to play.

I am secretly pleased to be the favoured one, but I am cautious. He is too unpredictable. Once, long ago, I was Daddy's girl, trainee trail-rider apprentice engineer. I try to remember the things I once loved about him.

There was a time when my father used to sit me on the back of his motor-bike – 'Take care, Kolyusha!' Mother would cry – and we would roar about the long, straight fenland lanes. The first bike he had was a 250cc Francis Barnett he rebuilt from scrap, each piece cleaned and restored by hand. Then a shiny black 350cc Vincent; then a 500cc Norton. I used to recite the names like a mantra. I remember how I would rush to the window when I heard the deep throb of the engine at the top of the road, and then he would come in, all wind-blown, with his goggles and his old Russian leather flying helmet, and say, 'Who wants to come for a ride?'

'Me! Me! Take me!'

But that was before he discovered I had no aptitude for engineering.

*   *   *

After lunch my father snoozes, and I find the secateurs and go out into the garden to cut some roses for my mother's grave. There has been rain, and the earth smells of roots and growth – a wild, disorderly growth. The red rose which rambles up the fence between us and the neighbours is strangled in bindweed, and nettles are sprouting up in patches where once the dill and parsley self-seeded. The lavender bushes my mother planted by the path have grown tall, sparse and leggy. Brown, rattling seed-heads of poppies and columbines jostle with willowherb in the flowerbeds, greedy for the black chocolate she fed them. Ah, she would sigh, there's always work to do in a garden. Always something growing and something to be cut down. A soul can't sit down for a moment.

The graveyard, too, is a place where life and death go side by side. A tortoiseshell cat has marked out his territory here, and patrols the hedge that separates the cemetery from the cornfields. A pair of fat thrushes are tugging at worms in the earth of a newly turned grave. Five more graves have appeared after hers; five more people have died in the village since she died. I read their tombstones. Dearly beloved . . . Mum . . . Sadly departed this life . . . Resting with Jesus . . . In eternity

A rabbit and a chicken

... A mole has been busy at work alongside the gravediggers, turning up mounds of earth here and there. There is a molehill above my mother's grave. I like to think of the sleek black mole snuggled up with her down below in the dark. At her funeral, the vicar said she was in heaven, but she knew she was going down here into the ground, to be eaten by worms. (Never harm a worm, Nadezhda, it is the gardener's friend.)

My mother understood about life and death. Once she brought a dead rabbit home from market, and skinned and gutted it on the kitchen table. She took out its red, bloody insides, pushed a straw into the windpipe, and blew into the lungs. Wide-eyed, I watched how the lungs went up and down.

'See, Nadezhda, this is how we breathe. We breathe and we live.'

Another time she brought home a live chicken. She took it into the back garden, gripped it between her knees as it struggled to get free and wrung its neck with a quick, light movement. The chicken twitched and went still.

'See, Nadezhda, this is how we die.'

Both the rabbit and the chicken were pot-roasted with garlic, shallots and herbs from the garden, and then when the meat was all eaten up, the bones were used for soup. Nothing was wasted.

*   *   *

I sit on the bench under the wild cherry tree in the cemetery and sort through my memories, but the harder I try to remember, the more I get confused about which are memories and which are stories. When I was little, my mother used to tell me family stories – but only the ones that had a happy ending. My sister also told me stories: her stories were strongly

47

formulaic, with goodies (Mother, Cossacks) and baddies (Father, communists). Vera's stories always had a beginning, a middle, an end, and a moral. Sometimes my father told me stories, too, but his stories were complicated in structure, ambiguous in meaning and unsatisfactory in outcome, with lengthy digressions and packed with obscure facts. I preferred my mother's and my sister's tales.

I too have a story to tell. Once upon a time we were a family, my mother and father, my sister and I – not a happy family nor an unhappy one, but just a family that pootled along while children grew up and parents grew old. I remember a time when my sister and I loved each other, and my father and I loved each other. Maybe there was even a time when my father and my sister loved each other – that I can't remember. We all loved Mother, and she loved all of us. I was the little girl with plaited hair gripping a stripy cat, whose photo stands on the mantelpiece. We spoke a different language from our neighbours and ate different food, and worked hard and kept out of everybody's way, and we were always good so the secret police wouldn't come for us in the night.

Sometimes, as a small child, I used to sit in the dark at the top of the stairs in my pyjamas, listening, straining to overhear my parents talking in the room below. What were they talking about? I could catch only phrases, fragments, but I caught the urgency in their voices. Or I would come into a room and notice the way their voices suddenly changed, their faces lighted into temporary smiles.

Were they talking about that other time, that other country? Were they talking about what happened in between their childhood time and mine – something so fearful that I must never know about it?

My sister is ten years older than me, and had one foot in the adult world. She knew things I didn't know, things that were whispered but never spoken about. She knew grown-up secrets so terrible that just the knowledge of them had scarred her heart.

Now that Mother has died, Big Sis has become the guardian of the family archive, the spinner of stories, the custodian of the narrative that defines who we are. This role, above all others, is the one I envy and resent. It is time, I think, to find out the whole story, and to tell it in my own way.

5

A short history of tractors in Ukrainian

What do I know about my mother? Ludmilla (Milla, Millochka) Mitrofanova was born in 1912 in Novaya Aleksandria, a small garrison town in what is now Poland, but was then on the western flank of the Russian Empire. Her father, Mitrofan Ocheretko, was a cavalry officer, a war hero, and an outlaw. Her mother Sonia was nineteen years old when Ludmilla was born, a trainee schoolteacher, a survivor.

The Ocheretkos were not gentry but wealthy peasants from the Poltava region of Ukraine, who lived on the edge of a *khutor* (settlement) and farmed some thirty hectares on the eastern bank of the Sula River. They were hard-working, hard-drinking Cossacks who had somehow amassed enough wealth to pay the necessary bribe to win a lucrative contract to supply horses to the Tsar's army. This in turn allowed them to save up enough to pay the considerably greater sum needed to secure for their eldest son, Mitrofan, a place in the military academy.

Mitrofan Ocheretko seems to have been a brilliant soldier: fearless and prudent, he loved life but respected death. Unlike officers drawn from the nobility, who hardly considered the peasants to be human, Ocheretko was mindful of the troops and careful with their lives, only taking risks when there was something to be gained. From the mud and slaughter of the Great War, he emerged covered in glory. His great moment came in 1916, on the Eastern Front, when he took a bullet in his thigh at Lake Naroch crawling through a bog to rescue the Tsar's cousin, who had become trapped as the spring thaw turned the shores of the lake into miles of churned-up mud. Ocheretko dragged the young aristocrat to safety and carried him in his arms through a hail of artillery fire.

For his bravery he was awarded the St George's Cross. The Tsar himself pinned it to his chest, and the Tsarina patted little Ludmilla on the head. Two years later, the Tsar and Tsarina were dead, and Ocheretko was an outlaw on the run.

After the revolution of 1917, Ocheretko joined neither the Russian White Army nor the Soviet Red Army. Instead, he took Sonia and the three children – my mother Ludmilla now had a younger sister and brother – back to Poltava and left them there in a tumbledown wooden cottage on the *khutor* while he went off to fight with the rebel Ukrainian National Republican Army. It was a moment to be seized: now while Russia was tearing herself apart, this might be the occasion for Ukraine to slip free of the imperial yoke.

Ludmilla hardly saw her father during those years. Sometimes he would arrive in the middle of the night, exhausted and hungry, and be gone again by the morning. 'Don't tell anyone Pappa was here,' her mother would whisper to the children.

The Civil War was waged through a succession of bloody massacres and reprisals so gruesome that it seemed as if the human soul itself had died. No town, not even the smallest village, no household was left untouched. The history books tell of ingenious new ways of inflicting painful lingering death. The gift of imagination, perverted by blood-lust, invented tortures undreamt of before, and former neighbours became enemies for whom mere shooting was too merciful. But my parents never talked to me about these horrors: I was their precious peacetime baby.

When Mother described her early childhood it was always as an idyll – long summers when the sun was hot and they ran barefoot in the fields and skinny-dipped in the Sula River, or took their cow off to the distant pastures and stayed outdoors from dawn to dusk. No shoes, no pants, no one to tell them what to do. And grass tall enough to hide in, such a merry green, sprinkled with red and yellow flowers. And the sky blue-blue, and cornfields like a sheet of gold stretching as far as eye could see. Sometimes, in the distance, they could hear shooting, and see curls of smoke rising from a burning house.

*   *   *

My father has positioned himself in front of the map of Ukraine, and is delivering an intense two-hour lecture to his captive one-man (Mike) audience about the history, politics, culture, economics, agriculture and aviation industry of Ukraine. His student is settled comfortably in the armchair facing the map, but his eyes are focused on a spot beyond the lecturer's head. His cheeks are very pink. In his hand he cradles a glass of Mother's home-made plum wine.

'It is often forgotten that the Civil War was more than a simple matter of whites against reds. No fewer than four foreign armies were in battle for control over Ukraina: Red Army of Soviets, White Russian Imperial Army, Polish army mounting opportunistic invasion, and German army propping up puppet regime of Skoropadski.'

I am in the kitchen cutting up vegetables for soup, listening with half an ear.

'The Ukrainians were led by former Cossack atmans, or grouped under the anarchist banner of Makhno. Their aim, at once both simple and impossible, was to free Ukraina of all occupying forces.'

The secret of my mother's fabulous soup was plenty of salt (they both suffered from high blood pressure), a big knob of butter (they didn't worry about cholesterol), and vegetables, garlic and herbs fresh from the garden. I cannot make soup like this.

'Nadezhda's grandfather, Mitrofan Ocheretko, joined a band under the leadership of Atman Tiutiunik, to whom he became second-in-command. They were fighting in a loose alliance with the "Ukrainian Directoire" of Simon Petlura. Ocheretko, by the way, was a very remarkable type with sweeping moustaches and eyes black like coal. I have seen his picture, though of course I have never met him.'

Into the soup, when it was simmering, she dolloped teaspoons of 'halushki' – a paste of raw egg and semolina, beaten together with salt and herbs – which fluffed up into dumplings that crumbled on your tongue.

'At end of the Civil War this Ocheretko fled to Turkey. Now Sonia's brother Pavel – he by the way was a very remarkable type, railway engineer who built first rail line from Kiev to Odessa – he was friend of Lenin. Because of this, some letters were written and Mitrofan Ocheretko was rehabilitated under amnesty, and obtained a job teaching sword-fencing in the military academy in Kiev. And it was here in Kiev that Ludmilla and I first met.'

His voice has gone all croaky.

'Come on, Pappa, Mike, lunch is ready!'

*   *   *

The time between Valentina's return to Ukraine and her re-entry into England was a time of great personal growth and intellectual activity for my father. He started pouring out poems again, which he left lying around the house on scraps of paper, all written in the same crabbed Cyrillic hand. I deciphered the word 'love' once or twice, but I couldn't bring myself to read them.

Every week he wrote to Valentina in Ukraine and in between letters he telephoned and talked, sometimes to her, sometimes to her intelligent-type husband. I know the phone calls were long because I saw the phone bill.

However, with my sister and me he was very cagey. He didn't want us telling him what to do. He had already made his mind up.

Vera went to visit him in September. She described her visit.

'The house is filthy. He eats off newspaper. He eats nothing but apples. I tried to persuade him to go into a sheltered housing scheme, but he says you dissuaded him. I can't imagine what you think you can gain from this, Nadezhda. I suppose you're worried that if he sells the house you won't be able to inherit your share. Really! Your obsession is going too far. The house is much too big for him now. I tried to get a home help, but he refuses. As for this other sordid business – I tried to find out what's going on with this tart, but he won't talk about it at all. He just changes the subject. I don't know what the matter with him is. He was behaving most oddly. We really should see the doctor about having him certified, don't you agree? He seems to be living in a world of his own.'

I held the phone away from my ear and let her rabbit on.

The next day he phoned me to describe Big Sister's visit.

'When I saw the car pulling into driveway and I saw her getting out and walking towards the house, can you imagine, Nadezhda, I performed involuntary excretion in my trousers.' He said it as though his bowels were not part of him but a discrete force of nature. 'You see, this Vera, she is terrible autocrat. Tyrant. Like Stalin. She is always pestering me. Must do this, must do that. Why must I always do as I'm told? Can I not make up my mind about something? Now she says I must have sheltered housing. I cannot afford sheltered housing. Too expensive for me. Better I stay here. Live here. Die here. You tell her I said so. Tell her I want her to visit me no more. You and Michael can visit.'

When Mike and I next visit, we find the house and garden much as my sister described. A thin veil of dust has greyed all the white paintwork and clings to cobwebs on the ceiling. The sitting-room is full of windfall apples collected from the ground and laid out in shallow boxes and cartons on the table, chairs, sideboard and even on top of the wardrobe, filling the house

with their fruity over-ripe smell. Fruit-flies hover over the
Grieves and Beauty of Bath apples which, being softer, have
already started to turn brown and bubble up in specks of
mould that my father is too short-sighted to notice. He sits at
one end of the table with his little knife, peeling, slicing and
sorting them into Toshiba-sized piles. I notice how much
better he himself is looking.

'Hallo! Hallo!' he greets us warmly. 'Well, nothing new
to report. Excellent apples! Look!' He offers us a dish of the
sticky Toshiba-cooked mixture. 'Today we must go to library.
I have ordered some books. I am becoming very interested in
this business of an engineering *Weltanschauung* as in ideology
incorporated into design of new machines.'

Mike looks impressed. I raise my eyes to the ceiling. My father
ploughs on, furrowing up trails of gleaming brown ideas.
   'You see as Marx said himself, the relations of production
are embedded in the machinery of production. Take for
example the tractor. In nineteenth century, early tractors were
made by the individual craftsman in his workshop. Now they
are produced on assembly lines, and at the end of assembly
line stands man with stopwatch. He measures the process.'
(The accent is on the second syllable – 'pro-*cess*'.) 'To make
more efficiency the worker must work harder. Now look
at a man who ploughs in the field. He sits alone in cab. He
moves levers and the tractor ploughs. He follows the gradi-
ent of terrain, he takes account of soil and weather. He believes he is master of the pro-*cess*. But at the end of the field
stands another man with stopwatch. He observes the tractor
driver, makes note of his lines and turns. So certain time is
allotted for the ploughing of a field, and man's wages fixed

accordingly. Now, you see, in this era of computerised numeri-cal control, even the man with stopwatch will be redundant, and stopwatch itself will be incorporated into dashboard equipment.'

He flourishes the little knife with manic energy. Curls of apple peel slide off the table on to the carpet, where they are trodden into a fragrant mush.

*   *   *

'It's the testosterone surge,' says Mike as we follow my father through the busy Saturday morning streets of Peterborough. 'Look, his back's straightened up, his arthritis is better. We can hardly keep up with him.'

It is true. My father is racing ahead of us, darting and dodging through the crowd with single-minded intent. He is heading for the public library to pick up his books. He walks in a kind of rapid shuffle, bending forward from the hips, hands at his sides, head stretched out in front, jaw set, peering straight ahead.

'Oh, you men are all the same. You think sex is the cure for everything.'

'It cures quite a lot of things.'

'It's funny, but when I talk about this business of my father and Valentina with my women friends, they're absolutely appalled. They see a vulnerable old man who's being exploited. Yet all the men I talk to – without any exception, Mike' (I wag my finger) 'they respond with these wry knowing smiles, these little admiring chuckles. Oh, what a lad he is. What an achievement, pulling this much younger bird. Best of luck to him. Let him have his bit of fun.'

'You must admit, it's done him good.'

'I don't admit anything.'

(It's much less satisfying arguing with Mike than with Vera or Pappa. He's always so irritatingly reasonable.)

'Are you sure you're not just being a bit puritanical?'

'Of course I'm not!' (So what if I am?) 'It's because he's my father – I just want him to be grown up.'

'He is being grown up, in his way.'

'No he's not, he's being a lad. An eighty-four-year-old lad. You're all being lads together. Wink wink. Nudge nudge. What a great pair of knockers. For goodness' sake!' My voice has risen to a shriek.

'But you can see it's doing him good, this new relationship. It's breathed new life into him. Just goes to show that you're never too old for love.'

'You mean for sex.'

'Well, maybe that as well. Your Dad is just hoping to fulfil every man's dream – to lie in the arms of a beautiful younger woman.'

'*Every* man's dream?'

That night Mike and I sleep in separate beds.

*   *   *

My father has ordered from the library several biographies of nineteenth-century engineers: John Fowler, David Greig, Charles Burrell, the Fisken brothers. Encouraged by Valentina's husband, the intelligent-type polytechnic director, he has started to research and write his great work: *A Short History of Tractors in Ukrainian*.

The first tractor was invented by a certain John Fowler, a Quaker, an intelligent and abstemious type. No vodka, beer, wine, not even tea crossed his lips, and for this reason his brain was extraordinarily clear. Some people may describe him as a genius.

Fowler was a good man, who saw in the tractor a means to emancipate the labouring masses from their life of mindless toil, and bring them to an appreciation of the spiritual life. He worked night and day to perfect his plans.

He writes in Ukrainian then translates it painstakingly into English (he studied English and German at high school) for Mike's benefit. I am surprised how good his written English is, though sometimes I have to help him with the translation.

The first tractor, which Fowler invented, was not strictly speaking a tractor at all, since it did not drag a plough. Nevertheless, it was an engine of amazing ingenuity. Fowler's tractor consisted of two engines positioned on opposite sides of the field, and connected by a looped cable, and to the cable were fixed the blades of a plough. As the engines turned, so the cable pulled the plough up and down the field, up and down. Up and down.

My father's voice drones up and down like a contented harvest bumble-bee. The room is warm and full of harvest smells. Outside the window, a purplish twilight is settling over the fields. A tractor is moving slowly up and down, already turning the burned-off stubble into the ground.

6

Wedding pictures

Despite Vera's and my efforts, Valentina and her son Stanislav came back to England on 1 March. They entered at Ramsgate, on six-month tourist visas. No one at the British Embassy in Kiev objected to their visa; no one at Ramsgate gave their passports more than a cursory examination. Once back in Peterborough, they moved in with Bob Turner. Valentina took a job at a hotel near the cathedral, and immediately went ahead with plans for the marriage to my father. This much I managed to piece together from hours of telephone conversations.

My father has tried to keep my sister and me in the dark about his plans. When we ask him a direct question he changes the subject, but he isn't a very good liar and is easily caught out. He forgets what he has told each of us, and he believes that we are still not on speaking terms. But we have started to share our information.

'Of course he sent her the eighteen hundred pounds in the end, Vera. He paid it into her bank account and she withdrew it all. And he was sending her regular payments all the time she was away.'

'Really! It's too much!' Big Sister's voice hits a note of high drama. 'That must have been most of his pension.'

'And he sent money for the coach tickets for her and Stanislav from Lviv to Ramsgate. And then she told him she needed extra money for an Austrian transit visa.'

'Of course Mother was absolutely right,' says Vera. 'He has no common sense.'

'He'll have to stop when he runs out of money.'

'Maybe. Maybe it's only just beginning.'

My father has not only rescued this beautiful destitute Ukrainian woman, but he is also in a position to foster the talents of her extraordinarily gifted son.

Stanislav, who is fourteen, has been to see an independent psychologist, who, for a modest fee, paid by my father, has tested his IQ, and written a certificate declaring him to be a genius. On the basis of this, the boy (also a very talented musician, by the way, plays piano) has been offered a place at a prestigious private school in Peterborough. (Of course he is much too intelligent for the local comprehensive, which is only fit for the sons and daughters of farm labourers.)

My sister, who paid good money to send her extraordinarily gifted daughters to a posh school, is outraged. I, who sent my own extraordinarily gifted daughter to the local comprehensive, am outraged too. Our rage bubbles merrily up and down the telephone lines. We have something in common at last.

And another thing. As Romeo and Juliet found to their cost, marriage is never just about two people falling in love, it is about families. Vera and I do not want Valentina in our family.

'Let's face it,' says Vera. 'We don't want someone so *common*' (*I* didn't say it!) 'to carry our name.'

'Oh, come on, Vera. Our family is not *un*common. We're just an ordinary family, like everybody else.'

I have started to challenge Big Sis's self-appointed guardianship of the family story. She doesn't like it.

'We come from solid bourgeois people, Nadezhda. Not *arrivistes*.'

'But the Ocheretkos were – what? Wealthy peasants . . .'

'Farmers.'

'. . . turned horse-dealers.'

'Horse-*breeders*.'

'Cossacks, anyway. A bit wild, you might say.'

'Colourful.'

'And the Mayevskyjs were teachers.'

'Grandfather Mayevskyj was Minister of Education.'

'But only for six months. And of a country that didn't really exist.'

'Of course Free Ukraine existed. Really, Nadia, why must you take such a *downbeat* view of everything? Do you think you are some kind of handmaid of history?'

'No, but . . .' (Of course this is exactly what I think.)

'When I was a little girl . . .' Her voice softens. I hear her fumbling for a cigarette. 'When I was a little girl, Baba Sonia used to tell me the story of her wedding. Now *that's* what a wedding should be like, not this pitiful charade that our father is being dragged through.'

'But just look at the dates, Vera. The bride was four months pregnant.'

'They were in love.'

What's this? Is Big Sis a closet romantic?

*   *   *

Mother's mother, Sonia Blazhko, was eighteen when she married Mitrofan Ocheretko in the gold-domed Cathedral of St Michael in Kiev. She wore a white dress and a veil, and a pretty gold locket hung around her neck. Her long brown hair was crowned with white flowers. Despite her slim build, she must have been visibly pregnant. Her oldest brother Pavel Blazhko, railway engineer, later friend of Lenin, gave her away, for her father was too frail to stand through the service. Her older sister Shura, recently qualified as a doctor, was maid of honour. Her two younger sisters, still at school, pelted her with rose petals, and burst into tears when she kissed the groom.

The Ocheretko men strode into the church in their riding-boots, embroidered shirts and outlandish baggy trousers. The women wore wide swinging skirts and boots with little heels and coloured ribbons in their hair. They stood together in a fierce bunch at the back of the church and left abruptly at the end without tipping the priest.

The Blazhkos looked down on the groom's family, whom they thought uncouth, little more than brigands, who drank too much and never combed their hair. The Ocheretkos thought the Blazhkos were prissy urbanites and traitors to the land. Sonia and Mitrofan didn't care what their parents thought. They had already consummated their love, and its fruit was on her way.

*   *   *

'Of course it was pulled down in 1935.'
  'What was?'
  'St Michael of the Golden Domes.'

'Who pulled it down?'

'The communists of course.'

Ha! So there is a subtext to this romantic story.

'Pappa and Valentina are in love, Vera.'

'How can you talk such nonsense, Nadia? Will you never grow up? Look, she's after a passport and a work permit, and what little money he has left. That's clear enough. And he's just mesmerised by her boobs. He talks of nothing else.'

'He talks about tractors a lot.'

'Tractors and boobs. There you have it.'

(Why does she hate him so much?)

'And what about our mother and father – do you think they were in love when they married? Don't you think that was, in its way, a marriage of convenience?'

'That was different. It was a different time,' says Vera. 'In times like that people did what they had to in order to survive. Poor Mother – after all she went through, to end up with Pappa. What a cruel fate!'

*   *   *

In 1930, when my mother was eighteen, her father was arrested. It was still several years before the purges were to reach their terrible climax, but it happened in the classic way of the Terror – a knock on the door in the middle of the night, the children screaming, my grandmother Sonia Ocheretko in her nightdress, her loose hair streaming down her back, pleading with the officers.

'Don't worry, don't worry!' my grandfather called over his shoulder as they bundled him away with just the clothes he stood up in. 'I'll be back in the morning.' They never saw him again. He was taken to the military prison in Kiev, where he was charged with secretly training Ukrainian Nationalist combatants. Was it true? We will never know. He never stood trial.

Every day for six months Ludmilla and her brother and sister would accompany their mother to the prison with a bundle of food. They handed it to the guard at the gate, hoping that at least some of it would get through to their father. One day the guard said: 'There's no need to come tomorrow. He won't be needing your food any more.'

They were lucky. In the later years of the purges, not only the criminal, but his family, friends, associates, anyone who could be suspected of complicity in his crime, would be sent away for correction. Ocheretko was executed, but his family was spared. Still, it was no longer safe for them to stay in Kiev. Ludmilla was expelled from her veterinary course at the university – she was now the daughter of an enemy of the people. Her brother and sister were removed from their school. They moved back to the *khutor* and tried to scratch a living.

And that was not easy. Although the Poltava farmland is some of the most fertile in the whole of the Soviet Union, the peasants faced starvation. In the autumn of 1932 the army seized the entire harvest. Even the seed corn for next year's planting was taken.

Mother said that the purpose of the famine was to break the spirit of the people and force them to accept collectivisation.

Stalin believed that the peasant mentality, which was narrow, covetous and superstitious, would be replaced by a noble, comradely, proletarian spirit. ('What wicked nonsense,' said Mother. 'The only spirit was to preserve one's own life. Eat. Eat. Tomorrow there may be nothing.')

The peasants ate their cows, chickens and goats, then their cats and dogs; then rats and mice; then there was nothing left to eat but grass. Between seven and ten million people died across Ukraine during the man-made famine of 1932–3.

Sonia Ocheretko was a survivor. She made watery soup from grass and wild sorrel that they gathered from the fields. She dug for roots of horseradish, and tuberous artichokes, and found a few potatoes in the garden. When those ran out they trapped and ate the rats that lived in the thatch of their roof, then the thatch itself, and they chewed on harness leather to quell the hunger pangs. When they were too hungry to sleep, they used to sing:

> 'There is a tall hill, and beneath it a meadow,
> A green meadow, so abundant
> You would think you were in paradise.'

In the next village, there was a woman who had eaten her baby. She had gone mad, and wandered through the lanes crying, 'But she died first. She was dead. What harm to eat? So plump! Why waste? I didn't kill! No! No! No! She died first.'

They were saved by the remoteness of their *khutor* – if anyone thought about them at all, they probably thought they were already dead. In 1933 they somehow obtained a travel permit and made the long journey to Luhansk, soon to be renamed Voroshilovgrad, where Sonia's sister Shura lived.

Shura was a doctor, six years older than Sonia. She had a dry sense of humour, dyed red hair, a taste for extravagant hats, a rattling laugh (she smoked hand-rolled cigarettes made with home-grown tobacco) and an elderly husband – a Party member and a friend of Marshal Voroshilov – who could pull strings. They lived in an old-fashioned wooden house on the edge of town, with carved eaves, blue-painted shutters, and sunflowers and tobacco plants in the garden. Shura had no children of her own, and fussed over Sonia's. When Sonia found a teaching job and moved into a small flat in town with the two younger children, Ludmilla stayed with Aunty Shura. Aunty Shura's husband found her a job in the locomotive factory in Luhansk, where she was to be trained as a crane operator. Ludmilla was reluctant. What did she want with cranes?

'Do it, do it,' urged Aunty Shura. 'You will become a proletarian.'

At first, mastery of those mighty machines that swung and turned at her command was thrilling. Then it became routine. Then deadly boring. She dreamed once more of becoming a vet. Animals smelled of life, and were warm to the touch, more exciting to handle and subdue than a mere machine that could be operated with levers. ('What a poor thing is the crane or the tractor compared to a horse, Nadia!') Veterinary surgeons at that time worked only with big animals – animals that had value – cows, bulls, horses. ('Just imagine, Nadia, these English people will spend one hundred pound to save the life of a cat or dog that can be pick up in street for nothing. Such foolish kind hearts!')

She wrote to the Institute in Kiev, and was sent a bundle of forms to fill in, asking her to detail her and her parents' and her grandparents' occupations – their position in the class structure. Only those from the working class were to study at university now. She sent the forms off with a heavy heart, and was not surprised to hear nothing. She was twenty-three, and it seemed as though her life had reached a dead end. Then a letter came from that strange boy she had been at school with.

*   *   *

Weddings, like funerals, provide the perfect arena for family drama: there are the rituals, symbolic costumes, and every opportunity for snobbery in its many guises. According to Vera, my father's family disapproved of the Ocheretkos. The girl, Ludmilla, was pretty enough, said Baba Nadia, but rather wild; and it was unfortunate, to say the least, that her father was an 'enemy of the people'.

Baba Sonia, for her part, found my father's family pretentious and peculiar. The Mayevskyjs were part of the small Ukrainian intelligentsia. Grandfather Mayevskyj, Nikolai's father, was a very tall man with flowing white hair and little half-glasses. In the brief flowering of Ukrainian independence in 1918 he was even Minister for Education for six months. After Stalin came to power and all ideas of Ukrainian autonomy were stamped out, he became the head teacher of the Ukrainian language school in Kiev, operating on voluntary subscription and under constant pressure from the authorities.

It was at this school that my mother and father first met. They were in the same form. Nikolai was always the first boy to put his hand up, always top of the class. Ludmilla thought him an insufferable know-all.

Nikolai Mayevskyj and Ludmilla Ocheretko were married in the register office in Luhansk in the autumn of 1936. They were twenty-four years old. There were no golden domes or bells or flowers. The ceremony was conducted by a plump female party official in a bottle-green suit and a not-very-clean white blouse. The bride was not pregnant and nobody cried, even though there was much more to cry about.

*   *   *

Did they love each other?

No, says Vera, she married him because she needed a way out.

Yes, says my father, she was the loveliest woman I had met, and the most spirited. You should see her dark eyes when she was in a rage. On the skating rink she glided like a queen. To see her on horseback was a wonder.

Whether they loved each other or not, they stayed together for sixty years.

'So, Pappa, what do you remember about Ludmilla? Tell me, what was she like when you first met?' (I am attempting some reminiscence therapy. I somehow hope that filling his mind with images of my mother will blot out the interloper.) 'Was it love at first sight? Was she very beautiful?'

'Yes, indeed. Quite beautiful in every way. But of course not as beautiful as Valentina.'

There he sits with a small secret smile on his face, wisps of silver hair straggling on to his frayed collar, his spectacles repaired with brown parcel tape balanced on the end of his nose so that I can't quite see his eyes, his hands swollen with arthritis cradling a mug of tea. I want to grab it from him and dash it in his face. But I realise that he has no idea, no idea at all, of the effect his words might have on me.

'Did you love her?' (I mean did he love her *more*.)

'Ah, love! What thing is love! No one can understand. On this point, science must concede to poetry.'

*   *   *

My father doesn't invite us to the wedding, but he lets slip the date. 'No need to visit now. Everything is OK. You can come after June first,' he says.

'We've got four weeks to stop her,' says my sister.

But I hesitate. I am touched by his joy, his new vitality. Also, I am mindful of Mike's opinion.

'Maybe it'll be OK. Maybe she'll look after him, and make him happy in his last years. It's better than going into a home.'

'For goodness' sake, Nadia. You don't think that kind of woman will be around when he's old and dribbling and incontinent. She'll take what she can, and be off.'

'But let's face it, neither you nor I are going to look after him in his old age, are we?' (Best to get it out into the open, even though the bluntness of it smarts.)

'I did what I could for Mother. Towards Father I feel a sense of obligation: nothing more.'

'He isn't so easy to love.' I'm not trying to sound accusing, but that's the way she takes it.

70

'Love has got nothing to do with it. I'll do my duty, Nadezhda. As I sincerely hope you will. Even if that means saving him from making an absolute idiot of himself.'

'It's true I couldn't look after him full-time, Vera. We'd argue all the time. It would drive me mad. But I want him to be all right – to be happy. If Valentina makes him happy . . .'

'It's not about happiness, Nadezhda, it's about money. Can't you see? I suppose with your leftish ideas you would welcome anyone who wanted to come and rip off hard-working people.'

'Leftish doesn't come into it. It's about what's best for him.' (Smug voice. See? *I* am not a fascist like my sister.)

'Of course it is. Of course it is. Did I ever suggest otherwise?'

*   *   *

My sister rings the Home Office again. They tell her she must put it in writing. She writes again, anonymously. She telephones the register office where their wedding will be recorded. The registrar gives her a sympathetic hearing.

'But you know, at the end of the day if he's determined to go ahead with it, there's absolutely nothing I can do,' the registrar says.

'But the divorce from her husband in Ukraine – it came through just like that at the last minute. And after they were divorced, she went back to stay with him.'

'I'll check the paperwork, but if it's all in order . . .'

'What about the translation? She had to have it translated at the last minute at an agency in London. They might have confused a decree absolute with a decree nisi.' My sister is an expert on divorce.

'Of course I'll look at it closely. But I don't read Ukrainian. I have to take it at its face value. He's an adult.'

'He's not behaving like one.'

'Ah, well.'

She sounded like a typical social worker bureaucrat, my sister tells me. She will do her best, but of course she must stay within the rules.

We have flights of imagination in which we turn up at the wedding, sneaking in half-way through the service, while the couple are at the altar.

'I will wear my black suit,' says Vera, 'which I wore to Mother's funeral. At the point when the priest says, "... *and if anyone knows of any just cause or lawful impediment* . . . ?" we will shout out from the back . . .' (I've always wanted to do that.)

'But what would we say?' I ask my sister.

We are both stumped.

*   *   *

My father and Valentina were married on 1 June at the Church of the Immaculate Conception, for Valentina is a Catholic. My father is an atheist, but he humours her. (It's natural for women to be irrational, he says.)

He has given her £500 for a wedding dress: cream polyester silk, tightly fitting around the waist and hips, with a plunging neckline trimmed in frilled lace, through which we catch a glimpse of those modestly nestled Botticellian breasts. (I have seen the wedding pictures.) I can just imagine how he fusses around to make sure the photographer he has hired gets the best angle. He wants to show her off, his trophy, to all those gossipy doubters who scorned her. She needs the photo for the immigration officials.

The priest was a young Irishman who, says my father, looked like a teenager with spots and sticking-up hair. What did he make of this oddly assorted couple as he blessed their union? Did he know that the bride was a divorcée? Did he feel just a twinge of unease? The Zadchuks, her only Ukrainian friends, are also Catholics from western Ukraine. All the other Ukrainians in the congregation, my mother's friends invited to the wedding by my father, are Orthodox from the east. I suppose the youth and spottiness of the priest confirmed all their suspicions about Catholicism.

Her uncle from Selby is in the group picture, and Stanislav, and some friends she met at work. They have that smug dressed-up look of people brazening out a sham. Bob Turner is not there.

After the wedding, people who some two years ago sat in our front room after my mother's funeral, now come back to the house again to toast the happy couple in vodka, nibble Tesco-bought snacks and talk about . . . I don't know, I wasn't there. But I can imagine the gossip, the scandal. Half his age. Look at her bosom – how she waves it under a man's nose. Greasepaint on her face. The old man making a fool of himself. The shame of it.

7

Crap car

It's three weeks after the wedding, and I still haven't met my new stepmother.

'So when can we come and meet the lucky bride?' I ask my father.

'Not yet. Not yet.'

'But when?'

'Not yet.'

'Why not yet?'

'She isn't here yet.'

'Not there? Where is she?'

'Never mind where is she. Not here.'

Stubborn old man. He won't tell me anything. But I find out anyway. I trick him.

'What kind of a wife is that? Won't even live with her husband?'

'Soon she will come. In three weeks. When Stanislav's school finishes.'

'What difference does it make when school term finishes? If she loved you she would be here right now.'

'But his house is right next to the school. It is more convenient for Stanislav.'

'Hall Street? Where Bob Turner lives? So she's still with Bob Turner?'

'Yes. No. But the relationship is quite Platonic now. She has assured me.' (He pronounces it with three syllables – a-shoo-red.)

Fool. Taken for a ride. No point in arguing with him now.

It's mid-August, and hot, by the time we go to visit. The fields are humming with combine harvesters that crawl up and down like great cockroaches. Some fields have already been harvested, and the huge round hay bales, wrapped in black polythene, lie randomly among the stubble like broken bits of giant machines – nothing picturesque about these Cambridge-shire harvests. The mechanical hedge cutters have already been out, slashing back the dog roses and brambles that crowd the hedgerows. Soon it will be time for stubble-burning in the cornfields, and potato and pea fields will be sprayed with chemical defoliants.

My mother's garden, however, is still a refuge for birds and insects. The trees are heavy with fruit – not ripe yet, give you tummy-ache – and wasps and flies are already gorging themselves on the windfalls, while greedy finches feast on gnats, blackbirds dig for grubs and fat buzzing bumble-bees thrust themselves into the open labia of foxgloves. Roses pink and red battle it out with bindweed in the flower-beds. The downstairs dining-room window that overlooks the garden is open and my father is sitting there with his glasses on and a book on his knees. There's a tablecloth on the table instead of newspaper, and some plastic flowers in a vase.

'Hi, Pappa.' I lean forward and kiss his cheek. Stubbly.

'Hi, Dyid,' says Anna.

'Hi, Nikolai,' says Mike.

'Aha. Very nice you come. Nadia. Anushka. Michael.'

Hugs all round. He looks well.

'How are you getting on with your book, then, Dyid?' asks Anna. She adores her grandfather, and thinks he is a genius. And for her sake I gloss over his peculiarities, his distasteful sexual awakening, his lapses of personal hygiene.

'Good. Good. I am soon coming to most interesting part. Development of caterpillar track. Significant moment in history of mankind.'

'Shall I put the kettle on, Pappa?'

'So tell me about the caterpillars,' says Anna without irony.

'Aha! You see in prehistoric times, great stones were moved on wooden rollers made out of tree-trunks. Look.' On the table he lines up a row of sharp-pointed 2H pencils, and puts a book on top of them. 'Some men are pushing the stone, but others – after the stone has passed over the roller – they must pick up the tree from the back of the stone and run round to put it in the front. In caterpillar track, this movement of rollers is done through chains and linkages.'

Pappa, Anna and Mike take turns pushing the book over the pencils, and moving the pencils from the back to the front, faster and faster.

I go into the kitchen and prepare teacups on a tray, pour milk into a jug and hunt for biscuits. So where is she? Is she at home? Is she still hiding from us? Then I see her – a large blonde woman, sauntering down the garden towards us on high-heeled peep-toe mules. Her gait is lazy, contemptuous, as though she can barely be bothered to stir herself to greet us. A denim mini-skirt rides high above her knees; a pink sleeveless top stretches around voluptuous breasts that bob up and down as she walks. I stare. Such a wanton expanse of dimpled, creamy flesh. Plump bordering on fat. As she comes closer I see that her hair, which tumbles Bardot-style in a tousled pony-tail over bare shoulders, is bleached, showing an inch of brown at the roots. A broad, handsome face. High cheekbones. Flared nostrils. Eyes wide set, golden brown like syrup, and outlined in black Cleopatra lines that flick up at the corners. The mouth curls into a pout that is almost a sneer, drawn in pale peach-pink lipstick that extends beyond the line of the lips, as though to exaggerate their fullness.

Tart. Bitch. Cheap slut. This woman who has taken the place of my mother. I stretch my hand out and bare my teeth in a smile.

'Hallo, Valentina. How nice to meet you at last.'

Her hand in mine is cold, limp, no grip. The long fingernails are varnished in peach-pink pearlised nail-polish to match the lips. I see myself through her eyes – small, skinny, dark, no bust. Not a real woman. She smiles at Mike, a slow, wicked smile.

'You like vodka?'

'I've made a pot of tea,' I say.

My father's eyes are fixed on her as she moves about the room.

When I was sixteen my father forbade me to wear make-up. He made me go upstairs and wash it off before I could go out.

'Nadia, if all women were to wear paint on their faces, just think, there could be no more natural selection. The inevitable result would be the uglification of the species. You wouldn't want that to happen, would you?'

Such an intellectual. Why couldn't he be like normal fathers, and just say he didn't like it? Now look at him drooling over this painted Russian tart. Or maybe he is now so short-sighted he can't see that she is wearing make-up. He probably thinks she was born with pale peach pearlised lips and black Cleopatra flick-ups at the corners of her eyes.

Now another figure appears in the doorway, a boy in his teens. A bit on the plump side, childish freckled face, chipped front tooth, curly brown hair, round glasses.

'You must be Stanislav,' I gush.

'Yes I am.' Charming chipped-tooth smile.

'Lovely to meet you. I've heard so much about you. Let's all have some tea.'

Anna looks him up and down, but her face gives nothing away. He is younger than she is, and therefore of no interest.

We sit awkwardly around the table. Stanislav is the only one who appears to be relaxed. He tells us about his school, his favourite teacher, his least favourite teacher, his favourite football team, his favourite pop group, his waterproof sports watch which he lost at Lake Balaton, his new Nike trainers, his favourite food, which is pasta, his concern that the other kids will tease him if he gets fat, the party he went to on Saturday, his friend Gary's new puppy. His voice is confident, pleasantly inflected, his accent delightful. He is perfectly at ease. No one else says anything. The heavy weight of all the unsaid things bears down on us like storm clouds. Outside, a few drops of rain fall and we hear thunder in the distance. My father closes the window. Stanislav carries on talking.

After tea I take the cups to the sink to wash up, but Valentina gestures me away. She pulls on rubber gloves over her plump peach-pearl-tipped fingers, puts on a frilly apron, and whips up a lather in the bowl.

'I do,' she says. 'You go.'

'We go to cemetery,' says my father.

'I'll come with you,' says Stanislav.

'No Stanislav, please, stay and help your mother.'

He will be telling us about his favourite graveyards next.

When we get back from the cemetery, we have another cup of tea, and then it's dinner time. Valentina will cook for us, my father says; she is a good cook. We sit around the table and wait. Stanislav tells us about a game of football in which he scored twice. Mike, Anna and I smile politely. My father beams with pride. Meanwhile Valentina puts on her frilly apron and busies herself in the kitchen. She reheats six ready-cooked chilled meals, roast meat slices in gravy with peas and potatoes, and places them on the table with a flourish.

We eat in silence. You can hear the scraping of the knives on the plates as we tackle the stringy reheated meat. Even Stanislav shuts up for a few minutes. When he gets to the peas, my father starts to cough. The skins catch in his throat. I pour him water.

'Delicious,' says Mike, looking round for assent. We all murmur in agreement.

Valentina beams triumphantly.

'I make modern cooking, not peasant cooking.'

After dinner there is raspberry-ripple ice-cream from the freezer.

'My favourite,' says Stanislav with a little giggle.

He tells us his order of preference for ice-cream flavours.

My father has been rummaging in a drawer, and now comes up with a sheaf of papers. It is the latest chapter of his book, which I have helped him to translate. He wants to read it to Mike, and to Valentina and Stanislav.

'You will learn something about the history of our beloved motherland.'

But Stanislav suddenly remembers that he has some home-work to catch up on, Anna has walked into the village to buy some milk, and Valentina is detained on the telephone in the next room, so it is just Mike and I who sit with him in the wide-windowed sitting-room.

In the history of Ukraina, the tractor has played a contradictory role. In former times, Ukraina was a country of peasant farmers. For such a country to develop the full potential of her agriculture, mechanisation is absolutely essential. But the method by which such mechanisation was introduced was truly terrible.

His voice has become heavy, dragging along all the unwritten and unspoken words that are compressed into the words he is reading.

After the Revolution of 1917, Russia started to become an industrial country with a growing urban proletariat. This proletariat was to be recruited from the rural peasants. But if the peasants were to leave the countryside, how would the urban population be fed?

Stalin's answer to this dilemma was to decree that the country-side must be industrialised too. So in place of peasant smallhold-ings, all land was collectivised into great farms, organised on the factory principle. The name for this was Kolkhoz, meaning collective husbandry. Nowhere was the principle of Kolkhoz applied more rigorously than in Ukraina. Where the peasant farmers used horses or oxen to plough, the kolkhoz was ploughed by the iron horse, as the first tractors were called. Crudely built, unreliable, with slatted iron wheels and no tyres, these early tractors could still do the work of twenty men.

The coming of the tractor was also of symbolic importance, for it made possible the ploughing up of boundary lands which separated the individual peasant strips, creating one large kolkhoz. Thus it heralded the end of the whole class of kulaks, those peasants who owned their own land, and were seen by Stalin as the enemy of the revolution. The iron horse destroyed the traditional pattern of village life, but the tractor industry in Ukraina flourished. However, the kolkhozy were not as efficient, and this is largely due to resistance from the peasants, who either refused to take part in the kolkhoz, or continued to cultivate their own plots on the side.

The retribution of Stalin was ruthless. Hunger was the tool he used. In 1932 the entire harvest of Ukraina was seized and transported to Moscow and Leningrad to feed the proletariat in the factories – how else was the revolution to be sustained? Butter and grain from Ukraina were on sale in Paris and Berlin, and well-meaning people in the West marvelled at this miracle of Soviet productivity. But in Ukrainian villages the people starved.

This is the great unrecorded tragedy of our history, which only now is coming to light . . .

He stops, and gathers together his papers quietly. His glasses are perched low on his nose, the lenses so thick I can hardly see his eyes, but I fancy I catch a glint of tears. In the silence that follows, I can hear Valentina still chatting on the phone next door, and a faint beat of music coming from Stanislav's room. In the distance, the clock on the village church strikes seven.

'Well done, Nikolai,' Mike applauds. 'Stalin had a lot to answer for.'

'Well done, Pappa.' My applause is more grudging than Mike's. All this Ukrainian nationalism bothers me – it seems outdated and irrelevant. Peasants in the fields, folk-songs at harvest, the motherland: what has all this got to do with me? I am a post-modern woman. I know about structuralism. I have a husband who cooks polenta. So why do I feel this unexpected emotional tug?

The back door clicks. Anna has come back. Valentina finishes her telephone conversation, and slips in to join in the applause, tapping her pearl-tipped fingertips delicately together. She smiles with satisfaction, as though she is person-ally responsible for this literary masterpiece, and kisses him on the nose. *'Holubchik!'* Little pigeon. My father glows.

Then it's time for us to go home. We all shake hands and put on an unconvincing display of cheek-pecking. The visit is deemed a success.

*   *   *

'So what was she like?' my sister asks, over the phone.

I describe the mini-skirt, the hair, the make-up. My tone is neutral, disciplined.

'Oh my God! I knew it!' Vera cries.

(And how I am enjoying my bitch-fest! What has happened to me? I used to be a feminist. Now I seem to be turning into Mrs *Daily Mail*.)

I tell her about the washing-up gloves, the pink-pearl-tipped fingers.

'Yes, Yes. I see everything.' Her voice wobbles with rage.

Our mother's hands were brown and rough from gardening and cooking. 'I can see what kind of woman she is. He has married a tart!' (*I* didn't say it!)

'But Vera, you can't judge someone by how they dress.' (Ha! Look how rational and grown up *I* am!) 'Anyway, that style of dress doesn't mean the same in Ukraine – it signifies a rejection of the peasant past, that's all.'

'Nadia, how can you be so naïve?'

'Not at all, Vera. I had a Ukrainian sociology professor visiting last year and she looked exactly like that. And she was upset that most of my friends wore no make-up and went around in jeans or tracksuit bottoms, when she yearned for designer clothes. She said it was a betrayal of womanliness.'

'Well, yes.'

My sister would rather be dead than be seen in jeans (apart from designer jeans of course) or tracksuit bottoms. Then again, she would rather be dead than be seen in high-heeled peep-toe mules and a denim mini-skirt.

I tell her about the pre-cooked chilled meal. We are on common ground here. 'The sad thing is, he probably doesn't notice the difference,' she murmurs. 'Poor Mother.'

*   *   *

The first crisis of their marriage comes shortly after our visit. Valentina is demanding a new car – not just any old car, either. Must be good car. Must be Mercedes or Jaguar at least. BMW is OK. No Ford please. The car will be used to drive Stanislav to his posh school, where other children are driven in Saabs and Range Rovers. My father has seen a second-hand Ford Fiesta in good condition, which he can afford. Valentina will not tolerate a Ford Fiesta. She will not even tolerate a Ford Escort. There is a blazing row.

'Tell me what you think, Nadezhda.' He phones me in an agitated state.

'I think the Ford Fiesta sounds just right.' (I drive a Ford Escort.)

'But she will not tolerate it.'

'Well, do what you like.' He will anyway.

My father has a bit of money in the bank. It is his Pensioners Bond, which matures in three years' time, but what the hell, the lady wants a new car and he wants to be generous. They settle on an old Rover, large enough to satisfy Valentina's aspirations, old enough for my father to afford. He cashes in his Pensioners Bond and gives most of it to Valentina for the car. He gives the £200 that is left to my daughter Anna, who has just passed her 'A' levels with flying colours, to help her on her way to university. I feel bad about this, but not too bad. I tell myself that if he didn't give it to Anna for university, he would only give it to Valentina for a Mercedes.

'It is to make up the difference from the codicil,' he says, 'this money will not be for Vera's daughters, only for Anna.'

I am uneasy, because I know Big Sister will hit the roof. But I want revenge for the codicil.

'That's great, Pappa. She'll need it when she goes to university.'

Now he is spent up – he has no money left.

Anna is thrilled when I tell her about her grandfather's gift.

'Oh! He's so cute. I wonder if he gave some to Alice and Lexy when they went to uni?'

'I expect so.'

Valentina is delighted with the Rover. It is sleek, shiny, metallic green in colour, with a 3-litre engine, leather seats that smell of expensive cigars, a walnut dashboard and 186,000 miles on the clock. They ride around town and park up beside the Saabs and the Range Rovers outside Stanislav's school. Valentina holds an international driver's licence issued in Ternopil, which is valid for a year. She has never taken a driving test, says my father, but she paid for the licence in pork cutlets from her mother's smallholding. They go to visit the Zadchuks and her friend Charlotte, and the uncle in Selby. Then the car breaks down. The clutch is shot. My father telephones.

'Nadezhda, please will you lend me a hundred pounds for repairs. Until I get my pension.'

'Pappa,' I say, 'you should have bought the Ford Fiesta.'

I send him a cheque.

Then he phones my sister. She phones me.

'What's going on with this car?'

'I don't know.'

'He wanted to borrow a hundred pounds to mend the brakes. I said to him, can't Valentina pay for it out of her earnings? She's earning enough.'

'So what did he say?'

'He won't hear of it. He's afraid to ask her. He says she needs to send money back to Ukraine for her sick mother. Can you imagine.' Her voice is crisp with irritation. 'Each time I criticise her he just springs to her defence.'

'Maybe he still loves her.' (I am still a romantic.)

85

'Yes, I suppose he does. I suppose he does.' She sighs a worldly sigh. 'Men are so stupid.'

'Mrs Zadchuk told her it was the husband's duty to pay for the wife's car.'

'Duty? How lovely! How quaint! He told you that?'

'He asked me what I thought. Apparently being a feminist makes me an authority on the rights of wives.' I'm not sure what my sister thinks of feminism.

'Our mother never liked the Zadchuks, did she?' Vera muses.

'I think it's his pride. He can't ask a woman for money. He thinks the man should be the provider.'

'He's just asked you and me, Nadezhda.'

'But we're not proper women, are we?'

Mike rings him up. They have a long conversation about the merits and drawbacks of hydraulic braking systems. They are on the phone for fifty minutes. Mike is silent most of the time, but occasionally he says, 'Mmm. Mmm.'

*   *   *

A month later there is another crisis. Valentina's sister is arriving from Ukraine. She is coming to see for herself the good life in the West that Valentina has described in her letters – the elegant modern house, the fabulous car, the wealthy widower husband. She must be met at Heathrow by car. My father says the Rover will not make it to London and back. Oil is leaking from the engine and fluid from the brakes. The engine smokes. One of the seats has collapsed. Rust has bubbled up through the dealer's patch and polish. Stanislav sums up the problem.

'Auto ne prestijeskiy.' He says it with that little sweet smile that is half-way to a sneer.

Valentina turns on my father.

'You no good man. You plenty-money meanie. Promise money. Money sit in bank. Promise car. Crap car.'

'You demand prestigious car. Prestijeskiy auto. Looks prestigious; doesn't go. Ha ha.'

'Crap car. Crap husband. Thphoo!' she spits.

'Where you learning this new "crap" word?' demands my father. He isn't used to being bossed about. He's used to getting his own way, to being wheedled and coaxed.

'You engineer. Why you no mending car? Crap engineer.'

My father has dismantled and reassembled engines in the garage for as long as I can remember. But he can't get down under the car any more: his arthritis won't let him.

'Tell your sister she is coming by train,' my father answers back. 'Train. Plane. All modern transport is better. Crap car. Of course is crap car. You wanted. Now you have.'

And there is another problem. Crap cooker. The cooker in the kitchen, which has been there since my mother's time, is getting old. Only two of the three rings will work, and the oven timer is gone, though the oven itself still works. On this cooker, heavenly delights of culinary art have been prepared for more than thirty years, but this will not impress Valentina's sister. The cooker is electric, and everyone but a fool knows that electricity is not as prestigious as gas. Did not Lenin himself admit that communism was socialism plus electricity?

My father agrees to buy a new cooker. He likes spending money, but he has no money left. The cooker will have to be bought on hire purchase. He has seen a special offer at the Co-op. Valentina puts Nikolai into crap car and drives him into town to buy prestigious cooker. Must be gas. Must be brown. Alas, the brown cooker is not included in the special offer. It costs twice as much.

'Look, Valenka, is exactly same cooker. Same knobs. Same gas. Same everything.'

'In former Soviet Union all cookers are white. Crap cookers.'

'But everything in kitchen is white – washing machine white, fridge white, freezer white, cupboards white – tell me what point is to having a brown cooker?'

'You plenty-money meanie. You want give me crap cooker.'

'My wife is cooking on her thirty years. Better than you cooking.'

'You wife peasant Baba. Peasant Baba, peasant cooking. For civilised person, cooker must be gas, must be brown.' She says this slowly and with emphasis, as if repeating a basic lesson to a nincompoop.

My father signs the hire purchase agreement for a civilised person's cooker. He has never borrowed money before in his life, and the illicit thrill makes him giddy with excitement. When Mother was alive, money was saved in a toffee tin hidden under a loose floorboard beneath the lino, and only when enough money was saved was anything purchased. Always in cash. Always at the Co-op. The Co-op stamps were stuck in a book, and this was kept under the floorboard too. In later years, when Mother discovered you could get interest if you put money in the building society, the building society deposits still started off as cash under the floorboard.

Another problem: the house is dirty. Crap Hoover. The vintage Hoover Junior is not picking up properly. Valentina has seen an advertisement for a civilised person's Hoover. Blue. Cylinder. See, no pushing about. Just suck, suck, suck. My father signs another hire purchase agreement.

My father told me this, so naturally he told me his side of the story. Maybe there is another version of events that is more favourable to Valentina. If so, I don't want to hear it. I imagine my father, bent and frail, shaking with impotent rage, and my heart fills up with righteous anger.

'Look, Pappa, you must stand up to her. Just tell her she can't have everything she wants.'

'Hmm,' he says. '*Tak*.' He says yes, but his voice lacks conviction. He likes to grumble to a sympathetic audience, but he won't do anything about it.

'She has unrealistic expectations, Pappa.'

'But for this she cannot be blamed. She believes all Western propaganda.'

'Well she'll just have to learn, won't she?' Acid in my voice.

'But still, better you not talk to Vera about this.'

'Of course not.' (I can't wait!)

'You see, Nadezhda, she is not a bad person. She has some incorrect ideas. Not her fault.'

'We'll see.'

'Nadezhda . . .'

'What?'

'You are not talking about this with Vera.'

'Why not?'

'She will laugh. She will say I have told you so.'

'I'm sure she won't.' (I know she will.)

'You know this Vera, what a type she is.'

Despite myself, I feel myself getting sucked into the drama, and back into my childhood. It has a hold of me. Just like civilised person's Hoover. Suck, suck, suck. And I am dragged up into the dustbag of the past, full of clotted greying memories, where everything is formless, indistinct, lumpy with obscure gobs of matter shrouded in ancient dust – dust everywhere, drowning me, burying me alive, filling my lungs and my eyes until I cannot see, cannot breathe, can barely cry out,

'Pappa! Why are you always so angry with Vera? What did she do?'

'Ah, that Vera. She was always autocrat, even when baby. Clinging to Ludmilla with fists of steel. Grip tight. Suck, suck, suck. Such a temper. Crying. Screaming.'

'Pappa, she was only a baby. She couldn't help it.'

'Hmm.'

My heart cries out, 'You should love us. You're supposed to love us, no matter how bad we are! That's what *normal* parents do!' But I can't say it aloud. And anyway, he can't help it, can he? Growing up with Baba Nadia with her thin soups and strict punishments.

'None of us can help how we are,' I say.

'Hmm. Of course this question of psychological' (he pronounces both consonants: p, s) 'determinism is very interesting to discuss. Leibniz, for example, who by the way was a founder of the modern mathematics, believed that all was determined in the moment of creation.'

'Pappa . . .'

'*Tak tak*. And smoking all the time. Smoking even by Milla's death-bed. What a powerful tyrant is a cigarette.' He realises my patience is running thin. 'Did I ever tell you, Nadia, that I almost died from cigarettes?'

Is this a crude changing-the-subject ploy? Or has he become completely unhinged?

'I didn't know you smoked.'

Neither of my parents smoked. Not only that, but they had kicked up such a dreadful fuss when I started smoking at the age of fifteen that I never got completely hooked, and gave up a few years later, having made my point.

'Ha! It was because I did not smoke that cigarettes saved my life, and for the same reason, they almost cost me my life.' He shifts his voice into an easy narrative gear. He is in control now, driving his tractor across the crumbling furrows of the past. 'You see, in that German labour camp where we found ourselves at ending of war, cigarettes were a currency followed by everybody. When we worked we got paid: so much bread, so much fat, so many cigarettes. So any person who did not smoke his cigarettes could exchange them for food, clothing, even luxuries such as soap or blankets. Because of cigarettes, we always had enough to eat, were always warm. That was how we survived through war.' He fixes his eyes on a spot behind my head. 'Vera, unfortunately, is now of course a smoker. Has she told you about her first encounter with cigarettes?'

'No, she didn't tell me anything. What do you mean?' My mind had wandered during his ramble. Now I realise I should have been paying attention. 'What happened with Vera and the cigarettes?'

There is a long silence.

'Can't remember.' He looks sideways out of the window and starts to cough. 'Did I tell you, Nadia, about the boilers of these ships, how gigantic they were?'

'Never mind about the boilers, Pappa. Please finish what you were saying about the cigarettes. What happened?'

'Can't remember. No point to remember. Too much in the past . . .'

Of course he can remember, but he won't say.

*   *   *

Valentina's sister arrives. She is met at Heathrow by a man from the village, who has been paid fifty pounds by my father to drive down to London in his Ford Fiesta and bring her back. She is not blonde, like Valentina, but dark and elaborately coiffed with a bunch of little ringlets on her nape. She wears a real fur coat and patent leather shoes, and her mouth is a small pouting scarlet bow. She casts a cool, twinkly eye over the house, the cooker, the Hoover, the husband, and announces that she will stay with her uncle in Selby.

8

A green satin bra

Another crisis. This time it's the telephone bill. It is more than seven hundred pounds, almost all of which is for phone calls to Ukraine. My father rings me.

'Can you lend me please five hundred pounds?'

'Pappa, this has to stop. Why should I pay for her to make telephone calls to Ukraine?'

'Not just she. Stanislav also.'

'Well, both of them. They can't just ring up and chat to their friends. Tell her she must pay it herself out of her wages.'

'Hmm. Yes.' He puts the phone down.

He telephones my sister.

She rings me.

'You've heard about the telephone bill? Honestly! Whatever next?'

'I told him he must get Valentina to pay. I'm not going to subsidise her.' My voice is Disgusted of Tunbridge Wells.

'Of course that's exactly what I said, Nadezhda.' My sister is even better at D. of T. W. than I am. 'And do you know what he said? He said, she can't pay for the telephone bill because she has to pay for the car.'

'But I thought he bought her the car.'

'Another car. A Lada. She's buying it to take back to Ukraine.'

'So she has two cars?'

'It seems so. Of course these people – they *are* communists. I'm sorry, Nadezhda. I know what you're going to say. But they've always had everything they wanted, every luxury, every privilege, and now they can't rip off the system any more over there, they want to come over here and rip off our system. Well, I'm sorry . . .'

'It's not quite as simple as that, Vera.'

'You see in this country, communists are harmless little people with beards and sandals. But once they get into power, suddenly a new vicious type of personality emerges.'

'No, it's the same people who are always in power, Vera. Sometimes they call themselves communists, sometimes capitalists, sometimes devoutly religious – whatever they need to be to hang on to power. The former communists in Russia are the same people who own all the industries now. They're the real rip-off merchants. But the professional middle classes, people like Valentina's husband, have been hardest hit.'

'Of course I knew you would disagree with me, Nadezhda, and really I don't want to argue about this. I know where your sympathies really lie. But I could see straightaway what kind of people they were.'

'But you haven't seen them yet.'

'But I can see from your description.'

Silly cow. No point in arguing with her. But still it irks me that she doesn't think twice about lashing out at me, even in our new alliance.

I telephone my father.

'Aha,' he says. 'Yes, the Lada. She bought it for her brother. You see her brother was living in Estonia, but he was expelled because he failed the Estonian Language examination. He is pure Russian, you see. Talks pure Russian. Couldn't speak one word of Estonian. But after independence, this new Estonian Government wants to expel all Russians. So her brother must go. Now Valentina, she speaks Ukrainian and Russian. Speaks both very good. Stanislav, too. Good vocabulary. Good pronunciation.'

'About the Lada.'

'Aha, yes, Lada. Her brother had a Lada, you see, which was smashed up. Smashed his face up, too. In a night, he went fishing, catching fish through a hole in ice. Very cold, sitting long time on a snow, waiting for some fish. Very cold in Estonia. So to make himself warm he drinks vodka. Now alcohol of course is not a combustion fuel in the way of kerosene or gasoline that is used for tractors, but it has certain warming properties. But at some cost. Well, cost is this. He drinks too much, skids on ice. Smashes up Lada. Smashes up his face, too. But I ask myself, why should I helping a man who is not only not a Ukrainian, but is so much a Russian that he fails Estonian Language examination? Tell me this.'

'So she bought him a new Lada?'

'Not new. Second-hand. Not too expensive, by the way. One thousand pounds. You see in this country Lada is not considered to be chic car.' (He pronounces it the French way – 'sheek'. He fancies himself as a bit of a francophone.) 'Too heavy body for engine size. Inefficient fuel consumption. Old-style transmission. But in Ukraina a Lada is good because plenty of spare parts. Maybe it isn't even for her brother. Maybe she will sell and make a good profit.'

'So she's driving about in two cars?'

'No. Lada sits in garage. Rover sits on drive.'

'But she has no money to pay the phone bill.'

'Aha. Telephone. Now here is a problem. Too much talking. Husband, brother, sister, mother, uncle, auntie, friend, cousin. Sometimes Ukrainian but mostly Russian.' As if he wouldn't mind paying the bill if it was for talking in Ukrainian. 'Not intelligent talking. Chatterbox talking.' He wouldn't mind paying the bill if it was for talking about Nietzsche and Schopenhauer.

'Pappa, tell her if she doesn't pay the phone will be cut off.'

'Hmm. Yes.' He says yes, but his tone says no.

He can't do it. He can't stand up to her. Or maybe he doesn't really want to. He just wants to complain, to have our sympathy.

'You must be firmer with her.' I can feel his resistance down the telephone line, but I plug on. 'She doesn't understand. She believes that in the West everyone is a millionaire.'

'Aha.'

A few days later he rings again. The Rover has broken down again. This time it's the hydraulic braking system. Oh, and it failed its MOT. He needs to borrow more money.

'Only until I get my pension.'

'You see?' I rage at Mike. 'They're both completely mad. Both of them. Why can't I come from a normal family?'

'Think how dull it would be.'

'Oh, I think I could put up with a bit of dullness. I just don't want all this – not at my time of life.'

'Well don't let yourself get too worked up about it, because one thing you can be certain of – it's going to get worse.' He takes a can of cold beer from the fridge and pours it into two glasses. 'You've got to give him a chance to have his bit of fun. You shouldn't interfere.'

Afterwards, I regretted that I hadn't interfered more, and earlier.

It's impossible, I realise, to keep tabs on things by phone. Time for another visit. I don't warn my father this time.

Valentina is out when we arrive, but Stanislav is there. He is up in his room doing his homework, bent low over the page. He works hard. Good boy.

'Stanislav,' I say, 'what's going on with this car? It seems to be causing a lot of trouble.'

'Oh, no trouble. It's all right now. All fixed.' He smiles his cute chipped-tooth smile.

'But Stanislav, can't you persuade your mother it would be better to have a smaller car that's more reliable than this big shiny monster that costs a fortune to run? My father hasn't got that much money, you know.'

'Oh, it's OK now. It's a very nice car.'

'But wouldn't you have been better off with something more reliable, like a Ford Fiesta?'

'Oh, Ford Fiesta is not a good car. You know, when we were coming here on the motorway we saw a terrible accident between a Ford Fiesta and a Jaguar, and the Ford Fiesta was quite crushed underneath the Jaguar. So you see the bigger car is much better.'

Is he serious?

'But Stanislav, my father can't afford a big car.'

'Oh, I think he can.' Sweet smile. 'He has enough money. He gave Anna some money, didn't he?' The spectacles slip down his nose. He pushes them back, and looks up at me, meeting my eyes with a cool stare. Maybe not such a good boy.

'Yes, but . . .' What can I say? '. . . that's up to him.'

'Exactly so.'

There are quick footsteps on the stairs and Valentina bursts into the bedroom. She chides Stanislav for talking to me. 'Stop talk this bad-news peeping no-tits crow.' She has forgotten that I speak Ukrainian, or she doesn't care.

'No matter, Valentina,' I say. 'It's you I want to talk to. Shall we go downstairs?'

She follows me down into the kitchen. Stanislav comes down too, but Valentina sends him into the next room where Pappa is explaining at length to Mike about the comparative safety features of different braking systems, stubbornly avoiding reference to the specific problems of the Rover, while Mike is striving against the odds to steer the conversation in this direction.

'Why you want for talk?' Valentina positions herself opposite me and a little too close. Her lipstick is an angry red smudge around the edges of her mouth.

'I think you know why, Valentina.'

'Know? Why I know?'

I had planned a rational discussion, a cool unfolding of logical arguments which would end up in a gracious admission of guilt on her part, a smiling, rueful acceptance that things would have to change. But all I feel is a burning, blinding rage and my arguments desert me. Blood beats in my head.

'Aren't you ashamed of yourself?' I have slipped into the mongrel language, half-English half-Ukrainian, fluent and snappy.

'Ah-shamed! Ah-shamed!' she snorts. 'You shame. No me shame. Why you no visit you mamma grave? Why you no crying, bringing flower? Why you making trouble here?'

The thought of my mother lying neglected in the cold ground while this usurper lords it in her kitchen drives me to a new pitch of fury.

'Don't dare to talk about my mother. Don't even say her name with your filthy-talking boil-in-the-baggage mouth!'

'You mother die. Now you father marry me. You no like. You make trouble. I understand. I no stupid.'

She speaks the mongrel language too. We snarl at each other like mongrels.

'Valentina, why are you driving around in two cars, when my father doesn't have enough money to pay for the repairs on one car? Why are you talking on the telephone to Ukraina while he's asking me for money to pay the bills? You tell me!'

'He give you money. Now you give him money,' the big red mouth taunts.

'Why should my father pay for your cars? For your telephone bills? You have work. You earn money. You should contribute something to the household.' I have worked myself up into a lather of righteous anger, and the words come pouring out, some English, some Ukrainian, mixed up any old how.

'You father buy me nothing!' She leans forward and shouts into my face so close that I can feel a fine shower of saliva on my skin. I can smell armpits and hair lacquer. 'No car! No jewel! No clothes!' (She pronounces it in two syllables – cloth-es.) 'No cosmetic! No undercloth-es!' She yanks up her t-shirt top to display those ferocious breasts bursting like twin warheads out of an underwired, ribbon-strapped, lycra-panelled, lace-trimmed green satin rocket-launcher of a bra.

'I buy all! I work! I buy!'

When it comes to bosoms, I have to admit defeat. I am lost for words. In the silence that falls, I hear my father's voice in the next room, droning on. He is telling Mike the story about pencils in space. I have heard it many times before. So has Mike.

'In early days of space travel, one interesting problem emerged from experiments with weightlessness. Americans found that for writing notes and keeping records, normal ink pen would not work without gravity feed. Scientists undertook intensive research, finally developed high-technology pen to work in conditions of no gravity. In Russia, scientists faced with same problem found different solution. Instead of pen, they used pencil. That is how Russians put pencils into space.'

How can my father be so blind to what is happening to him?

I turn on Valentina.

'My father is an innocent man. Stupid but innocent. You spend all your money on tart underwear and tart make-up! Is it because my father's not enough for you, ey? Is it because you're after another man, or two or three or four, ey? I know what you are, and soon enough my father will know. Then we'll see!'

Stanislav exclaims,

'Wow! I didn't know Nadezhda could speak such Ukrainian!'

Then the doorbell rings. Mike answers. It's the Zadchuks. They're standing on the doorstep with a bunch of flowers and a home-made cake.

'Come in! Come in!' says Mike. 'You're just in time for tea.'

They hover in the doorway. They have caught sight of Valentina's thunderous face. (The breasts are re-covered.)

'Come in,' says Valentina with a pout. They are her friends, after all, and she may need them.

'Come in,' I say, 'I'll put the kettle on.' I need time to rally, to get my breath back.

Although it is October, the weather is mild and sunny. We will drink tea in the garden. Mike and Stanislav set out deck-chairs and an old wonky camping table under the plum tree.

'Good you come,' says Pappa to the Zadchuks, settling back into the creaking canvas. 'Good cake. My Millochka used to make like this.'

Valentina takes this as a slight.

'In Tesco is better.'

Mrs Zadchuk is offended.

'I like baking cake better.'

Mr Zadchuk springs to her defence.

'Why you buying cake in Tesco, Valentina? Why you no baking? Woman should bake.'

Valentina is still in full eruption-mode from her encounter with me.

'I no time to baking. All day working for money. Buy cake. Buy clothes. Buy car. No-good meanie husband give no money.'

I am afraid the t-shirt will come up again, but she satisfies herself with a dramatic bosom-lunge in my father's direction. Alarmed, he looks to Mike for help. Mike, not knowing enough Ukrainian to understand what is going on, fatally returns to the subject of cake, and ingratiates himself with Mrs Zadchuk by helping himself to another large slice.

'Mmm. Delicious.'

Mrs Zadchuk's pink cheeks glow. She pats his thigh.

'You good eat. I like man good eat. Why you no eat more, Yuri?'

Mr Zadchuk takes this as a slight.

'Too much cake make fatty tum. You fatty, Margaritka. Little bit fatty.'

Mrs Zadchuk takes this as a slight.

'Better fatty than skinny. Look Nadezhda. She starving Bangladesh-lady.'

I take this as a slight. Righteously, I draw in my stomach. 'Thin is good. Thin is healthy. Thin people live longer.'

All of them turn on me with howls of derisive laughter.

'Thin is hunger! Thin is famine! Everybody thin drop over dead! Ha ha!'

'I like fatty,' says my father. He places a placatory wizened hand on Valentina's breast and gives it a little squeeze. Blood rushes to my head. I jump up and accidentally catch the leg of the table, sending the teapot and the remains of the cake sliding on to the ground.

The tea party has not been a success.

After the Zadchuks have gone, there is still the washing-up to be done, and some dirty linen to be washed. Valentina pulls on rubber gloves over pearlised-pink-tipped fingers. I shove her aside.

'I'll do it,' I say. 'I don't mind getting my hands dirty. You're obviously too fine for this, Valentina. Too fine for my father, don't you think? Not too fine to spend his money, though. Eh?'

She lets out a shriek. 'Vixen! Crow! You get out my kitchen! Out my house!'

'Not your house! My mother's house!' I shriek back.

My father comes running into the kitchen.

'Nadezhda, why you poking your nose in here? Not your business!'

'Pappa, you crazy man. First you say Valentina spends all your money. Lend me a hundred pounds. Lend me five hundred pounds. Then you say I shouldn't poke my nose in. Make your mind up.'

'I say lend money. I no say poke nose in.' His jaw is clenched. His fists are clenched. He is beginning to shake. I remember when this look used to strike terror in me, but I am taller than he is now.

'Pappa, why should I give money for you to spend on this grasping deceitful painted . . .' Bitch, bitch, bitch! I think. But my feminist mouth won't say it.

'Go out! Go out and never come back! You are not my daughter Nadezhda!' He fixes me with pale demented eyes.

'Fine,' I say. 'Fine by me. Who wants you for a Dad anyway? You cuddle up with your fat-bosom wife and leave me out of it.'

I grab my things and rush out to the car. After a few moments, Mike follows.

As we leave the outskirts of Peterborough and head out for the open country, Mike ventures, in a jocular sort of way, 'What a crazy bunch you are.'

'Shut up!' I shriek. 'Just shut up and keep your nose out of it!' Then I feel ashamed. I have surrendered to the madness. We drive home in silence. Mike searches the radio waves for soothing music.

9

Christmas gifts

Very late one evening, not long after our visit, Stanislav phones my sister. He found her number in Father's phone book.

'Please. You must do something . . . these terrible rows . . . shouting all the time . . .' he sobs down the telephone.

Vera does something. She telephones the Home Office. They tell her to put it in writing. She telephones me in a fury.

'This time we're both going to do it, and we're both going to sign it. I'm not having him playing us off one against the other. I'm not having you keeping in his good books by doing nothing, while I do all the work and then end up getting cut out of his will.'

'Maybe,' I say. 'I'll phone him first. See if I can find out what's going on. I don't want to do something we're both going to regret.' I feel guilty that I haven't been vigilant enough on his behalf.

I phone my father. I hear the phone crackle, then his breathless panting as he picks it up.

'Hallo? Ah, Nadezhda. Good you phoned.'

'What's up, Pappa?'

'Well, not so good with Valentina. Some problems. She is now acting as if she rather dislikes me . . . telling me I am inferior being . . . insect to be squashed . . . imbecile to be locked away . . . dead corpse to be put in ground . . . other things like this.' He mumbles incoherently and coughs a lot. His voice is croaky, as if dragging the words out is causing him pain.

'Oh, Pappa.' I don't know what to say, but he hears reproof in my voice.

'Of course it is not entirely her fault. She has been placed under severe pressure by delays from Home Office. And besides this her work is very hard, in day working at nursing-home, in evening working at hotel. She gets tired, and when tired is easily angry.'

I am filled with rage – rage against her and rage against him.

'But Pappa, anybody could see this was going to happen. Anybody but you.'

'Don't tell Vera, will you? She will say . . .'

'Pappa, Vera knows. Stanislav telephoned her.'

'Stanislav telephoned to Vera?'

'He was crying down the telephone.'

'Too bad. Too bad. Well, whatever happens . . . at least until her Appeal we will stay together . . . after that they will go and I will be left in peace.'

But my sister and I will take no chances. I draft a letter to the Home Office Immigration Department at Lunar House, Croydon, setting out the story of Valentina's marriage to our father and her relationship with Bob Turner. I don't care about being a good liberal any more. I want this woman taken away. I describe the living arrangements – separate beds – and the fact that the marriage has not been consummated, because I believe the Establishment will take the view that penetrative sex is what marriage is all about. I am pleased with the primness of the letter.

Earlier this year Mrs Dubova obtained a second 6 months visa and arrived via Ramsgate in March. She once more moved into Mr Turner's house. She and my father were married at the Immaculate Conception in Peterborough in June.

After the wedding Mrs Dubova did not move in with our father, but carried on living at Hall Street in Mr Turner's house. When the school term ended, Mrs Dubova (now Mayevska) and Stanislav moved into our father's house. However, she did not share a room with our father, and the marriage has never been consummated.

At first things seemed to be working out all right. We believed that although Mrs Dubova (now Mrs Mayevska) might not love our father in a romantic sense, she would at least be kind and caring to a frail elderly man in his last years. However, after only a few months, things have begun to go very wrong.

As I write I feel a terrible sense of guilt, and also a sweet secret feeling of release. The Judas kiss in the garden, the bliss of malice without accountability. My father must never know. Mike and Anna must never know. Valentina will suspect, but will never know for sure.

I ask the secret correspondent at the Home Office to protect our anonymity. I sign the letter and post it to my sister. She signs it and posts it to the Home Office. There is no reply. My sister rings a couple of weeks later and is told the letter has been filed.

Next time I phone my father to ask how things are, he is evasive.

'Everything OK,' is all he will say. 'Nothing out of normal.'

'No more arguments?'

'Nothing out of normal. Husband wife. Quarrelling is normal. Not too bad.' Then he starts to talk about aviation. 'You see, in love as in aviation, all is a matter of the balance. Uplift is greater in a long thin wing, but at cost of greater weight. So in same way, argument and occasional bad temper is a cost of the love. In design of aircraft wing, the secret of success is to achieve correct ratio between lift and drag. Is same with Valentina.'

'You mean she has plenty of uplift but she's a bit of a drag.' (Ha ha.)

There is a long silence on the other end of the phone as he tries to puzzle out what I have said.

'Pappa,' I say, 'that's enough about aviation. Can't you see I'm worried about you?'

'I'm all right. But my arthritis is coming back. This wet weather.'

'Would you like me and Mike to come up and see you?'

'No, not now. Later, maybe. After a while.'

My sister gets even shorter shrift.

'He won't answer any of my questions. He just rambles on about this and that, on and on. I really think his mind's going,' she says. 'We should see the doctor to get him certified insane. Then we could say he was of unsound mind when he entered into the marriage.'

'He's always been like that. He's no worse now than he was. You know he's always been a bit mad.'

'Of course that's true. Quite mad. But somehow I feel this is worse. Does he talk to you about Valentina?'

'Not really. He says they have their arguments, but nothing out of the normal. Remember the arguments he used to have with Mother? Either things have settled down, and they're getting on OK, or he doesn't want us to know how bad it is. He's worried that you'll laugh at him, Vera.'

'Well of course I'll laugh at him. What does he expect? But still, he's our father. We can't let this frightful woman do this to him.'

'He says everything's all right. But he doesn't sound all right.'

'Maybe she listens to him when he talks on the phone. Just a thought.'

Christmas gives us the excuse we need for a visit.

'It's Christmas, Pappa. Families always get together at Christmas.'

'I'll see what Valentina says.'

'No, just tell her we're coming.'

'All right then. But no presents. No presents for me, and I get none for you.'

This 'no presents' idea comes from his mother, Baba Nadia. I was named after her. She was a village schoolteacher, a stern and pious woman, with straight black hair that didn't go grey until she was seventy (a sure sign of Mongolian ancestry, said my mother), and a great follower of Tolstoy and his cranky ideas that captivated the Russian intelligentsia of the time: the spiritual nobility of the peasantry, the beauty of self-denial, and other such nonsense (said my mother, who had suffered her mother-in-law's pronouncements on marriage, child-rearing, and the best way to make dumplings). And yet. And yet when I was a child my father had made me such wonderful gifts. There were model aeroplanes made from balsa wood and powered with rubber bands – and all the street turned out to watch them fly. There was a garage with an inspection pit made from wood and riveted aluminium, with a lift operated by a rubber-band that raised the dinky-cars on to the roof, and a curved ramp so that you could roll them down again. One Christmas there was a farmyard, a *'khutor'* like the one that was home in Ukraine – a sheet of green-painted hardboard surrounded by a painted wall, with a hinged gate that opened, a farmhouse with windows and a door that opened and a little byre with a sloping roof for the die-cast cows and pigs. I remember these gifts with wonder. It is so long since I remembered the things I once loved about my father.

'But Valentina and Stanislav – maybe they would like presents,' he says. 'They are really quite traditional, you know.' Ha! Not the Nietzsche-reading intellectuals he took them for.

I enjoy choosing presents for Valentina and Stanislav. For Valentina, I wrap a particularly cheap and nasty bottle of perfume which I got free in a supermarket promotion. For Stanislav I choose a mauve polyester jumper my daughter once brought home from a school jumble sale. I wrap them elaborately, with little bows. We get my father some chocolates and a book about aeroplanes. He always really likes presents, even though he says he doesn't.

We drive over on Christmas afternoon. It's one of those grey, penetratingly cold days that seem to have taken over from white Christmases. The house is gloomy, cheerless and dirty, but my father has hung a few Christmas cards (including some saved from last year) on a string across the ceiling to brighten things up. There is no food in the house. For Christmas dinner they ate reheated microwave packs of sliced turkey breasts with potatoes, peas and gravy. There are not even any left-overs. In a pot on the stove are some greying cold boiled potatoes and the remnants of a fried egg.

I remember when Christmas dinner was a big fat bird with salt-crisped skin and oily juices oozing out of it, fragrant with garlic and marjoram and kasha stuffed in its plump tummy and roasted shallots and chestnuts round the side, and home-made wine that made us all tipsy, and a white cloth and flowers on the table, even in winter, and silly presents, and laughter and kisses. This woman who has taken the place of my mother has stolen Christmas and replaced it with boil-in-the-bag food and plastic flowers.

'Why don't we all go out for a meal,' says Mike.

'Good idea,' says my father. 'We can go to Indian restaurant.'

My father likes Indian food. There is a restaurant called the Himalaya in the desolate concrete shopping parade that was added on to the village in the 1960s. For a while, after our mother died, he lived on take-outs which they delivered, and he got to know the proprietor.

'Better than Meals on Wheels,' he would say, 'better taste.' Until one day he overdosed on vindaloo, with unpleasant consequences that he took great pleasure in describing to anyone who would listen. ('Hot on way in. Hot hot on way out.')

We are the only people in the restaurant, Mike, Anna and I, and Pappa, Valentina and Stanislav. The heating has been turned down and the room is chilly. There is a smell of rising damp and stale spices. We choose a table nearest to the window, but there is nothing to see outside except the glint of frost on car roofs and the glare of a street-light across the road. The restaurant has maroon flock wallpaper and parchment light-shades with Indian motifs. Jazzed-up Christmas carols from a local pop radio station play in the background.

The proprietor greets my father like a long-lost friend. My father introduces me and Mike and Anna. 'My daughter, husband, granddaughter.'

'And these?' The proprietor indicates Valentina and Stanislav. 'Who are they?'

'This lady and her son are coming from Ukraine,' says Pappa.

'And who is she? Wife?' It's obvious that word has gone around the village, and now he wants confirmation of the scandal. He wants his own bit of hot gossip.

'They are from Ukraine,' I say. I cannot bring myself to say, Yes, wife. 'Can we see the menu?'

Thwarted, he fetches the menu and plonks it on the table.

'Could we have a bottle of wine?' asks Mike, but the restaurant is unlicensed.

We will have to make our own cheer.

We order. My father loves lamb bhuna. My daughter is a vegetarian. My husband likes dishes that are very hot. I like oven-baked dishes. Valentina and Stanislav have never eaten Indian food before. They are wary, condescending.

'I want only meat. Plenty meat,' says Valentina. She chooses a steak from the English selection. Stanislav chooses roast chicken. We wait. We listen to the pop music and the babble of the DJ. We watch the frost glint on the car roofs. The proprietor stands behind the bar and watches us discreetly. What is he waiting for?

Anna squeezes up beside Mike and starts to fold his napkin into an elaborate origami flower. She is a Daddy's girl, as I once was. Watching them together makes me feel sad and happy at the same time.

'Well,' says Mike. 'Christmas again. Isn't it good to go out for a meal together? We should do it more often.'

'Great,' I say. He doesn't know about the letter to the Home Office.

'Did you get any nice presents, Stanislav?' asks Anna, her voice bubbling with Christmas excitement. She doesn't know, either.

Stanislav got socks, soap, a book about aeroplanes and some tapes. Last year he got a black jacket with a fur collar. Real fur. The year before he got skates from his father.

'Is better in Ukraina, Christmas,' says Valentina.

'Well why don't you . . .' I try to stop myself, but Valentina knows what I am saying.

'Why for? For Stanislav. All is for Stanislav. Stanislav must have good opportunity. Is no opportunity in Ukraina,' she turns on me loudly. 'Is only opportunity for gangster prostitute in Ukraina.'

Mike nods sympathetically. Anna goes quiet. Stanislav smiles his cute chip-toothed smile. Behind the bar the proprietor has gone very still. My father looks as if he is miles away, on a tractor somewhere.

'Was it better under communism?' I ask.

'Of course better. Was good life. You no understand what type of people is rule country now.'

Her syrup-coloured eyes have a heavy, glazed look. Today is her first day off work in two weeks. The black eyeliner has smudged and run into the wrinkles below her eyes. If I'm not careful, I will begin to feel sorry for her. Tart. Slut. Boil-in-the-bag cook. I think of Mother and harden my heart.

'My school was better,' says Stanislav. 'More discipline. More homework. But now in Ukraina you have to pay the teachers if you want to pass the exams.'

'No different to your new school then,' I say drily. Mike kicks me under the table.

'No different to my school,' chirps Anna. 'We're always having to bribe our teachers with apples.'

Stanislav looks astonished.

'Apples?'

'Just a joke,' says Anna. 'Don't children in your country give their teachers apples?'

'Apples never,' says Stanislav. 'Vodka, yes.'

'You in university teacher?' Valentina asks me.

'Yes.'

'I want for help Stanislav in OxfordCambridgeUniversity. You working CambridgeUniversity. So you help?'

'Yes, I work in Cambridge, but not at Cambridge University. I am at the Anglia Polytechnic University.'

'Angella University? What is this?'

My father leans across and whispers, 'Polytechnic.'

Valentina raises both eyebrows and mutters something that I cannot understand.

Our meals arrive. The proprietor seems to hover for a long time around Valentina as he sets out the dishes before her. She manages to flash her syrupy eyes his way, but it is a half-hearted flirtation. It is late and we are all too hungry for courtesies. The lamb bhuna is stringy, and we have to cut it up into tiny pieces for my father. The vegetable curry has no vegetables in it apart from cabbage. Mike's hot curry is too hot. Stanislav's oven-cooked chicken is dry and tough. Valentina's steak is like a slab of wood.

'Everything all right?' asks the proprietor.

'Lovely,' says Mike.

Afterwards, Mike drives my father and Anna and Stanislav home in the car and I walk home with Valentina. The pavements are icy, and we cling on to each other, first for balance, but after a while the clinging becomes companionable. Despite the dismal meal, some seasonal cheer has rubbed off on us. Peace on earth, goodwill to all men, sing the Christmas angels in the crispy sky. I realise there will not be another opportunity like this.

'How are things going?' I ask.

'Good. Everything good.'

'But what about the arguments? You seem to have a lot of arguments.' I keep my voice neutral, friendly.

'Who telling you?'

'Valentina, it's obvious to anybody.' I don't want to betray Stanislav, and I don't want to land my father in it.

'You father is no easy man,' she says.

'I know.' I know that I couldn't put up with my father day in day out as she does. I begin to regret my letter to the Home Office.

'All time he making trouble for me.'

'But Valentina, you worked in an old people's home. You know old people can be difficult.'

What did she expect? A refined elderly gentleman who

would shower gifts on her, and pass away quietly one night? Not my tough cantankerous stubborn old father.

'You father more difficult. Trouble with cough cough cough. Trouble with nerves. Trouble with bath. Trouble with pi-pi.' As she turns towards me, the moonlight catches her handsome Slavic profile, the high cheekbones, the curved mouth. 'And all time, you know, kiss kiss, touching here, here here . . .' Her gloved hands caress her breasts, thighs, knees through the thick coat. (My father does that?) I feel like gagging, but I keep my voice steady.

'Be kind to him. That's all.'

'I kind,' she says. 'As my own father. You no worry.'

She slips on the ice and grips my arm tighter. I feel her warm sensuous bulk rest briefly against me and smell the strong sugary perfume, my Christmas gift, which she has sprayed on to her neck and throat. This woman who has taken the place of my mother.

10

Squishy squashy

My father is excited. The inspector from the Immigration Service has come to call. Soon Valentina's immigration status will be confirmed and their love will be sealed for ever. Without the fear of deportation hanging over them, the cloud of misunderstanding will lift and it will once more be as when they were first in love. Maybe even better. Maybe they will start a new family. Poor Valentina has been so anxious and this has sometimes made her irritable, but soon their troubles will be at an end.

The inspector is a middle-aged woman with flat lace-up shoes and parted hair. She carries a brown briefcase, and refuses my father's offer of tea. He shows her around.

'This is my room. This is Valentina's room. This is Stanislav's room. You see, plenty room for everybody.'

The inspector makes notes of where everyone lives.

'And this is my table. You see, I prefer to eat by myself. Stanislav and Valentina eat in the kitchen. I cook for myself – look, Toshiba apples. Cooked by Toshiba microwave. Full of vitamins. You like to try?'

The inspector refuses politely, and makes more notes.

'And will I be able to meet Mrs Mayevska? When does she come back from work?'

'She is always coming at different time. Sometimes early, sometimes late. Better you telephone first.'

The inspector makes another note, then she puts her notebook away in her brown briefcase and shakes my father's hand. He watches her small turquoise Fiat disappear around a bend in the road, and telephones me with the news.

A fortnight later Valentina gets a letter from the Home Office. Her application for leave to stay in Britain has been refused. The inspector has found no evidence of a genuine marriage. She flies into a rage at my father.

'You foolish idiot man. You giving all wrong answer. Why you no show her you love-letter poem? Why you no show her wedding picture?'

'Why should I show her a poem? She did not ask to see poem, she asked to see bedroom.'

'Hah! She see you no good man to go into woman bedroom.'

'You no good woman shut husband out of bedroom.'

'What you want in bedroom, eh? Thphoo! You squishy squashy. You flippy floppy. Squishy squashy flippy floppy!' she taunts. She puts her face close to his, and her voice gets louder and louder. 'Squishy squashy! Flippy floppy!'

'Stop! Stop!' my father cries. 'Go! Go! Go away! Go back to Ukraina!'

'Squishy squashy flippy floppy!'

He pushes her away. She pushes him back. She is bigger than he is. He stumbles, and bangs his arm against the corner of the dresser. A livid bruise rises.

'Look what you done!'

'Now you go crying to daughter! Help, help, Nadia

Verochka! Wife beating me! Hah hah! Husband should beat wife!'

Maybe he would beat her if he could, but he cannot. For the first time, he realises how helpless he is. His heart fills with despair. Next day, when she is at work, he telephones me and tells me what happened. His words come stumbling, limping out, as though just speaking it aloud hurts. I express concern, but I feel smug. Wasn't I was right about the official view of penetration?

'You see, this matter of erectile dysfunction, Nadia. Sometimes it happens to the male.'

'It doesn't matter, Pappa. She shouldn't mock you like that.' Stupid man, I think. What did he expect?

'Don't tell Vera.'

'Pappa, we may need Vera's help.'

I had thought this story was going to be a knockabout farce, but now I see it is developing into a knockabout tragedy. He hasn't told me before because she listens when he talks on the telephone. And because he doesn't want Vera to know.

I resist the temptation to say 'I told you so, stupid man'. But I telephone Vera, and she says it for me.

'But really I blame you, Nadezhda,' she adds. 'You stopped him going into sheltered housing. None of this would have happened if he had gone into sheltered housing.'

'Nobody could have predicted it . . .'

'Nadia, *I* predicted it.' Her voice rings with Big Sis triumph.

'OK, so you're so clever. How are we going to get him out of it?' I pull a mocking face that she can't see on the phone.

'There are two possibilities,' says Vera. 'Divorce or deportation. The first is expensive and uncertain. The second is also uncertain but at least Pappa doesn't have to pay for it.'

'Can't we go for both?'

'How you've changed, Nadia. What's happened to all your feminist ideas?'

'Don't be so spiteful, Vera. We should be allies, but you just can't bring yourself to be civil to me, can you? I can understand why Pappa never tells you anything.'

'Yes, well he's another idiot. Mother and I were the practical people in the family.'

See how she claims Mother's legacy? It's not just the cupboard full of tins and jars, nor the gold locket, nor even the money in the savings account she's after: no, it's the inheritance of character, of nature, that we fight over.

'We never were a very practical family.'

'What is the word you social workers use? A *dysfunctional* family. Maybe we should apply for a grant from the council.'

Despite getting off to a shaky start, we manage to agree a division of labour. Vera, as the family expert on divorce, will contact solicitors, while I will find out the law relating to immigration and deportation. It feels uncomfortable at first to step out of my soft-soled liberal shoes into the stilettos of Mrs Flog-'em-and-send-'em-home of Tunbridge Wells, but after a while the new shoes mould to my feet. I discover that Valentina has the right to appeal, and then if she is refused she has the right to appeal again to a tribunal. And she is also entitled to legal aid. She is obviously going to be here for some time.

'Maybe we should write to the *Daily Mail*.' I am expanding into my role.

'Good idea,' says Vera.

On the divorce front, my sister has a cunning plan. A contested divorce is going to be complex and expensive, she has discovered, so she hits on the idea of annulment – the no-consummation-therefore-no-marriage angle so popular with European royalty in the sixteenth century.

'You see the marriage never really existed so there is no need for a divorce,' she explains to the wet-behind-the-ears trainee solicitor in the Peterborough practice. He has not come across this before, but he promises to look it up. He mumbles and stammers as he tries to get the details of the non-consummation from my sister over the phone.

'Good heavens,' she says, 'just how much detail do you need?'

But although it worked for European royalty, it isn't going to work for Pappa – it is only if one party complains about the other party's inability or refusal to consummate the marriage that non-consummation becomes a ground for annulment or divorce, the trainee solicitor writes in a clumsily worded letter.

'Well, I never knew that,' says Vera, who thought she knew everything about divorce.

Valentina laughs out loud when Pappa suggests a divorce. 'First I get passport visa, then you get divorce.'

Pappa, too, has gone off the idea of divorce. He is afraid that they will question him about squishy squashy. He is afraid the whole world will find out about flippy floppy.

'Better think of something else, Nadia,' he says.

*   *   *

Despite the stress he is under, he has managed to finish another chapter of his history, but it has taken on a sombre tone. When Mike and I visit at the beginning of February, he takes us into the sitting-room, still full of last year's apples and as chilly as a cold store, and reads aloud to us.

The early makers of the tractor dreamed that swords would be turned into ploughshares, but now the spirit of the century grows dark, and we find that, instead, ploughshares are to be turned into swords.

The Kharkiv Locomotive Factory, which once produced 1,000 tractors a week to feed the demands of the New Economic Plan, was relocated to Chelyabinsk beyond the Urals and converted to produce tanks by decree of K. J. Voroshilov, the People's Commissar for Defence.

The chief designer was Mikhail Koshkin, who was educated at the Leningrad Institute and worked at the Kirov Plant until 1937. He was a moderate, cultured type, whose genius was used, one might say abused, by Stalin to create the Soviet Union's military supremacy. Koshkin's first tank, the A20, ran on the original cater-pillar tracks, with a 45-mm gun and armour that would withstand a hit by a shell. This was renamed the T32 when the gun size was increased to 76.2 mm and the armour was also made thicker. The T32 saw action in the Spanish Civil War, where the thinness of the armour plating made it vulnerable, though its manoeuvrability was much admired. Out of this was born the legendary T34, which many credit with having turned the tide of the war. It had even thicker armour, and to compensate for the additional weight, was the first locomotive to be fitted with a cast aluminium engine.

His voice is weaker, more quavery, and he has to keep stopping for breath.

In the ferocious weather of February 1940, the first T34 was driven to Moscow to be paraded before the Soviet leadership. It made a huge impression, not least because of the way it rolled so smoothly over the rutted, cobbled, snow-bound streets of the capital.

However, poor Koshkin did not live to see his creation in production. On this trip, being exposed for many hours to the abominable weather, he contracted pneumonia, and died some months later.

The design was completed by his pupil and colleague Aleksandr Morozov, a dashing and handsome young engineer. Under his guidance, the first T34 tanks rolled off the assembly line in August 1940, as they were soon to roll off in their hundreds and thousands. In honour of this, the town of Chelyabinsk, formerly most noted for production of tractors, was renamed Tankograd.

Outside the window, the sun sinks into the frosted furrows which have not thawed all day. The wind that nips the branches has blown in from the flatlands of the East Anglia coast, and beyond that from the steppes, and beyond the steppes from the Urals.

My father is warmly wrapped against the cold with fingerless gloves and a woollen hat and three pairs of socks. He leans forward in his chair, reading through his thick glasses. Behind him on the mantelpiece sits a portrait of my mother. She is looking over his shoulder, out towards the fields and the horizon. Why did she marry him, this musing brown-eyed young woman with coiled, plaited hair and a mysterious smile? Was he a dashing and handsome young engineer? Did he seduce her with talk of automatic transmission and gifts of engine oil?

*   *   *

'Why did she marry him?' I ask Vera.

Mrs Divorce Expert and Mrs Flog-'em-and-send-'em-home have been swapping notes on the phone, and the tone between us has become quite cordial. We moved from talking about our father's marriage to Valentina to our parents' marriage, and now I see the door to the past has opened a crack, and I want to push.

'It was after the submarine commander was killed at Sebastopol. I suppose she was frightened of being on her own. It was a frightening time.'

'What submarine commander?'

'From the Black Sea Fleet. Whom she was engaged to.'

'Mother was engaged to a submarine commander?'

'Didn't you know? He was the love of her life.'

'Not Pappa?'

'What do *you* think?'

'I don't know,' Bogey-nose whines, 'no one ever told me anything about it.'

'Sometimes it's better not to know.'

With a snap, Big Sis closes the door to the past and turns the key.

II

Under duress

A date has been set for Valentina to appeal against the Immigration Service decision. Suddenly my father realises he is not so powerless after all. The appeal is to be held in Nottingham in April.

'I'm not going,' says Pappa.

'Yes you go,' says Valentina.

'You go by yourself. Why I shall travel to Nottingham?'

'You foolish man. If you no go, immigration bureaucraczia will say, where you husband? Why you no husband?'

'Tell bureaucraczia I am sick. Tell them I will not go.'

Valentina gets advice from her solicitor in Peterborough. He tells her that her case will be seriously compromised if her husband does not go, unless she can produce evidence of his illness.

'You sick in head,' says Valentina to my father. 'You causing too much trouble. Too much crazy talking. Too much kiss kiss. No good eighty-four-year man. Doctor must write letter.'

'I am not sick,' says Father. 'I am poet and engineer. By the way, Valentina, you should remember that Nietzsche himself was considered to be mad by those who were his intellectual inferiors. We will go to Doctor Figges. She will tell you I am not sick in head.'

The village doctor, a softly spoken woman approaching retirement, has treated my mother and father for twenty years.

'Good. We go to Doctor Figges. Then I tell Doctor Figges about oralsex,' says Valentina. (What? Oral sex? My father?)

'No no! Valya, why you must talk about this to everybody?' (He doesn't seem to mind talking to me!)

'I will tell her eighty-four-year husband want make oralsex. Squishy squashy husband want make oralsex.' (Please Pappa – this is making me feel a bit queasy.)

'Please, Valenka.'

Valentina relents. They will go to a different doctor instead. Valentina and Mrs Zadchuk bundle my father into Crap car. They are in such a hurry to get to the surgery before he changes his mind that his coat is buttoned up out of kilter and his shoes are on the wrong feet. Instead of his distance glasses he is still wearing his reading glasses, so everything passes in front of his eyes in a blur – the rain, the flicking of the windscreen wipers, the misted-up car windows, the smear of hedgerows as they pass. Valentina sits in the front, driving in her wild self-taught way, while Mrs Zadchuk sits in the back hanging tightly on to Nikolai, in case he decides to open the door and fling himself out. So they career around the narrow country lanes, splashing through puddles, sending a couple of pheasants running for their lives.

They do not take him to Doctor Figges at the village practice, but to a neighbouring village where there is another branch of the same practice, but staffed by a different GP. They are expecting to see the middle-aged Indian doctor, but instead there is a locum. Doctor Pollock is young, red-haired and very pretty. My father does not want to discuss his problems with her. He peers at her myopically through his misted-up reading glasses, and tries to change his shoes around without her noticing. Valentina does all the talking. She is sure the young woman will be sympathetic to her case, and she goes into some detail about my father's strange behaviour – the coughing, the Toshiba apples, the tractor monologues, the persistent sexual demands. Doctor Pollock looks intently at my father, notices the odd shoes, the staring eyes, the mis-buttoned coat, and asks him a number of questions:

'How long have you been married? Are you experiencing sexual difficulties? Why exactly have you come to see me?'

My father answers, 'I don't know,' to all of them. Then he turns to Valentina with a dramatic gesture: 'Because she has brought me! This fiend out of hell!'

Doctor Pollock declines to write a letter to the Immigration Service telling them that my father is too sick to attend Valentina's appeal. But she does tell my father that she will make an appointment for him to see a consultant psychiatrist at the Peterborough District Hospital.

'See!' says Valentina triumphantly. 'Doctor say you crazy!'

My father is silent. This is not the outcome he wanted.

'Do you think I am crazy, Nadia?' he asks me, over the telephone next day.

'Well, Pappa, to be honest, I do a bit. I thought you were crazy to marry Valentina – didn't I say so at the time?' (I want to say Hah hah! Told you so! But I bite my tongue.)

'Ah, that was not crazy. That was a simple mistake. Anyone can make mistake.'

'That's true,' I say. I am still angry with him, but I am also sorry for him.

*   *   *

'What is all this about oral sex?' I ask Vera. We are swapping notes again. It is getting quite pally.

'Oh, it's some sordid idea from Margaritka Zadchuk. Apparently Valentina told her we were looking for an annulment on the grounds of non-consummation.'

'But did they . . . ?'

'I'm sorry, Nadezhda. It's too disgusting to talk about.'

I find out from Pappa anyway. Valentina has been talking to her friend Margaritka Zadchuk, who has a thing or two to tell her. Old Mrs Mayevska was a cunning and thrifty woman, she says. When she died, she had saved up a huge fortune. Hundred thousand of pound. All is hidden somewhere in house. Why is that meanie husband not giving it to her? Meanie husband chuckles when he tells me this. She will pull up the whole house and she will not find a penny.

Mrs Zadchuk has taught Valentina a new word: oralsex. Is very popular in England, Mrs Zadchuk says. You can read about it in all English newspaper. Good Ukrainian people are not making oralsex. Meanie husband has lived too long in England, reads English newspaper, gets English oralsex idea. Oralsex is good, says Mrs Zadchuk, because with oralsex everyone knows is genuinely marriage, meanie husband cannot say is no genuinely marriage.

And another thing Mrs Zadchuk tells her – if she gets a divorce from that meanie wife-beating husband of hers, because of oralsex, she will be sure to get half of the house. That is the law in England. Fired up with dreams of unimaginable riches, she confronts my father.

'First I get passport visa, then I get divorce. When I get divorce I will have half of house.'

'Why not start now?' he says. 'We will divide up house. You and Stanislav will have upstairs, I will have downstairs.'

Now my father starts drawing – ground-floor plans, upper-floor plans, doors that will be blocked, openings that will be made. He covers sheets of graph paper with spidery drawings. With help from the neighbours he brings his bed down into the apple-filled sitting-room, the room in which Mother died. He tells Vera it is because he has difficulty climbing the stairs.

But the room is too cold, and he is reluctant to turn the heating up because of the apples. He starts to cough and wheeze, and Valentina, fearful that he will die before her British passport is consummated (so he says), takes him to Doctor Figges. The doctor tells him he needs to keep warm at night. His bed is moved into the dining-room next to the kitchen, where the central heating boiler can be kept on day and night. It was open-plan before, but he asks Mike to put a door up for him, because he is afraid Valentina will murder him in the night (so he says). In this room he sits, sleeps, eats. He uses the small downstairs toilet and shower room that was put in for Mother. His world has contracted into a span of one room, but his mind still roams freely across the ploughed fields of the world.

*   *   *

Ireland, like Ukraina, is a largely rural country which suffers from its proximity to a more powerful industrialised neighbour. Ireland's contribution to the history of tractors is the genius engineer Harry Ferguson, who was born in 1884, near Belfast.

Ferguson was a clever and mischievous man, who also had a passion for aviation. It is said that he was the first man in Great Britain to build and fly his own aircraft in 1909. But he soon came to believe that improving efficiency of food production would be his unique service to mankind.

Harry Ferguson's first two-furrow plough was attached to the chassis of the Ford Model T car converted into a tractor, aptly named Eros. This plough was mounted on the rear of the tractor, and through ingenious use of balance springs it could be raised or lowered by the driver using a lever beside his seat.

Ford, meanwhile, was developing its own tractors. The Ferguson design was more advanced, and made use of hydraulic linkage, but Ferguson knew that despite his engineering genius, he could not achieve his dream on his own. He needed a larger company to produce his design. So he made an informal agreement with Henry Ford, sealed only by a handshake. This Ford-Ferguson partnership gave to the world a new type of Fordson tractor far superior to any that had been known before, and the precursor of all modern-type tractors.

However, this agreement by a handshake collapsed in 1947 when Henry Ford II took over the empire of his father, and started to produce a new Ford 8N tractor, using the Ferguson system. Ferguson's open and cheerful nature was no match for the ruthless mentality of the American businessman. The matter was decided in court in 1951. Ferguson claimed $240 million, but was awarded only $9.25 million.

Undaunted in spirit, Ferguson had a new idea. He approached the Standard Motor Company at Coventry with a plan, to adapt the Vanguard car for use as tractor. But this design had to be modified, because petrol was still rationed in the post-war period.

The biggest challenge for Ferguson was the move from petrol-driven to diesel-driven engines and his success gave rise to the famous TE-20, of which more than half a million were built in the UK.

Ferguson will be remembered for bringing together two great engineering stories of our time, the tractor and the family car, agriculture and transport, both of which have contributed so richly to the well-being of mankind.

*   *   *

My father goes to Nottingham for Valentina's appeal after all. How does she persuade him? Does she threaten to tell the bureaucraczia about oralsex? Does she cradle his bony skull between her twin warheads and whisper sweet nothings into his hearing aid? My father is silent about this, but he has a cunning plan.

They travel to Nottingham by train. Valentina has bought herself a new outfit for the occasion; it is a navy suit with a pink polyester silk lining that matches her lipstick and fingernails. Her hair is piled up on top of her head in a yellow beehive, secured with a clip and sprayed with lacquer to hold it in place. My father wears the same suit he wore at his wedding and a crumpled white shirt with a frayed collar and the two top buttons sewn on with black thread. On his head he wears a green peaked cap which he refers to as his 'lordovska kepochka' (meaning 'cap as worn by aristocracy') which he bought in the Co-op in Peterborough twenty years ago. Valentina trims his hair with the kitchen scissors to tidy him up a bit, straightens his tie, and even gives him a peck on the cheek.

They are ushered into a cheerless beige-painted room where two men in grey suits and a woman in a grey cardigan sit behind a brown table on which are some sheafs of paper and a decanter of water with three glasses. Valentina is called to speak first, and is taken through a series of questions in which she details how she and my father met at the Ukrainian Club in Peterborough, how they fell in love at first sight, how he wooed her with poems and love letters, how they were married in church, and how happy they are together.

When it is my father's turn to speak, he asks in a quiet voice whether he may go into a separate room. There is some discussion among the Immigration panel, but their conclusion is that no, he must speak in front of everybody.

'I will speak under duress,' he says. They take him through the same series of questions, and his replies are just the same as Valentina's. At the end when he has finished he says, 'Thank you. Now I want you to record that all I have said is spoken under duress.'

He is taking a gamble on her lack of English.

There is a flurry of note-taking, but none of the panel members looks up for a moment or meets my father's eye. Valentina raises one eyebrow by a fraction, but maintains her fixed smile.

'What it mean, this dooh-ress word?' she asks him, as they are waiting for the train to take them home.

'It means love,' my father says. 'Like the French, *tendresse*.'

'Ah *holubchik*. My little pigeon.' She beams, and gives him another peck on the cheek.

12

A half-eaten ham sandwich

'How do you suppose Mrs Z knew about the annulment plan?' Vera asks. Mrs Divorce Expert and Mrs Flog-'em-and-send-'em-home are putting their heads together again.

'Valentina must have seen the letter from the solicitor.'

'She's going through his mail.'

'Looks like it.'

'I must say, with her devious criminal bent, I'm not in the least surprised.'

'It's a game two can play.'

Next time we visit, I abandon Mike to field the tractor mono-logues in the apple-filled sitting-room, while I disappear upstairs to rummage through Valentina's room. She has taken over the room which used to be my parents' bedroom. It is a sombre, ugly room with heavy 1950s oak furniture, the ward-robe still full of my mother's clothes, twin beds with yellow candlewick covers, mauve, yellow and black curtains in a startling modernist design of my father's choosing, and a square of blue carpet in the middle of the brown lino. To me this room, this inner sanctum of my parents' relationship, has always been a place of mystery and trepidation. So I am startled to find that Valentina has transformed it into a Holly-wood-style boudoir, with pink nylon fur-fabric cushions, quilted and frilled holders for tissue paper, cosmetics and cotton wool, pictures of wide-eyed children on the walls, cuddly toys on the bed, and bottles of perfume, lotions and creams on the dressing-table. It seems they have all come from mail-order catalogues, several of which lie open on the floor.

But the most remarkable thing about the room is the mess. There is a chaos of papers, clothes, shoes, dirty cups, nail varnish, pots of cosmetics, crusts of toast, hairbrushes, beauty appliances, toothbrushes, stockings, packets of biscuits, jewellery, photographs, sweet wrappers, knick-knacks, used plates, underwear, apple cores, sticking plasters, catalogues, wrappings, sticky sweets, all jumbled together on the dressing-table, the chair, the spare bed, and overflowing on to the floor. And cotton wool, everywhere blobs of cotton wool covered with red lipstick, black eye make-up, orange face make-up, pink nail varnish, strewn on the bed, on the floor, trodden into the blue carpet, jumbled up with the clothes and food.

There is a strange odour, a mixture of sickly-sweet scent and industrial chemical, and something else – something organic and bacterial.

Where to start? I realise I don't know what exactly I'm looking for. I reckon I have an hour before Valentina gets back from work, and Stanislav gets home from his Saturday job.

I start with the bed. There are some photos, a few official-looking papers, an application for a provisional driver's licence, a P45 from her job at the nursing-home (I notice that the surname is spelt differently on both documents), an application form for a job at McDonald's. The photographs are interesting – they show Valentina in a glamorous off-the-shoulder evening gown, elaborately coiffed, standing beside a dark stocky middle-aged man who is a couple of inches shorter than she. Sometimes he has his arm around her shoulder; sometimes they hold hands; sometimes they smile at the camera. Who is the man? I study the picture closely, but it does not look like Bob Turner. I pick one of the photos and slip it into my pocket.

Under the bed, in a Tesco's carrier bag, I make my next discovery: it is a bundle of letters and poems in my father's crabbed hand. Interspersed with the letters and poems, someone has supplied an English translation. My darling . . . beloved . . . beautiful goddess Venus . . . breasts like ripe peaches (for goodness' sake!) . . . hair like the golden wheat fields of Ukraina . . . all my love and devotion . . . yours until death and beyond. The handwriting of the translations looks like a child's, with large rounded letters, and the *i*'s dotted with little circles. Stanislav? Why would he do this? Who is the intended reader of these translations? One of the letters, I notice, has numbers as well as words. Curious, I pull it out. My father has set out his income, giving details of all his pensions and all his savings accounts. The spidery numbers crawl up and down the pages. It is a modest amount, but enough to live comfortably, and all will be yours, my beloved, he has written at the bottom. All this has been neatly transcribed in the childish hand.

I read it through again, my irritation rising. My sister is right – he is a fool. I should not blame Valentina for taking his money – he has more or less thrust it upon her.

Now I turn my attention to the drawers. Here the same chaos prevails. I sift through the jumble of underwear, outerwear, sticky sweet wrappers, bottles of lotions, cheap perfume.

In one drawer, I find a note. '*See you on Saturday. All my love, Eric.*' Beside it, buried in a pair of knickers, is a half-eaten ham sandwich, its crusts grey and curled back, the pink dark-dry sliver of ham poking out obscenely.

At that moment, I hear the sound of a car pulling up. Quickly, I sneak out of Valentina's room and into Stanislav's. This used to be my room, and I still keep some things in the wardrobe, so I have an excuse to be there. Stanislav is tidier than Valentina. It does not take me long to realise that he is a fan of Kylie Minogue and of Boyzone. This 'musical genius' has a roomful of tapes of Boyzone! On the table under the window are some school books, and a writing pad. He is writing a letter in Ukrainian. Dear Daddy . . .

Then I realise there are two new voices – it is not Mike and my father, it is Valentina and Stanislav talking to each other in the kitchen. I close Stanislav's door behind me quietly and tiptoe downstairs. Valentina and Stanislav are in the kitchen poking at some boil-in-the-bag delicacies bubbling away on the cooker. Under the grill, two shrivelled sausages are starting to smoke.

'Hallo Valentina. Hallo Stanislav.' (I'm not sure of the etiquette here: how are you supposed to talk to someone who is beating up your father, and whose room you have been rifling through? I opt for the English way: polite conversation.) 'Had a hard day at work?'

'I always working hard. Too much hard,' Valentina replies grumpily. I notice how fat she has grown. Her stomach has swelled like a balloon, and her cheeks have stretched and bulged. Stanislav, on the other hand, seems to have grown thinner. My father is lurking in the doorway, emboldened by Mike's presence.

'Sausages burning, Valentina,' he says.

'You no eating, you shut up mouth.' She flicks a wet tea-towel in his direction.

Then she throws the boil-in-bags on to a plate and slits them with a knife, spewing out their indeterminate contents, slaps the sausages down beside them, splatters some ketchup on top, and stomps back up to her bedroom. Stanislav follows mutely.

*   *   *

The pen is mightier than the tea-towel, and Father writes his own revenge.

Never was the technology of peace, in the form of the tractor, transformed into a weapon of war, more ferociously than with the creation of the Valentine tank. This tank was developed by the British, but produced in Canada, where many Ukrainian engineers were skilled in the production of tractors. The Valentine tank was so named because it was first born into the world on the day of St Valentine in 1938. But there was nothing lovely about it. Clumsy and heavy with an old-fashioned gearbox, it was nevertheless deadly, indeed a true killing machine.

*   *   *

'Ugh!' exclaims Vera, when I tell her about the ham sandwich. 'But of course, what else would one expect from such a slut?'

I cannot describe the smell. I tell her about the cotton wool.

'How simply ghastly! In Mother's bedroom! But didn't you find anything else? Was there nothing from the solicitor about her immigration status, or any advice about divorce?'

'I couldn't find anything. Maybe she's keeping it at work. There's no trace in the house.'

'She must have hidden it. Of course it is only what one would expect from a highly developed criminal mind like hers.'

'But listen to this, Vera. I had a look in Stanislav's room, and guess what I found.'

'I haven't a clue. Drugs? Counterfeit money?'

'Don't be silly. No, I found a letter. He's writing to his Dad in Ternopil, saying he's really unhappy over here. He wants to go home.'

13

Yellow rubber gloves

Of course Valentina finds out the true meaning of 'duress'. Stanislav tells her. Worse, she finds out on the same day that a letter comes from the Immigration Service, telling her that her appeal has been refused once more.

She corners my father as he is coming out of the toilet, bent over, fumbling with his flies.

'You living corpse!' she screeches. 'I will show you dooh-ress!'

She is wearing yellow rubber gloves, and has in her hands a tea-towel, wet from washing up, which she starts to flick at him.

'You useless shrivel-brain shrivel-penis donkey.' Flick flick. 'You dried shrivelled relic of ancient goat turd!'

She flicks at his legs and at his hands that are stretched out for protection or in supplication. He backs away and finds himself pressed up against the kitchen sink. Over her shoulder he can see a pan of potatoes bubbling on the stove.

'You creeping insect I will stamp on.' Flick flick! The steam from the potatoes is misting his glasses and there is a slight smell of scorching.

'Dooh-ress! Dooh-ress! I show you dooh-ress!' Emboldened she starts to flick at his face. Flick flick. The corner of the tea-towel catches the bridge of his nose, and sends his spectacles skittering across the floor.

'Valechka, please . . .'

'You morsel of old gristle that dog chewed dog spat out! Thphoo!'

She pokes him in the ribs with a yellow rubber finger.

'Why you still living? You should be long ago lying beside Ludmilla, dead beside dead.'

His body is shaking and he can feel the familiar churning in his bowels. He is afraid he is about to soil himself. The stench of the burning potatoes fills the air.

'Please Valechka, darling, little pigeon . . .' She closes in on him, the yellow fingers now prodding, now slapping. The pan of potatoes is beginning to smoke.

'Soon you will return where you belong! Under ground. Under dooh-ress! Hah!'

He is saved by Mrs Zadchuk, ringing at the doorbell. She comes in, sizes up the situation and lays a plump restraining hand on her friend's arm.

'Come, Valya. Leave this no-good meanie oralsex maniac husband. Come. We go shopping.'

As Crap car disappears round the corner, my father rescues the burnt potatoes and creeps into the bathroom to relieve himself. Then he phones me. His voice is shrill and breathy.

'I think she means to kill me, Nadia.'

'She really said that, about returning to the graveyard?'

'In Russian. Said all in Russian.'

'Pappa, the language doesn't matter . . .'

'No, on contrary, language is supremely important. In language are encapsulated not only thoughts but cultural values . . .'

'Pappa, listen. Please listen.' He is still rabbiting on about the differences between Russian and Ukrainian while my mind is fixed on Valentina. 'Just listen for a moment. Although it is difficult for you, the good news is that she has not been granted leave to remain. That means that maybe soon she will be deported. If only we knew how long it was going to be . . . But in the meantime, if you feel afraid of being in the house with her, you must come and stay with me and Mike.' I know he will not come and stay unless he is really desperate – he hates any disruption to his routine. He has never spent a night under my sister's roof or mine.

'No, no. I will stay here. If I leave house, she will change lock. I will be out, she will be in. She is already talking like that.'

After my father has said goodbye and retreated behind his bolted door, I make three phone calls.

The first is to the Home Office: Lunar House, Croydon. I imagine a vast pock-marked moonscape, empty and silent except for the eerie ringing of unanswered telephones. After about forty rings the phone is picked up. A remote female voice advises me to put the information in writing, and informs me that files are confidential and cannot be discussed with a third party. I try to explain my father's desperate situation. If only he could have some idea what was happening, whether Valentina can appeal again, when she will be deported. I plead. The remote voice relents and suggests I try the local immigration service for the Peterborough area.

Next I telephone the police station in the village. I describe the incident with the wet tea-towel and explain the danger he's in. The policeman isn't impressed. He has come across much worse.

'Look at it this way,' he says. 'It could just be a marital tiff, couldn't it? Happens all the time. If the police got involved every time a married couple fell out – well, there'd be no end to it. If you don't mind me saying so, you seem to be interfering in his affairs when he hasn't asked you to. You obviously don't see eye to eye with this lady he's married to. But if he wanted to make a complaint, he would have telephoned himself, wouldn't he? For all we know, he's been having the time of his life with her.'

In my mind's eye I see a picture of my aged father, bent over, skinny as a stick, cowering under the blows of the wet tea-towel, and Valentina, large, voluptuous, gloved in yellow rubber, standing over him laughing. But the policeman has a different image in mind. Suddenly it's clear.

'You think it was a sex-game – the wet tea-towel.'

'I didn't say that.'

'No but you thought it, didn't you?'

The policeman has been trained to deal with people like me. Politely, he diffuses my anger. In the end, he agrees to drop by when he is doing his rounds, and we leave it at that.

The third call is to my sister. Vera understands instantly. She is outraged.

'The bitch. The criminal slut. But what a fool he is. He deserves everything.'

'Never mind what he deserves, Vera. I think we need to get him out.'

'It would be better if we could get *her* out. Once he is out, he will never be able to go back, and she will have the house.'

'Surely not.'

'You know what they say – possession is nine tenths of the law.'

'That sounds like a leaf from Mrs Zadchuk's law book.'

'It was the same with me – when Dick started to turn nasty, I just wanted to run away, but my solicitor advised me to sit tight, else I could lose the house.'

'But Dick wasn't trying to kill you.'

'Do you think Valentina wants to kill Pappa? I think she just wants to frighten him.'

'She's certainly succeeded there.'

There is a silence. In the background I can hear jazz playing on the radio. The music ends. There is a round of applause. Then Vera says in her Big Sis voice, 'Sometimes I wonder, Nadia, whether there is not such a thing as a victim mentality – you know, as in the natural kingdom there is a hierarchy of dominance in every species.' (There she goes again.) 'Maybe it is in his nature to be bullied.'

'You mean it's the victim's fault?'

'Well, yes, in a way.'

'But when Dick got nasty – that wasn't your fault.'

'Of course that was different. In relation to a man, a woman is always the victim.'

'That sounds dangerously feminist, Vera.'

'Feminist? Oh dear. I just thought it was common sense. But when a man allows himself to be beaten by a woman, you must admit, there's something wrong.'

'You mean it's OK if the husband beats the wife? That's just what Valentina said.' I can't help myself. I still wind her up. If I'm not careful, this conversation will end, as in the old days, with one of us slamming the phone down. 'Of course, you could have a point, Vera. But it might just be a matter of size and strength, rather than personality or gender,' I appease.

There is a pause. She clears her throat.

'This is all getting very confusing, Nadia. Maybe it's not a victim mentality, then. Maybe it's just Pappa who attracts violence. Did Mother never tell you the story of what happened when they first met?'

'No. Tell me.'

⋆　　⋆　　⋆

One Sunday in February 1926, my father set out across the city with his ice skates slung around his neck and a hardboiled egg and a slab of bread in his pocket. The sun was out, and a fresh fall of snow lay light on the ornate balconies and carved caryatids of the fin-de-siècle houses on Melnikov Avenue, muffled the Sunday bells that rang out from the golden domes, and settled as innocent as a baby's pillow on the slopes of Babi Yar.

He had just crossed Melnikov Bridge and was heading towards the sports stadium when a snowball lobbed from the other side of the street whistled past his ear. As he turned to see where it had come from, another hit him full in the face. Nikolai gasped for breath and scrabbled in the snow for his cap. 'Hey hey Nikolashka! Nikolashka cleverdick! Who do you fancy, Nikolashka? Who do you think of when you wank?'

His tormentors were two brothers called Sovinko, who had left school a couple of years before. They must have been about thirteen or fourteen – the same age as my father. They were big shaven-headed lads who lived with their mother and three sisters in two rooms behind the railway station. Their father had died in a forestry accident near Gomel. Mrs Sovinko eked out a living doing people's laundry, and the boys wore cast-offs that their mother rescued from the laundry-bags of her clients.

'Hey brain-arse! D'yer fancy Lyalya? D'yer fancy Ludmilla? Bet you fancy Katya. Have you showed her your dick?'

The bigger boy lobbed another snowball.

'I don't fancy anybody,' said my father. 'I am interested in languages and mathematics.'

The boys pointed their red-cold fingers and bayed derision.

'Hey, he dun't fancy girls: D'yer fancy the boys, then?'

'Just because I don't fancy the girls, it does not follow logically that I must fancy boys.'

'D'yer hear that? Dun't follow logically! D'yer hear that? He's got a logical dick! Hey hey Nikolashka, show us your logical dick.'

They had crossed the road, and were following him along the pavement, getting closer.

'Let's cool his dick down a bit!'

They broke into a careful run. The younger brother sneaked up and shoved a handful of snow down the back of his trousers. Nikolai tried to get away, but the pavement was treacherous. He fell on his face. The two boys pinned him down and straddled him shoving handfuls of snow into his face, down his neck, down his trousers. They started to pull his trousers down. The bigger brother grabbed his skates and began to tug. Nikolai, terrified, screamed and flailed about in the snow.

Just at that moment, three figures appeared at the top of the street. From where he was lying, face down in the snow, he made out a tall girl holding two smaller children by the hand.

'Help me! Help me!' cried Nikolai.

The three hesitated when they saw the fracas. Should they run away or should they intervene? Then the small boy dashed forward.

'Geroff him!' he yelled, hurling himself at the legs of the smaller of the two brothers. The tall girl pitched in, and started to pull the bigger boy's hair. 'You geroff, you fat bully! Leave him alone!'

He shrugged off her assault and seized her wrists with both hands, allowing Nikolai to wriggle free.

'Is he yer boyfriend, then? D'yer fancy him?'

'Geroff or I'll call my Dad, and he'll slice your fingers off with his sabre and stuff 'em up your nose.' Her eyes blazed.

The small girl rubbed handfuls of snow into their ears.

'Stuff 'em up your nose! Stuff 'em up your nose!' she shrilled.

The brothers squirmed and thrashed about, grinning and grabbing at the girls. There was nothing they liked more than a good fight, and they didn't feel the cold. The sky above them was blue as a robin's egg and the sun sparkled on the snow. Then adults appeared on the scene. There was shouting and sticks were waved. The Sovinkos pulled their caps over their ears and darted away, fast and agile as snow hares, before anyone could catch them.

'Are you all right?' asked the tall girl. It was his classmate Ludmilla Ocheretko, with her younger sister and brother. They had their skates slung round their necks too. (Of course the Sovinkos were too poor to have skates of their own.)

In winter, the sports stadium in Kiev was sprayed with water which froze instantly into an outdoor ice rink, and all the young people in Kiev got their skates on. They whizzed about, showed off, fell, pushed, glided and tumbled into each other's arms. It didn't matter what was happening in Moscow or on the many bloody fronts of the Civil War: people still met, skated a couple of laps together, and fell in love. So Nikolai and Ludmilla grasped each other's mittened hands and spun around and around on their skates – the sky and the clouds and the golden domes spun with them – faster and faster, laughing like kids (they were still only kids) till they fell in a dizzy heap on the ice.

14

A small portable photocopier

Next time I visit my father it is mid-week, mid-morning, and I come without Mike. It is a mild luminous spring day, with tulips bursting out in front gardens and new growth greening the tips of trees. In Mother's garden, the peonies are already out, thrusting up their crimson fists through the rampant weeds in the flower-beds.

As I pull up outside the house, I notice a police panda car parked there. I walk into the kitchen to find Valentina and the village policeman sharing a joke over a cup of coffee. After the freshness of the spring air, it is unbearably hot indoors, with the gas boiler belting away and all the windows closed. The two look up at me resentfully, as though I have disturbed a private tryst. Valentina, wearing a lycra denim mini-skirt and a fluffy baby-pink jumper with a white satin heart for the pocket, is perched on a high stool, with her legs crossed and her peep-toe mules casually dangling on her bare toes. (Slut!) The policeman lounges on a chair against the wall with his legs spread. (Slob!) They fall silent as I come in. When I introduce myself, the policeman pulls himself up and shakes my hand. It is the village constable, the same man I spoke to on the telephone about the wet tea-towel incident.

'Just dropped by to check on your Dad,' he says.

'Where is he?' I ask.

Valentina gestures towards the makeshift door which Mike put up, separating the kitchen from the dining-room, which is now his bedroom. My father has locked himself into his room, and is refusing to come out.

'Pappa,' I coax, 'It's me, Nadia. You can unlock the door now. It's OK. I'm here.'

After a long while, there is a rattling of the bolt being pulled, and my father peeps round the door. I am shocked by what I see. He is terribly thin – emaciated – and his eyes have sunk back into their sockets so that his head looks almost like a death's head. His white hair is long and straggles down his nape. He is wearing no clothes below the waist. I take in the terrible shrunken nakedness of his shanks and knees, livid white.

Just at that moment, I catch the policeman and Valentina exchanging glances. Valentina's glance says: See what I mean? The policeman's glance says: Blimey!

'Pappa,' I whisper, 'where are your trousers? Please put on your trousers.'

He indicates a pile of clothes on the floor, and he doesn't need to say anything else, for I can already smell what has happened.

'He shit himself,' says Valentina.
    The policeman tries to conceal an involuntary smirk.
    'What happened, Pappa?'
    'She . . .' He points at Valentina. 'She . . .'
    Valentina raises her eyebrows, re-crosses her legs, and says nothing.

'What did she do? Pappa, tell me what happened.'

'She throw water at me.'

'He was shout at me,' pouts Valentina. 'Shout bad thing. Bad language speaking. I say shut up. He no shut up. I throw water. Is only water. Water no hurt.'

The policeman turns towards me.

'Seems like it's six of one and half a dozen of the other,' he says. 'Usually the case in domestics. Can't take sides.'

'Surely you can see what's going on?' I say.

'As far as I'm aware, no crime has been committed.'

'But isn't your job to protect the vulnerable? Just look – use your eyes. If you can't see anything else, you can see that there's a difference in size and strength. They're not exactly evenly matched, are they?' I notice once more how much weight Valentina has put on, but despite this, or maybe because of it, there is a kind of magnetism about her.

'You can't arrest someone because of their size.' The police-man can hardly take his eyes off her. 'Of course I'll continue to keep an eye, if your dad would like me to.' He looks from Valentina to me to my father.

'You are no different to Stalin's police,' my father suddenly bursts out in a high quavery voice. 'Whole system of state apparatus is only to defend powerful against weak.'

'I'm sorry if you think that, Mr Mayevskyj,' the policeman says politely. 'But we live in a free country and you are free to express your opinion.'

Valentina swings herself down heavily from the stool.

'I time go working now,' she says. 'You clean up you Pappa shit.'

The policeman, too, makes his goodbyes and leaves.

My father sinks down in his chair, but I do not let him rest.

'Pappa, please put on some trousers,' I say. There is something so horrifying about his corpse-like nakedness that I cannot bear to look at him. I cannot bear the look in his eyes – at once defeated and dogged. I cannot bear the stench coming from his room. I have no doubt that Valentina cannot bear it either, but I have hardened my heart: it was her choice.

While my father is cleaning himself up, I search the house again. Somewhere there must be letters from her solicitor, information about her immigration appeal. Where does she keep her correspondence? We need to know what she is planning to do, how long she will be here. To my surprise, I find in the sitting-room, on the table amid the rotting apples, a small portable photocopier. I had overlooked it before, thinking it was some part of a computer, maybe belonging to Stanislav.

'Pappa, what's this?'

'Oh, this is Valentina's new toy. She uses it to copy letters.'

'What letters?'

'It is her latest craze, you know. Copying this, copying that.'

'She copies your letters?'

'Her letters. My letters. Probably she thinks it is very modern. All letters she copies.'

'But why?'

He shrugs. 'Maybe she thinks to have photocopier is more prestigious than writing by hand.'

'Prestigious? How stupid. That can't be the reason.'

'Do you know the theory of panopticon? English philosopher Jeremy Bentham. Is design for the perfect prison. Jailer sees everything, from every angle, and yet himself remains invisible. So Valentina knows everything about me, and I know nothing about her.'

'What are you talking about, Pappa? Where are all the letters and copies?'

'Maybe in her room.'

'No, I've looked. Not in Stanislav's room either.'

'I don't know. Maybe in car. I see she takes everything to car.'

Crap car is sitting on the driveway. But where are the keys?

'No need for keys,' says my father. 'Lock is broken. She locked keys inside boot. I break lock with screwdriver.'

I notice that the car also has no tax disc. Maybe she had second thoughts about driving off in it while the policeman was here. In the boot I find a cardboard box, bursting with papers, files and photocopies. This is what I have been looking for. I bring them into the sitting-room, and sit down to read.

There is so much paper here that I am overwhelmed. I have gone from having no information at all, to suddenly having far too much. As far as I can tell, the letters are not ordered or sorted in any way, not by date or correspondent or content. I start to pull them out at random. Near the front of the box, a letter from the Immigration Service catches my eye. It is the letter setting out their reasons for refusing to grant her leave to remain after her appeal – there is no reference to my father's statement under duress, but there is a paragraph explaining her rights to a further appeal to a tribunal. My heart sinks. So the last appeal was not the end of the road. How many more appeals and hearings will there be? I make a copy of the letter on the small portable photocopier, so that I can show it to Vera.

Now here are some copies of my father's poems and letters to her, including the letter setting out the details of his savings and pensions – both the original Ukrainian texts and the translations have been photocopied and stapled together. Why? For whom? Here is a letter to my father from the consultant psychiatrist at the Peterborough District Hospital, offering him an appointment. The appointment is for tomorrow. My father has not said anything about this. Did he receive the letter? She has copied the letter (why?) but she has not returned the original.

There are some letters from Ukraine, presumably from her husband, but I can only read Ukrainian character by character, and I haven't got time to read them now.

There is more of my father's correspondence – here is the letter from the trainee solicitor about the difficulty of obtaining an annulment. Here is a letter he has written to whom it may concern at the Home Office declaring his love for her, and insisting that the marriage is genuine. It is dated 10 April – shortly before the appeal panel in Nottingham. Was it also written under duress? Here is a letter from his GP, Doctor Figges, advising him that he needs to call in for a new prescription.

In a brown envelope I find some copies of the wedding pictures – Valentina smiling to camera, bent low towards my father so that her fabulous cleavage is revealed, and my father wide-eyed, grinning like a dog with two tails. In the same envelope are a copy of the marriage certificate and an information sheet from the Home Office regarding naturalisation.

Now here at last is the letter I have been looking for – it is a letter from Valentina's solicitor, dated only a week ago, agreeing to act for her in relation to her Immigration Tribunal hearing in London on 9 September and advising her to apply for legal aid. September! My father will never be able to hold out so long. The letter ends with a caution:

You are advised that you should avoid at all costs giving your husband grounds for divorce, as this could seriously jeopardise your case . . .

I am so deeply engrossed that I almost miss the sound of the back door opening. Someone is in the kitchen, I realise. Quickly, I bundle together all the letters and papers, shove them back into the box and look for somewhere to put them. In the corner of the room is the big chest freezer where my mother kept all her vegetables and herbs, and where Valentina now keeps her boil-in-the-bag dinners. I stick them in there. The door opens.

'Oh, you here still,' says Valentina.

'I'm just doing a bit of tidying up.' My voice is placatory (no point in upsetting her – I will be gone soon, and then she will be left with my father) but she takes this as a slight.

'I too much working. No time house working.'

'Quite.' I lean casually on the freezer.

'You father – he no give me money.'

'But he gives you half his pension.'

'Pension no good. What can buy with pension?'

I don't want to argue with her. I just want her to go, so I can get on with looking through the papers. But then I realise she may have come back for her boil-in-the-bag lunch.

'Would you like me to make lunch for you, Valentina? You

can go upstairs and have a rest, while I get the lunch ready.'

She is surprised and mollified, but declines my offer.

'I no time eating. Only sandwich' (she pronounces it san-yeedge). 'I come get car. After finish working I go Peter-borough with Margaritka shopping.'

She bangs the door and drives off in the car, and I am left with a box of frozen documents.

I make a copy of the solicitor's letter, but then I see that there are only two sheets of copier paper left, so I stop. I slip one of the wedding photos into my handbag, as well as the copies I have made. Then I put the rest of the papers back into the box.

As I am doing so, another paper catches my eye. It is a letter from the Institute of Feminine Beauty in Budapest, typed on thick cream paper, with a gold-embossed border, to a Mrs Valentina Dubova at Hall Street, Peterborough. It thanks her, in English, for her esteemed custom and acknowledges the payment of three thousand US dollars in respect of breast enhancement surgery. It is signed with a flourish by a Doktor Pavel Nagy. From the date, I work out that it must have taken place a few months before their marriage, during her trip to Ukraine. My mind goes back to the fat brown envelope. Three thousand US dollars is a little over £1,800. So my father must have known what it was for. Must have known, and must have been eager to pay it.

'Pappa,' I call him, softly, so as not to reveal the extent of my rage. 'Pappa, what is this?'

'Mmm. Yes.' He looks at the letter and nods. There is nothing he can say.

'You *are* crazy. Lucky you have an appointment with the psychiatrist tomorrow.'

I stow the box of frozen letters under my father's bed, with strict instructions that he must replace them in the boot of her car at the earliest opportunity, without her seeing. I suppose I should stay and do it myself, but it is already early evening, and I just want to get away, to get home to kind, sane Mike and my orderly house. I cook him macaroni cheese – maggot-white, tasteless, but he can eat it without his false teeth. We eat in silence. There is nothing left to say. When he has finished, I say goodbye. As I turn from the lane into the main road, a car careers wildly round the bend in the other direction. One headlamp is broken. In the front are two grinning figures: Valentina and Margaritka returning from their shopping trip.

15

In the psychiatrist's chair

My father's visit to the psychiatrist is a triumph. The consultation lasts a whole hour, and the consultant hardly gets a word in edgeways. He is a most cultured and intelligent type, my father says. An Indian, by the way. He is fascinated by my father's theory of the relationship between mechanical engineering as applied to tractors and the psychological engineering advocated by Stalin, as applied to the human soul. He is sympathetic to Schopenhauer's observation of the connection between madness and genius, but reluctant to be drawn into a debate about whether Nietzsche's supposed madness was an effect of syphilis, though he admits under pressure that there is some merit in my father's case that Nietzsche's genius was merely misunderstood by less intelligent types. He asks my father whether he believes that he is being persecuted. 'No, no!' my father exclaims. 'Only by her!' He points at the door behind which Valentina is lurking. (The doctor wanted to discover whether I am suffering from a paranoia, my father said, but of course I did not fall for this trick.)

Valentina is miffed at being excluded from the consultation, since she believes it was she who first brought my father's madness to the attention of the authorities. She is even more miffed when my father emerges with a beam of triumph on his face.

156

'Very intelligent doctor. He says I not crazy. You crazy!'

She barges into the psychiatrist's office and starts to berate him in a variety of languages. The doctor calls the hospital porters and she is asked to leave. She flounces out throwing offensive remarks about Indians over her shoulder.

'OK, Pappa, so the visit to the psychiatrist was a success. But what happened to your head? Where did you get that cut?'

'Ah, this too is Valentina's doing. After she failed to have me certified as insane, she attempted to murder me.'

He describes another ugly scene as they emerge from the porticoed entrance of the hospital, still shouting at each other. She pushes him, and he loses his footing and falls down the stone steps, banging his head. It starts to bleed.

'Come,' says Valentina, 'You foolish falling-on-ground man. Get in car quick quick quick we go home.'

A small crowd has gathered around them.

'No, go away, murderer!' my father cries, flailing his arms about. 'I will not go home with you!' His glasses have fallen off and one of the lenses is smashed.

A nurse steps out of the crowd, and looks at my father's head wound. It is not deep, but it bleeds copiously. She takes him by the arm.

'Might be just as well to pop into Casualty and have it looked at.'

Valentina grabs his other arm.

'No, no! He my husband. He OK. He coming home in car.'

There is a tug of war between the two women, my father in the middle, all the time protesting 'Murderer! Murderer!' The crowd of onlookers has swelled. The nurse calls the hospital security guards and my father is taken to Accident & Emergency, where his wound is dressed, Valentina still stubbornly clinging to his arm. She will not let him go.

But my father refuses to leave A & E with Valentina. 'She wants to murder me!' he calls out to anyone who comes within earshot. In the end, a social worker is called, and my father, his head dramatically bandaged, is admitted to a residential hostel for the night. Next day, he is escorted home in a police car.

Valentina is waiting for him when he arrives, all smiles and bosom.

'Come, *holubchik*, my little pigeon. My darling.' She pats his cheek. 'We will not argue any more.'

The policemen are charmed. They accept her offer of tea, and sit around in the kitchen far longer than is necessary, discussing the vulnerability and foolishness of old people, and how important it is that they be properly looked after. The policemen advance instances of elderly people who have been duped by doorstep criminals and knocked over in the street by muggers. Not all old people are so lucky as to have a loving wife to care for them. Valentina expresses horror at these wanton instances of brutality.

And maybe she is genuinely repentant, says my father, for after the policemen have gone she does not turn on him in a fury, but takes his hand and places it on her breast, stroking it with her fingers, chiding him gently for mistrusting her and allowing this shadow to fall between them. She does not even abuse him for taking her box of papers and hiding it under his bed. (Of course she found them – of course my father did not manage to return them to the boot of the car.) Or maybe someone (Mrs Zadchuk?) has explained to her the meaning of the last sentence of the solicitor's letter.

*   *   *

I have sent Mrs Divorce Expert a copy of the solicitor's letter, and she has sent Mrs Flog-'em-and-send-'em-home a newspaper cutting. It tells the story of a man from the Congo who has lived in the UK for fifteen years, who is now to be deported because he entered the country illegally all those years ago, even though he has established a life for himself, built up a business, become a figure in the local community. The local church has mounted a campaign on his behalf.

'I think the tide is turning,' says Vera. 'People are waking up at last.'

I have come to quite the opposite conclusion – people are falling asleep over this issue, not waking up. The remote voices in Lunar House are asleep. The blue-chip voices in far-flung consulates are asleep. The trio on the immigration panel in Nottingham are asleep – they are just going through the motions like sleepwalkers. Nothing will happen.

'Vera, all this stuff about deportation, and these high-profile cases with campaigns and letters to newspapers – it's just to create an illusion of activity. In reality, in most cases – nothing happens. Nothing at all. It's just a charade.'

'Of course that is what I would expect you to say, Nadezhda. Your sympathies have always been quite clear.'

'It's not a matter of sympathies, Vera. Listen to what I'm saying. Our mistake has been to think that they would remove her. But they won't. *We* have to remove her.'

Wearing the stilettos of Mrs Flog-'em-and-send-'em-home

has altered the way I walk. I used to be liberal about immigration – I suppose I just thought it was all right for people to live where they wanted. But now I imagine hordes of Valentinas barging their way through customs, at Ramsgate, at Felixstowe, at Dover, at Newhaven – pouring off the boats, purposeful, single-minded, mad.

'But you always take her side.'

'Not any more.'

'I suppose it's because you're a social worker, you can't help it.'

'I'm not a social worker, Vera.'

'Not a social worker?' There is silence. The phone crackles. 'Well what are you?'

'I'm a lecturer.'

'So – a lecturer! What do you lecture about?'

'Sociology.'

'Well that's it – that's what I mean.'

'Sociology's not the same thing as social work.'

'No? Well what is it?'

'It's about society – different forces and groups in society and why they behave as they do.'

There is a pause. She clears her throat.

'But that's fascinating!'

'Well, yes. *I* think so.'

Another pause. I can hear Vera lighting a cigarette on the other end of the line.

'So why is Valentina behaving as she is?'

'Because she's desperate.'

'Ah, yes. Desperate.' She draws a deep breath, sucking in smoke.

'Remember when we were desperate, Vera?'

The hostel. The refugee centre. The single bed we shared. The terraced house with the toilet in the back yard and the squares of torn newspaper.

'But how desperate must one be to become a criminal? Or to prostitute oneself?'

'Women have always gone to extremes for their children. I would do the same for Anna. I'm sure I would. Wouldn't you do the same for Alice or Lexy? Wouldn't Mother have done the same for us, Vera? If we were desperate? If there was no other way?'

'You don't know what you're talking about, Nadia.'

*   *   *

I lie in bed in the small hours thinking about the man from the Congo. I imagine the knock on the door in the night, the heart jumping against the rib-cage, the predator and prey looking into each other's eyes. Gotcha! I imagine the friends and neighbours gathered on the pavement, the Zadchuks waving hankies which they press to their eyes. I imagine the cup of coffee, still warm, left on the table in the haste of departure, which goes cold, then gathers a skin of mould and then finally dries into a brown crust.

Mike does not like Mrs Flog-'em-and-send-'em-home. She is not the woman he married.

'Deportation's a cruel nasty way of dealing with people. It's not the solution to anything.'

'I know. I know. But . . .'

Next morning I telephone the number at the top of the letter Valentina got from the Immigration Advisory Service. They give me a number at East Midlands Airport. Amazingly, I get through to the woman with the brown briefcase and blue Fiat who visited the house after their marriage. She is surprised to hear from me, but she remembers my father straightaway.

'I had a gut feeling something wasn't right,' she says. 'Your Dad seemed so, well . . .'

'I know.'

She sounds nice – much nicer than my father's description of her.

'It wasn't just the bedrooms – it was the fact that they didn't seem to do *anything* together.'

'But what will happen now? How will it end?'

'That I can't tell you.'

I learn that the deportation, if there is to be one, will be carried out not by the Immigration Service but by the local police, instructed by the Home Office. Every region has police officers who are located within local police stations but who specialise in immigration matters.

'It's been interesting talking to you,' she says. 'We visit people, and we file these reports, and then they disappear into thin air. We don't often find out what happens.'

'Well, nothing's happened yet.'

I phone the central police station in Peterborough, and ask to speak to the specialist immigration officer. They refer me on to Spalding. The officer whose name they have given me is not on duty. I phone again next day. I was expecting a man, but Chris Tideswell turns out to be a woman. She is matter-of-fact, when I tell her my father's story.

'Yer poor Dad. Yer get some right villains.' Her voice sounds young and chirpy, with a broad fenland accent. She doesn't sound old enough to have carried out many deportations.

'Listen,' I say, 'when all this is over, I'm going to write a book about it, and you can be the heroic young officer who finally brings her to justice.'

She laughs. 'I'll do my best, but don't hold yer breath.' There is nothing she can do until after the tribunal. Then there may be leave to appeal on compassionate grounds. Only after that will there be a warrant to deport, maybe.

'Phone me a week or so after the hearing.'

'You can have a starring role in the film. Played by Julia Roberts.'

'Yer sound as if yer a bit desperate.'

*   *   *

Will Valentina be able to keep up this regime of little-pigeon cooing and bosom-stroking until September? Somehow I doubt it. Will my father, thin as a stick, frail as a shadow, be able to survive on his diet of tinned ham, boiled carrots, Toshiba apples and the occasional beating? Seems unlikely.

I telephone my sister.

'We can't wait until September. We've got to get her out.'

'Yes. We've tolerated this for far too long. Really, I blame . . .' She stops. I can almost hear the screech of verbal brakes being slammed on.

'We need to work together on this, Vera.' My voice is placatory. We are getting on so well. 'We'll just have to persuade Pappa to reconsider his objections to divorce.'

'No, something more immediate. We must apply for an ousting order to get her out of the house at once. The divorce can come later.'

'But will he go along with it? Now they're back on bosom-fondling terms, he is quite unpredictable.'

'He's mad. Quite mad. In spite of what the psychiatrist said.'

*   *   *

This is not the first time my father has been given the all-clear by a psychiatrist. It happened at least once before, some thirty years ago, when I was in what he described as my Trotskyist phase. I found out about it by chance. My parents were out, and I was rooting through their bedroom – the same room with the heavy oak furniture and discordantly patterned curtains that Valentina has now converted into her boudoir. I can't remember what I was looking for, but I found two things that shocked me.

The first, lying on the floor under one of the beds, was a crumpled rubber sac full of whitish sticky fluid. I stared at it in horror. This most intimate outpouring. This shameless evidence that my parents had performed the sex act on more than the two occasions on which Vera and I had been conceived. My father's semen!

The second was a report from a psychiatrist at the Infirmary dated 1961. It was among some papers hidden in a drawer in the dressing-table. The report noted that my father had asked to see a psychiatrist because he believed he was suffering from a pathological hatred of his daughter (me, not Vera!). So obsessive and all-consuming was this hatred that he feared it was a sign of mental illness. The psychiatrist had talked to my father at length, and had concluded that in view of my father's experience of communism it was not at all surprising, natural in fact, that he should hate his daughter for her communist views.

I read it with growing astonishment, and then with rage, both at my father and at this anonymous psychiatrist, who had taken the easy option, who hadn't heard my father's call for help. Stupid – both of them. My mother, whose family had suffered unspeakable wrongs, who had far more reason to hate me for being a communist, had somehow never stopped loving me even through my wildest years, even though the things I said must have hurt her to the quick.

I put the papers back in the drawer. I wrapped the used condom in some newspaper and put it in the bin, as though I could somehow protect my mother from its shameful contents.

16

My mother wears a hat

Aunty Shura delivered my mother's first baby. Vera was born in Luhansk (Voroshilovgrad) in March 1937. She was a miserable baby whose high-pitched gasping cries, as though she was about to stop breathing at any moment, drove Nikolai to distraction. Aunty Shura doted on Ludmilla, but she did not like Nikolai, and neither did her Communist-Party-member-friend-of-Marshal-Voroshilov husband. Life at Aunty Shura's became tense. Tempers flared, doors were slammed, voices were raised, and the wooden house reverberated like a sound box. After a few weeks, Ludmilla, Nikolai and baby Vera decamped to live with Ludmilla's mother (now she was a grandmother they called her Baba Sonia) in her new three-roomed concrete-built apartment on the other side of the city.

It was a tight squeeze in the apartment. Nikolai, Ludmilla and the baby occupied one room; in another room lived Baba Sonia; the third room was rented out to two students. The younger brother and sister were away at college, but when they came back, they shared with their mother. There was no hot water – sometimes no cold water, either – and although the famine had eased, food was still scarce. The new baby grizzled and whined constantly. She sucked fiercely at the breast, but Ludmilla, sick and anaemic, had little milk to give her.

Baba Sonia would take the whining baby on to her knee, bounce her up and down, and sing:

'Beyond the Caucasus we stood up for our rights,
stood up for our rights. Hey!
There the Magyars were advancing, were advancing. Hey!'

Aunty Shura said: 'Take an apple, push iron nails into it, leave it overnight, then take the nails out and eat it – that way you get both vitamin C and iron.'

Nikolai could not find a suitable job in Luhansk and mooched around the flat writing poems and getting under everyone's feet. The constant crying of the baby got on his nerves, and he got on Ludmilla's nerves. In the winter of 1937 he returned to Kiev.

*   *   *

That same year, Ludmilla was finally offered a place at the veterinary college in Kiev. Maybe the crane-operating job had done the trick, and turned her into a proletarian after all. But now it seemed like a cruel joke. With a new baby and her husband at work, it would be impossible.

'Go! Go!' said Aunty Shura. 'I'll look after Verochka.'

Ludmilla had to choose: husband and veterinary college, or baby daughter. Aunty Shura bought her a new coat and a train ticket, and gave her an extravagant hat with silk flowers and a veil. Ludmilla kissed her mother and her aunt goodbye at the station. Little Verochka clung to her sobbing. They had to hold her back while Ludmilla boarded the train.

'So when did you see her again?'

'It was nearly two years,' says Vera. 'She stayed in Kiev right up until the start of the war. Then she came to get me. Kharkiv was too dangerous. We went to Dashev, to stay with Baba Nadia. It would be safer in the village.'

'You must have been glad to see her.'

'I didn't recognise her.'

One day a thin dishevelled-looking woman arrived on the doorstep, and grabbed Vera in her arms. The child started to scream and kick.

'Don't you recognise your mother, Verochka?' said Aunty Shura.

'She's not my mother!' cried Vera. 'My mother wears a hat.'

*   *   *

We still have a picture of Mother in the hat, with the veil pulled back and a girlish smile on her face. My father must have taken it shortly after she arrived in Kiev. I found it in a bundle of old photographs and letters in that same drawer where I once found the letter from the psychiatrist. The letter has long since been lost, but the photographs are in an old shoe box in the sitting-room, along with the fragrant rotting apples, the freezer full of boil-in-the-bag dinners, the small portable photocopier and the civilised person's Hoover, which being of a foreign make for which no dust bags are available in this country, now sits abandoned in the corner with its cover open and debris spilling from its civilised insides.

This room is still disputed territory. When Valentina is at home, she sits in here with the television on at full blast, and an electric bar fire (my father has fixed the radiator so that it doesn't come on, in order to protect his apples). My father does not understand television; most of the content is completely meaningless to him. He sits in his bedroom and listens to classical music on the radio, or reads. But when she is out at work, he likes to sit in here with his apples and his photographs and the view over the ploughed fields.

We are sitting in here together this wet afternoon in May drinking tea, watching the rain stream down the windows and lash the lilac trees in the garden, while I try to work the conversation away from the development of jet propulsion in Ukraine in the 1930s, and towards a discussion of divorce.

'I know you don't like the idea, Pappa. But I think it's the only way you will be free again.'

He stops and looks at me with a frown. 'Why you are now talking about divorce, Nadia? That is Vera, who is such enthusiast for the divorce. Cigarettes and divorce. Pah!'

His jaw is set, his arthritic fingers knotted in his lap.

'Vera and I are both agreed about this, Pappa. We think Valentina will continue to abuse you, and we are worried about your safety.'

'Did you know, when Vera first discovered there was such thing as divorce, she immediately tried to convince Ludmilla to divorce me.'

'Really?' This is the first I have heard about this. 'I'm sure she didn't mean it. Children say all sorts of strange things.'

'She did mean it. Indeed she did. All her life she has tried to make divorce between Millochka and me. Now between Valentina and me. Now you too, Nadia.'

He fixes me with that stubborn look. I can see this conversation is going nowhere.

'But Pappa, you lived with Mother for sixty years. Surely you can see that Valentina is not the same as Mother.'

'Clearly this Valentina, she is of quite different generation. She knows nothing of history, even less about recent past. She is daughter of the Brezhnev era. In times of the Brezhnev, everyone's idea was to bury all gone-by things and to become like in West. To build this economy, people must be buying something new all the time. New desires must be implanted as fast as old ideals must be buried. That is why she is always wanting to buy something modern. It is not her fault; it is the post-war mentality.'

'But Pappa, this is no excuse for her to mistreat you. She cannot abuse you like this.'

'One can forgive a beautiful woman many things.'

'O, Pappa! For goodness' sake!'

His glasses have slipped down his nose, and sit at a crazy angle. His shirt is unbuttoned at the throat, showing the white hairs that sprout around his scar. He has a sour, unwashed smell. He isn't exactly your Don Juan, but he has no idea.

'This Valentina, she is beautiful like Milla, and like Milla she has strong spirit, but also with an element of cruelty in her nature unknown to Ludmilla, which by the way is character-istic of the Russian type.'

'Pappa, how can you compare her with Mother? How can you even say her name in the same breath?'

It is his disloyalty that I cannot forgive.

'You made Mother's life a misery, and now you abuse her memory. Vera's right – Mother should have divorced you long ago.'

'Misery? Memory? Nadia, why you always want to make a drama out of something? Millochka died. That is sad, of course, but is now in the past. Now is time for new life, new love.'

'Pappa, it's not me making the drama. It's you. All my life, all Mother's life, we had to live with your crazy ideas, your dramas. Do you remember how upset Mother was when you invited all the Ukrainians to come and live with us? Do you remember how you bought the new Norton, when Mother needed a washing machine? Do you remember when you left home and tried to catch the train back to Russia?'

'But that was not because of Millochka. That was because of you. You were then a crazy Trotskyist.'

'I wasn't a Trotskyist. And even if I was, I was only *fifteen*. You were an adult – supposedly.'

It's true, though, that it was because of me that he tried to leave home and catch the train back to Russia. He packed his brown cardboard suitcase – the very same one that had travelled with him when he left Ukraine – and stood on the platform at Witney railway station. I can just imagine him pacing up and down, muttering to himself and looking impatiently at his watch from time to time.

Mother had to go and plead with him.

'Nikolai! Kolya! Kolyusha! Come home now! Kolka, where are you going?'

'I'm waiting for the train to Russia!' Picture the dramatic gesture of his head, his blazing eyes. 'Why not? It's all the same. Now they are bringing in communism here, I don't know why I ever left Russia. I don't know why I risked everything. Now even my own daughter is helping to bring in communism here.'

Yes, it was all my fault. I went down to Greenham Common with my friend Cathy in 1962. (I went again in 1981, but that's

a different story.) We went to protest about the planned
deployment of H-bombs at the nuclear base, and we got ourselves arrested. There we were in our drainpipes and head-
bands and groovy shades, sitting out on the newly laid approach
road. I was reading Julius Caesar's *De Bello Gallico* (GCE set
text) while the police came and carried us away one by one. I
may have been challenging the state through non-violent civil
disobedience, but I was still my father's daughter, and I did
my Latin homework.

Some people were strumming Spanish guitars, and everyone
started to sing:

> 'Don't you hear the H-bombs thunder,
> Sounding like the crack of doom?
> While they tear the heavens asunder,
> Fall-out makes the earth a tomb.'

Yes, I could hear the H-bombs. I could see the fall-out glimmer-
ing in the air, I could feel the strange rain falling. I did believe
I would never live to grow up if we didn't get rid of those
H-bombs. But still, I was hedging my bets and doing my
GCEs.

All the other people there were older than Cathy and me.
Some had long stringy hair and bare feet, and wore faded
jeans and dark glasses. Others were nice Quakerly types with
sensible shoes and cardigans. They carried on singing as the
police picked them up by their arms and legs and put them
into furniture vans (they seemed to have run out of Black
Marias). Cathy and I didn't sing – we didn't want to look daft.

An impromptu courtroom had been set up in the local primary school. We sat on infant-sized chairs, and were called to the bench one by one. Each person made a speech about the wickedness of war, and was fined £3, with £2 court costs. When it was my turn, I couldn't think of anything to say, so I was only fined £3. (A bargain!) I had lied about my age, because I didn't want my parents to find out, but they found out anyway.

'Kolya,' pleaded my mother, 'she's not a communist, she's just a silly girl. Come home now.'

My father said nothing, but stared at a fixed point down the railway line. The next train was in forty minutes, and that went to Eynsham and Oxford, not to Russia.

'Kolyusha, it's a long way to Russia. Look, at least come home and have something to eat first. I've got a lovely beetroot soup. And *kotletki* – your favourite *kotletki*, with spinach and beans from the garden, and little potatoes. Just come and fill your belly, then you can go to Russia.'

So, still muttering his rage, he allowed himself to be led back along the muddy path between the brambles and nettles, to the pebble-dash semi where we lived. Grudgingly he bowed his head over the steaming soup bowl. Later, she coaxed him up to bed. So he didn't leave home after all.

Instead, I left. I ran away to live at Cathy's house. They lived in a long low Cotswold stone cottage at White Oak Green, full of books and cats and cobwebs. Cathy's parents were left-wing intellectuals. They didn't mind Cathy going on marches, in fact they encouraged her. They talked about grown-up things like whether Britain should join the EEC and who created God. But the house was cold, and the food tasted funny, and the cats jumped on you in the night. After a few days my mother came and coaxed me home, too.

Years later I can still remember the smell of hot sun on freshly laid tarmac at Greenham Common, and the musty smell of Cathy's bedroom. Only the image of my father is unclear, as if something obscure but vital has been blotted out, and only the raging surface is left. Who is he, this man whom I have known and not known all my life?

'But this is all in past, Nadia. Why you have such bourgeois preoccupation with all personal history?'

'Because it's important . . . it defines . . . it helps us understand . . . because we can learn . . . Oh, I don't know.'

17
Lady Di and the Rolls-Royce

Valentina and Stanislav have been given a cat. They call it Lady Di, after Diana Princess of Wales, whom they admire greatly. She came from Mrs Zadchuk's neighbour, and she is more of a kitten than a cat – and not nearly as pretty as her namesake. She is black with random white splodges, pale pink-rimmed eyes and a wet pale pink nose.

Lady Di (they pronounce it Lyé Dee Dee) sets to, shredding all the soft furnishings in the house. After a few weeks, it turns out that she is a boy-cat, not a girl-cat (my mother would never have made that mistake) and starts pissing everywhere. Now, to the smell of rotting apples, mouldering half-eaten boil-in-the-bag dinners, cheap perfume, and the odour of unventilated old-man's room, is added the scent of tomcat's piss. Not just piss, either. No one has taught Lady Di to use a litter tray, and no one clears up after him when, on wet days, he decides he is too royal to go in the garden.

My father, Valentina and Stanislav all adore Lady Di, who has a neat way of scampering up curtains, and can jump four feet in the air to catch a bit of paper dangled on a string. Only Vera and I don't like him, and we don't live there, so what does it matter what we think?

Lady Di has become a surrogate child to them. They sit

together holding hands and marvelling over his brilliance and beauty. It is surely only a matter of time before he is taught to prove Pythagoras from first principles.

* * *

'He won't even consider a divorce, Vera. They sit there holding hands cooing over that nasty little cat.'

'Really, it's too much! I told you we should have had him certified,' says Big Sis.

'That's what Valentina thinks.'

'Well she's quite right, wicked though she is. She's obviously got him eating out of her hands again, until she gets her passport. Men are so stupid.'

'Vera, what's all this about you wanting Mother to divorce him?'

'What do you mean?'

'He says you tried to persuade Mother to divorce him.'

'Did I? I can't remember. What a pity I didn't succeed.'

'Anyway, the upshot is, it's put him right off the idea of divorce.'

'I can see I'm going to have to come and talk to him myself.'

* * *

However, something soon happens which makes him change his mind. Early one morning, he telephones and starts ranting some nonsense about a big roller. I am in a hurry to get to work so I urge him to ring later. But he finally gets the words out:

'It's the roller sitting in the front garden, on the lawn.'

'Pappa, what do you mean? What roller?'

'Roller! Rolls-Royce!'

Valentina has achieved the apogee of her dreams of life in the West – she is the owner of a Rolls-Royce. It is a 4-litre sedan, sold to her by Eric Pike for the knock-down price of £500 (paid by my father). She now has a Lada in the garage, a Rover on the drive, and a Roller on the lawn. None of the cars is licensed or insured. She has still not passed her driving test.

'Who is this Eric Pike, Pappa?' I remember the note I found tucked up in the knicker drawer with the half-eaten ham sandwich.

'Actually, this is a most interesting type. Once he was pilot in RAF. Jet propulsion fighter pilot. Now he is used car dealer. He has superb moustaches.'

'And is he very friendly with Valentina?'

'No no. I think not. They have nothing in common. She has no interest whatsoever in motors, except as vehicle for self-display. Actually is quite nice car. Came from estate of Lady Glaswyne. I believe was used for many years as farm vehicle, transporting hay, sheep, fertiliser bags, anything you like. Almost like tractor. Now is in need of some repairing.'

Mike bursts out laughing when he sees the Roller. It flops crookedly on the grass in front of the sitting-room window like a swan with a broken wing. It looks as if the suspension is gone. Brown fluid seeps from its underbelly, poisoning the grass. The paintwork which was once white is now a patchwork of touch-up paint, filler, and rust. He and my father walk round and round it, patting it and poking it here and there, shaking their heads.

'She wants me to repair her,' says my father with a helpless little shrug, as if he is the fairytale prince set an impossible task as a test of love by the beautiful princess.

'I think it's past repair,' says Mike. 'Anyway, where would you get the parts?'

'True, she is needing some parts, and even then it is by no means any certainty that she will run,' says my father. 'Such is a pity. Car like this should run for ever, but she has clearly suffered from some abuses in her past. Nevertheless, what beauty . . .'

Just at that moment, Valentina emerges from the house. Although it is June, and the weather is warm, she is wearing a huge pinch-waisted wide-shouldered fur coat, which she wraps around herself with her hands in the pockets, movie-star style. She has grown so fat that the coat hardly meets in the middle. Around her neck twinkle some sparkly beads which in a poor light could be mistaken for diamonds. Stanislav, in a short-sleeved shirt, walks behind her carrying her bag.

She stops when she sees the three of us standing in the garden looking at her Roller.

'Is nice car, yes?' She addresses all of us, but looks to Mike for a reply.

'Yes, a very nice car,' says Mike, 'but possibly more of a museum piece or a collector's item than an on-road vehicle.'

'Hallo, Valentina,' I smile ingratiatingly. 'You're looking very elegant. Are you going out?'

'Verk.' One word. She doesn't even turn her head towards me.

'What do you think, Stanislav? Do you like the car?'

'Oh yes. It's better than a Zill.' Flash of chipped tooth. 'Valentina always gets what she wants in the end.'

'Car is kaput,' says my father.

'You mend car,' she snaps. Then remembering she is

supposed to be nice to him, she bends forward and pats his cheek. 'Mr Engineer.'

Mr Engineer draws himself up to his full crooked height.

'Rolls-Royce kaput. Lada kaput. Soon Rover kaput. Only walking is not kaput. Ha ha.'

'Soon you kaput,' says Valentina. Then she catches my eye and gives a little laugh as if to say, only joking.

She drives off with Stanislav in the Rover, leaving behind a cloud of smoke and a smell of burning. While Mike and my father continue to pore over the Roller, I go inside and search the Yellow Pages.

'Hallo, is that Mr Eric Pike?'

'How can I help?' The voice is both oily and gritty, like burnt engine oil.

'I'm the daughter of Mr Mayevskyj. You sold him a car.'

'Ah yes.' Gritty chuckle. 'Valentina's Roller. Came from the Glaswyne estate, you know.'

'Mr Pike, how could you do a thing like that? You know the car doesn't even go.'

'Well now, Miss er . . . Mrs er . . . You see Valentina said that her husband was a wizard engineer. Aeronautics. You see I happen to know a bit about planes.' The oily gritty voice becomes confiding. 'You see some of the world leaders in aeronautics in the 1930s were Ukrainian. Sikorsky – invented the helicopter. Lozinsky – worked on the MiG. Saw them in action myself in Korea, you know. Fine little fighters. So when Valentina told me about her husband, how he promised her he would get it going in no time . . . Believe me, I had my doubts, but she was very persuasive. You know what she's like.'

'My father's looked at it, and he says he can't fix it. Perhaps you could just take it away and give him his money back.'

'Five hundred quid is a very good price for a vintage Roller.'

'Not if it doesn't go.'

There is silence on the other end of the phone.

'Mr Pike, I know what's going on. I know about you and Valentina.'

Silence again, then a soft click. Then the dialling tone.

*   *   *

Lady Di likes the Roller. There is a window on the rear passenger side that does not fully close, where he can squeeze in. He invites his friends round, too, and they party all night on the sumptuous leather seats, and then spray a bit of piss around to mark that they were there. Lady Di's girlfriend is a shy skinny tabby, who, it soon becomes apparent, is pregnant, and who likes to curl up on the driver's seat, sinking her claws into the soft leather.

It is unseasonably wet in June. It rains and rains until the lawn is a sea of mud. The Roller sinks deeper and deeper; grass and weeds grow tall around it. Lady Di's girlfriend has her babies on the front seat of the Roller – there are four of them – blind, soft, mewing bits of fluff that suck at their skinny mother, pawing her belly in rhythm. Pappa, Valentina and Stanislav are enchanted with them, and try to bring them into the house, but the girlfriend moves them all back, carrying them one by one by the scruff of the neck.

*   *   *

Vera's visit to Pappa comes very shortly after the kittens are born. She drives up from Putney in her battered open-top Golf

GT, a love-gift from Big Dick in the days when he still loved her (of course it wasn't battered then). She arrives in the middle of the afternoon, while Stanislav and Valentina are out, and Pappa is snoozing in his armchair with the radio on full blast. He wakes up to find her standing over him, and lets out an involuntary scream: 'No! No!'

'Oh, for goodness' sake be quiet, Pappa. We've had quite enough melodrama this week already, thank you,' Vera barks in her Big Sis voice. 'Now!' She looks around, as though Valentina might be hiding in a corner. 'Where is she?'

Father sits in the armchair gripping the armrests and saying nothing.

'Where is she, Pappa?'

He bites his lips together theatrically and stares straight ahead.

'Pappa, for goodness' sake, I've driven all the way up from Putney to try to get you out of this mess you've got yourself into, and you can't even bring yourself to talk to me.'

'You tell me to be quiet, so I am quiet.' He clamps his lips together again.

Big Sis marches through every room in the house, slamming doors as she goes. She even looks in the outhouse and the greenhouse. Then she goes back into the room where my father is sitting. He hasn't moved. His lips are still pressed tight.

'Really, Nadia,' she tells me, 'I could quite understand why Valentina threw a cup of water at him. I felt like doing just the same. I suppose he was trying to demonstrate how clever he was.' I say nothing. My lips are clamped tight. I am trying not to laugh. 'Of course it was easy to get him talking again.

I just asked him about Korolev and the space programme.'

'And what happened in the end? Did you meet Valentina?'

'But I thought she was quite wonderful. So . . . *dynamic.*'

Apparently, Big Sis and Valentina got on like a house on fire. Valentina admired Vera's style and panache. Vera admired Valentina's up-front sexuality and her ruthlessness. They both agreed that Father is pathetic, crazy and contemptible.

'But the peach pearlised nail-polish? The high-heeled peep-toe mules? The Roller on the lawn?'

'Ah yes. Of course she is a tart. And a criminal. But still, I had to admire her.'

My heart sinks. I have been so looking forward to this con-frontation: the Zadchuk matrimonial canon v. Mrs Divorce Expert; the green satin rocket-launcher v. the Gucci handbag. I realise how much I have been depending on Big Sis to take on Valentina. Now I recognise that in some ways they are two of a kind.

'Poor Pappa. I know he's a bit eccentric, but I wouldn't call him contemptible.'

'Look at all the trouble he has caused everybody – us, the authorities, even Valentina. In the end, she will realise that she would have been better latching on to somebody else. It would have been better if he could just have said no right from the beginning. He thinks he really is a suitable match for a tarty thirty-six-year-old. If that isn't contemptible, tell me what is.'

'But she led him on. She flattered him. She made him feel young and sexy.'

'He let himself be flattered, because in his heart he believes that he is rather superior. He thinks he's so clever he can outwit the system. It's not the first time he's done something like this.'

'What do you mean?'

'There are a lot of things you don't know, Nadia. Did you know, he almost had Baba Sonia sent off to Siberia?'

'I remember a story Pappa told me – it was all about the Ukrainian pioneers of aircraft design. And I remember Mother's story about how Baba Sonia got her front teeth knocked out.'

*   *   *

After he graduated from the Aeronautical Institute at Kiev in 1936, my father wanted to go to the University of Kharkiv, where Lozinsky and others were pioneering developments in jet propulsion. But instead he was sent east to Perm, in the foothills of the Urals, to teach in a Soviet air force training college. He hated Perm: full of drunken soldiers; no intellectual or cultural life; thousands of miles away from home; thousands of miles from Ludmilla, who was now pregnant with their first child. How to get himself sent home? Nikolai had a cunning plan. He would fail the security check. On one of the reams of forms which had to be filled in, he told the authorities that he was married to an enemy of the people. And just to put himself in an even worse light, he invented an older brother for Ludmilla, a counter-revolutionary terrorist living in Finland, dedicated to the overthrow of the Soviet state.

The authorities could hardly believe their luck. Naturally they wanted to know more about this counter-revolutionary brother. They arrested Baba Sonia and subjected her to several days of intensive interrogation and beatings. Where was this older son? Why was he not mentioned on any of her paperwork? What else did she have to hide? Was she, like her late husband, a traitorous enemy of the people?

Sonia Ocheretko had been lucky to escape in 1930, when her husband was taken away and shot. But those were just the first ripples of the purges. By 1937, the waves of arrests were mounting. Now shooting was too good for the enemies of the people – they were to be sent away to camps in Siberia for corrective re-education through labour.

Aunty Shura came to the rescue. She told the examiner how, as a young trainee doctor, she had travelled to Novaya Aleksandria in 1912 to deliver her sister's first baby, my mother Ludmilla. She signed a sworn statement that Sonia Ocheretko had been a primigravida. It helped that Shura's husband was a friend of Voroshilov.

But Sonia the survivor never recovered from her six days of interrogation. Her forehead was scarred above the eye and her front teeth were knocked out. Her movements which had been quick and lithe became lumbering and painful, and she blinked nervously all the time. Her spirit was broken.

*   *   *

'Of course Aunty Shura threw him out after that. They had nowhere else to go, so they went back to live with Baba Sonia in her flat. Really, it was unforgivable.'

'But Baba Sonia forgave him.'

'She forgave him for Mother's sake. But Mother never forgave him.'

'She must have forgiven him in the end. She stayed with him for sixty years.'

'She stayed with him for our sake. For you and me, Nadia. Poor Mother.'

I wonder – is this true? Or is Vera projecting her own drama into the past?

'But Vera, does that mean you're going to sit back and let Valentina abuse our father? Rip him off? Maybe even murder him?'

'No of course not. Really, Nadezhda, I can't understand how you could want me to sit back and do nothing in such a situation. We have to defend him, for Mother's sake. Useless though he is, he is still our family. We can't let her win.'

(So Big Sis is still on board!)

'Vera, why does Father always go on about you smoking? He's got a thing about cigarettes.'

'Cigarettes? He talked to you about cigarettes?'

'He says you're obsessed with divorce and cigarettes.'

'What else did he say?'

'Nothing else. Why?'

'Forget it. It doesn't matter.'

'Obviously it *does* matter.'

'Nadia, why do you always go scrabbling around in the past?' Her voice is tense, brittle. 'The past is filthy. It's like a sewer. You shouldn't play there. Leave it alone. Forget it.'

18

The baby alarm

Valentina has received a wedding invitation from her sister in
Selby. She has shown it to my father, waving it under his nose
with a few nasty gibes. The accompanying letter describes the
husband-to-be as a doctor, forty-nine years old, married (no
longer married, of course) with two children of school age
(both in private school) and a good house with good garden
and double garage. The no-tits wife is making plenty trouble
but husband is too much in love, no problem.

In double garage is Jaguar and second car Renault. Jaguar is
good, says Valentina, but not as good as Rolls-Royce. Renault
is little better than Lada. Nevertheless, her sister's letter has
fired up in Valentina a new dissatisfaction with her plenty-
money-meanie no-good husband and the second-rate life-style
he has condemned her to.

As my father burbles on down the phone, stopping from time
to time for a violent fit of coughing, I cannot help glancing
across at Mike, who is sitting there with his feet up and a glass
of beer in his hand, watching the Channel Four News. He looks
so decent, so nice, greying a bit, with the slight beginnings of
a paunch, but handsome still, so loved, so – *husbandly*. But . . .
an anxious thought brushes my mind.

The baby alarm

What is it with men?

And now, with another fit of coughing, my father comes to the nub of his telephone call. Valentina requires more money, and he must liquidate some assets. But what assets does he have? Only the house. Ah! At the back of the house is a large area of land which is good for nothing. This he could sell. (He is talking about Mother's garden!)

He has had a discussion with a neighbour, and the neighbour is willing to take it off his hands for a sum of three thousand pounds.

My heart is pounding now, my eyes so misted with rage that I can hardly see, yet I must control my voice.

'Don't rush into anything, Pappa. There's no hurry. Maybe this sister's husband-to-be will turn out to be a meanie as well. After all he must provide for his wife and his private-school children. Maybe the wife will get the Jaguar, and the sister will have the Renault. Maybe Valentina will realise how lucky she is. Just wait and see.'

'Hmm.'

As for selling Mother's garden – my jaw is clenched tight so that I can barely get the words out through my teeth – these things are often more complicated than they seem. The deeds would have to be redrawn. Probably most of the money would be swallowed up in solicitors' fees. And the offer from the neighbour – well that is quite a paltry amount. If he had planning permission to build another house there, why the plot of land would fetch ten times as much. Just imagine how pleased Valentina would be. (And planning permission takes ages and ages.)

Would he like me to ask a solicitor? Would he like me to contact the council about planning permission? Should I talk to Vera?

'Hmm. Solicitor yes. Council yes. Vera no.'

'But probably Vera will find out. Imagine how *upset*' (he knows I mean furious) 'she will be.'

*   *   *

Vera did find out. I told her. She was both upset and furious.

It took her two hours to drive from Putney to Peterborough. She was still wearing her house slippers when she arrived (an unusual lack of attention to detail). She marched straight up to the neighbour's house (it is an ugly mock-Tudor house, much larger than my parents'), banged on the door and confronted him. ('You should have seen the look on his face.') The neighbour, a retired businessman and gardening amateur of the Leylandii-and-bedding-plants school, cowered under the onslaught.

'I was only trying to be helpful. He said he was having financial difficulties.'

'You're not being helpful. You're making things worse. Of course he's having financial difficulties, because of that bloodsucking wife of his. You should be keeping an eye on him, not encouraging him. What sort of neighbour are you?'

His wife has heard the row, and comes to the door, twin-setted and pearled, with a gin and tonic in her hand (it is these neighbours who witnessed the codicil to Mother's will).

'What's going on, Edward?'

Edward explains. His wife raises her eyebrows.

'That's the first I've heard of this. I thought we were saving to go on a cruise, Edward.' Then she turns to Vera. 'We were worried about Mr Mayevskyj, but we didn't like to get involved. Did we, Edward?'

Edward nods and shakes his head at the same time. Vera needs to keep them on side, so she softens her tone.

'I'm sure it was all a misunderstanding.'

'Yes, a misunderstanding.'

Edward seizes the lifeline and retreats behind his wife, who has comes forward to take her husband's place on the doorstep.

'She doesn't seem a very nice sort of lady,' she says. 'She sunbathes in the garden wearing . . . wearing . . .' She steals a backward glance at her husband, her voice drops to a whisper, 'I've seen him watching out of the upstairs window. And another thing,' her tone is confidential, 'I think she's having an affair. I've seen a man . . .' – she purses her lips – '. . . who calls for her in a car. He parks up under the ash tree – where Mr Mayevskyj can't see from the window – and beeps his horn and waits for her. She comes running out, all dressed up to the nines. All fur coat and no knickers, as my mother used to say.'

'Thank you for telling me this,' says Vera. 'You've been *so* helpful.'

*   *   *

Valentina must have seen Vera's car, for she is waiting for her in the doorway blocking the way, arms at her waist, ready for a fight. She looks Vera up and down. Her eyes rest momentarily on Vera's slippered feet, and a quick smile flickers across her mouth. Vera looks down too. ('It was only then that I realised what a mistake I had made.') Valentina is wearing a pair of stiletto shoes, which make her bare muscular calves bulge like a boxer's biceps.

'What you go for next-door, nose-pock?' Valentina demands.

Vera ignores her, and pushes past into the kitchen, which is full of steam, the windows all misted up. There is a pile of washing-up in the sink, and a smell of something disgusting. Pappa is hovering by the door, wearing a pair of navy blue nylon dungarees, the straps criss-crossed over his thin crooked back.

'I've spoken to the people next door, Pappa. They are no longer interested in buying Mother's garden.'

'Vera, why must you do this? Why can you not leave me alone?'

'Because if I leave you alone, Pappa, this vulture will peck out your liver.'

'Eagle. Eagle.'

'Eagle? What are you talking about?' ('Really, Nadia, I thought he had completely flipped.')

'Eagle pecked out liver of Prometheus because he has brought fire.'

'Pappa, you are not Prometheus, you are a pitiful, confused old man, who through your own idiocy have fallen prey to this she-wolf . . .'

Valentina, who has been listening with a storm gathering in her face, lets out a low howl, and flexing her arms shoves Vera hard in the chest. Vera staggers back, but doesn't fall.

'Valya, please, no violence,' Father pleads, trying to get between them. He is way out of his depth.

'You dog-eaten-brain old bent stick, you go in room you shut up.' Valentina gives him a shove too, and he stumbles against the frame of the door which Mike put in, and leans there crookedly. Valentina produces a key from her pocket and dangles it in front of Father's nose.

'I have room key ha ha I have key room!'

Father makes a grab for it, but she holds it just above his reach.

'Why you want with key?' she taunts. 'You go in room. I lock unlock.'

'Valya, please give key!' He makes a pathetic little jump as he attempts to grab, then falls back with a sob.

Vera tries to make a grab, too – 'How dare you!' – but Valentina pushes her away.

'I have a microphone!' cries Vera. 'I will get evidence of your criminal activities!'

Out of her handbag she takes a small hand-held Dictaphone (you have to admire her!) and switches it on, holding it up above Valentina's head.

'Now, please, Valentina, give my father back the key to his room, and try to behave in a calm and civilised manner,' she says in a clear dictating voice. She is taller than Valentina, but Valentina has the advantage of heels. She grabs for the Dictaphone, and would have got it, but her attention is distracted, as at that moment Father makes a snatch at the key in her other hand. Attacked on both fronts, she shrieks and jumps into the air ('It was just like one of those Kung Fu films that Dick used to watch') and comes down with a crash, the stiletto heel of one shoe landing on Vera's slippered foot, the other heel catching Father's shin just below the knee. Father and Vera both buckle. The Dictaphone falls and skids across the floor under the cooker. Vera makes a dive for the Dictaphone. Valentina pushes Father through the door of his room, wrestles the key out of his hand and locks the door. Vera falls upon Valentina, pulling, twisting – they are both on the floor now – and tries to wrest the key from her hand, but Valentina is stronger, and grips the key in a fist behind her back, pulling herself up off the floor. Defeated, Vera wields the Dictaphone:

'I have it all on tape! Everything you say is on tape!'

'Good!' says Valentina, 'this is what I want say you bitch vixen no-tits. You have no tits, you jealous.' She puts her hands under her breasts, pressing them obscenely up and together, and makes little pouting kisses with her mouth. 'Man like tits. You Pappa like tits.'

'Please, Valentina,' says Vera, 'control yourself. There is no need for foul language.'

But she knows she is defeated. She holds her head high, but humiliation sits heavy in her heart.

On the other side of the locked door, Father is scratching and whimpering like a whipped dog.

*   *   *

'Oh Vera! You did your best. You are magnificent. A heroine. Have you got the tape?'

'There was no tape in the Dictaphone. It was all a bluff. What else could I do?'

Later on, before she went out, Valentina unlocked the door of Father's room, but she kept the key.

Father had soiled himself again.

'He can't help it. He really shouldn't wear dungarees.'

'Oh yes, he can help it – not the incontinence, of course, but the obsession. He clings to it against all reason – the excitement, the glamour of it. He still defends her against me, you know.'

'I know.'

'And do you know what else I found? Plugged in to the socket under his bed was a baby alarm.'

'Goodness. What does he need that for?'

'She, not he. The other one's plugged in upstairs in her room. It's one of those clever things that works on the mains circuit. It means she can hear everything he says in his room.'

'But does he talk to himself?'

'No, stupid, when he talks to us on the phone.'

'Ah.'

19

The Red Plough

I think it was the baby alarm that finally did the trick. Father has agreed to a divorce. I am charged with finding a suitable solicitor – someone who is authoritative enough to stick up to Valentina's army of legal-aid lawyers, someone who will fight my father's corner, not just go through the motions and collect the fees.

'Not the youth I spoke to about the annulment. He was useless,' Mrs Divorce Expert says. 'It must be a woman – she will be outraged by what has happened. Not the biggest firms, because they will pass the smaller cases on to a junior. Not the smallest firms, because they will have no expertise.'

I wander up and down the streets of Peterborough's legal district, looking at the names on the brass plates. What can you tell from a name? Not a lot. That's how I find Ms Laura Carter.

The first time I meet her, I almost get up and walk straight out of the room. I am sure I have made a mistake. She seems far too young, far too nice. How am I going to be able to talk to her about bosom-fondling, about oralsex, about squishy squashy? But I am wrong – Ms Carter is a tigress: a blonde-haired, blue-eyed, pert-nosed English rose of a tigress. As I talk, I see her pert nose twitching with anger. By the time I have finished, she is furious.

'Your father is at risk. We must get her out of the house as soon as possible. We'll apply for an injunction immediately, and we'll file for divorce at the same time. The three cars are good. The note from Eric Pike is good. The episode in the hospital is excellent, because it is a public place, and there were plenty of witnesses. Yes, I think we can get something in place by the tribunal appeal in September.'

The first time I take my father to meet Ms Carter in her office, he wears the tattered suit he wore for his wedding and the same white shirt with the black-stitched buttons. He bows so low over her outstretched hand, in the old Russian way, that he almost topples over. She is charmed.

'Such a nice gentleman,' she murmurs to me in her English-rose voice. 'Such a shame that someone would take advantage.'

He, however, has reservations. He tells Vera on the phone,

'Looks like young girl. What does she know?'

'What do *you* know, Pappa?' Big Sis retorts. 'If you knew anything, you wouldn't be in this pickle.'

Ms Carter also throws light on the mystery of the small portable photocopier and the missing medical appointments.

'She may want to show that your father is ill – too ill to attend a tribunal. Or she may be getting evidence that he is of unsound mind – confused, doesn't know what he's doing.'

'And the translated poems?'

'That will be to demonstrate that it is a bona-fide relationship.'

'The scheming vixen!'

'Oh, I expect her solicitor told her to do it.'

'Solicitors do that?'

Ms Carter nods. 'And worse.'

It's mid-July now, and the September tribunal hearing, having seemed an eternity away, suddenly seems very close. Ms Carter arranges for a private detective to serve the papers.

'We'll have to make sure the divorce petition is served on her in person. Otherwise she can claim she never received it.'

Vera has volunteered to be there on the day, to make sure that Valentina receives it in person. Now there is to be some action, she doesn't want to miss out. My father insists that she does not need to come, that he is after all an intelligent adult and can handle this himself; but he is overruled. The trap is set.

At the pre-ordained time, the detective, a tall dark louche-looking man with plenty of five-o'clock shadow, turns up at the house and hammers on the door.

'Oh, it must be the postman!' cries Vera, who has been up since six o'clock anticipating the excitement. 'It could be a parcel for you, Valentina.'

Valentina rushes to the door. She is still wearing her frilly pinafore and her yellow rubber gloves from washing up the breakfast things.

The detective thrusts the envelope into her hands. Valentina looks confused.

'Divorce pepper? I no want divorce.'

'No,' says the detective, 'the petitioner is Mr Nikolai Mayevskyj. *He* is divorcing *you.*'

She stands for a moment in stunned silence. Then she explodes in a ball of fury.

'Nikolai! Nikolai! What is this?' she screams at my father. 'Nikolai, you crazy dog-eaten-brain graveyard-deadman!'

My father has locked himself in his room and turned the radio on full volume.

She swings round again to confront the private detective, but he is already slamming the door of his black BMW and driving away with a screech of tyres. She turns on Vera.

'You she-cat-dog-vixen flesh-eating witch!'

'I'm sorry, Valentina,' says Big Sis, in a voice which she later describes to me as calm and rational, 'but this is no more than you deserve. You cannot come to this country and deceive and cheat people, however stupid they are.'

'I no cheat! You cheat! I love you Pappa! I love!'

'Don't be silly, Valentina. Now, go and see your solicitor.'

* * *

'Oh Vera, that's wonderful! Did it all go so smoothly?'

If I feel a moment's pity for the trapped bewildered Valentina, it is only fleeting.

'So far so good,' says Mrs Divorce Expert.

* * *

But Valentina's solicitor has a trick up his sleeve that Ms Carter has not foreseen. The first court hearing, at which the injunction will be served to oust Valentina from the house, has been brought forward at Ms Carter's request. Neither my sister nor I can be there, so we only have Laura's account of what happened. She and my father arrive early at the court. The judge arrives. Valentina and Stanislav arrive. The judge opens the proceedings. Valentina stands up.

'I no understand English. I must interpreter.'

There is consternation in the court. Clerks rush around,

hurried phone calls are made. But no Ukrainian-speaking interpreter can be found. The judge adjourns the hearing, and a new date is set. We have lost two weeks.

'Oh, bother!' says Ms Carter. 'I should have thought of that.'

In early August, the same group reassembles, but this time with a middle-aged woman from the Ukrainian Club in Peterborough, who has agreed to act as an interpreter. My father will pick up the tab. She must know about the story of Valentina and my father – all the Ukrainians for miles around know about it – but she is po-faced, and reveals nothing. I have taken the day off to be there too, to give Laura and Pappa moral support. It is a blazing hot day, just over a year since they were married. Valentina is wearing a navy-blue pink-lined suit – maybe the same one she wore for the immigration panel. My father is wearing his wedding suit again and the white shirt stitched with black button thread.

Ms Carter describes the incidents with the wet tea-towel, the glass of water, and the hospital steps. Her voice is low and clear, dense with suppressed emotion, solemn at the awfulness of the things she describes. She seems almost apologetic, as with her head bowed and her eyes downcast, she produces her *coup de grâce*: a report from the psychiatrist. Valentina protests vigorously and colourfully that my father has told a malicious pack of lies, that she loves her husband, and that she has nowhere else to live with her son.

'I am not bad woman. He has a paranoia!'

She tosses her hair from side to side and whips the air into a lather with her hands as she appeals to her audience. The interpreter translates it all into bland third-person English.

Now my father stands up and answers questions in a voice so faint and quavery the judge has to ask him to repeat himself several times. His English is correct and formal, engineer's English, yet there is a clever touch of drama in the way he raises his shaking hand and points at Valentina: 'I believe she wishes to murder me!' He looks small, wizened and bewildered in his crumpled suit and thick glasses; his frailty speaks volumes. The judge orders that Valentina and Stanislav must leave the house within a fortnight, taking all their possessions with them.

That evening, my father and I open a four-year-old bottle of my mother's purple plum wine, to celebrate. The cork bursts out and hits the ceiling with a thwack, leaving a dent in the plaster. The wine tastes like cough-medicine and goes straight to the head. My father begins to tell me about his days at the Red Plough Factory in Kiev, which, apart from today, he declares, were the happiest days of his life. Within thirty minutes we are both fast asleep, my father in his armchair, I slumped across the dining-table. Some time very late during the night, I am woken by the sounds of Stanislav and Valentina letting themselves into the house and creeping upstairs, talking in quiet voices.

*   *   *

Although the psychiatrist pronounced my father all-clear, Valentina may have been closer to the truth than she realised, for only someone who has lived in a totalitarian state can appreciate the true character of paranoia. In 1937, when my father returned to Kiev from Luhansk, the whole country was bathed in a miasma of paranoia.

It seeped everywhere, into the most intimate crevices of people's lives: it soured the relations between friends and colleagues, between teachers and students, between parents and children, husbands and wives. Enemies were everywhere. If you didn't like the way someone had sold you a piglet, or looked at your girlfriend, or asked for money you owed, or given you a low mark in an exam, a quick word to the NKVD would sort them out. If you fancied someone's wife, a word to the NKVD, a stint in Siberia, would leave the coast clear for you. However brilliant, gifted, or patriotic you might be, you were still a threat to somebody. If you were too clever you were sure to be a potential defector or saboteur; if you were too stupid, you were bound to say the wrong thing sooner or later. No one could escape the paranoia, from the lowliest to the greatest; indeed the most powerful man in the land, Stalin himself, was the most paranoid of all. The paranoia leached out from under the locked doors of the Kremlin, paralysing all human life.

In 1937 the arrest of the renowned aircraft designer Tupolev, on suspicion of sabotage, shocked the world of aviation. He was imprisoned not in the gulag but in his own institute in Moscow, along with his entire design team, and forced to continue his work under conditions of slavery. They slept in dormitories under armed guard, but were fed the finest meat and plenty of fish, for it was believed that the brain needed good nourishment in order to perform. For an hour or so each day, the engineers were allowed out into a caged enclosure on the roof of the institute for recreation. From here they could sometimes watch the aeroplanes they had designed wheeling in the sky high above them.

'And not only Tupolev,' says my father, 'but Kerber, Lyulka, Astrov, Bartini, Lozinsky, even the genius Korolev, father of space flight.' Suddenly aviation was a dangerous endeavour.

'And such imbecile types now in control! When the engineers proposed to build a small two-stroke emergency gasoline engine in place of bulky four-stroke engine, to run the aeroplane's electrical system if generators should fail, they were forbidden, on grounds that switching from four-stroke to two-stroke in one step would be too risky. They were ordered to build three-stroke engine! Three-stroke engine! Ha ha ha!'

Maybe it was the arrest of Tupolev, or maybe it was the poisonous effect of the paranoia, but it was now that my father began to switch his allegiance from the soaring firmament of aviation to the humble earth-bound world of tractors. So he found his way to the Red Plough Factory in Kiev.

The Red Plough was a paranoia-free zone. Nestled in a curve of the Dnieper River, away from the main political centres, it got on with its humble work of producing agricultural implements, construction machinery, boilers and vats. Nothing had military implications. Nothing was secret or state-of-the-art. Thus it became a haven for scientists, engineers, artists, poets and people who just wanted to breathe free air. My father's first design project was a concrete mixer. It was a beauty. (He whirls his hands around to demonstrate its motion.) Then there was a twin-furrow plough. (He slides his hands up and down, palms outward.) On summer evenings after work, they would strip off and swim in the wide sandy-bottomed river that looped around the factory precinct. (He demonstrates vigorous breast-stroke. The plum wine has really gone to his head.) And they always ate well, for as a sideline they repaired bicycles, motors, pumps, carts, whatever anyone brought to the back door, and took payment in bread and sausages.

My father worked at the Red Plough from 1937 until the outbreak of war in 1939, while my mother attended the Veterinary Institute on the outskirts of Kiev. They lived in a two-roomed apartment on the ground floor of an 'art nouveau' stuccoed house on Dorogozhitska Street, which they shared with Anna and Viktor, a couple of friends they knew from university. At the bottom of their road was Melnikov Street, a wide boulevard which leads down past the old Jewish cemetery into the steep wooded ravine of Babi Yar.

*　　*　　*

I awake late next morning with a splitting headache and a stiff neck. My father is already up, fiddling about with the radio. He is in excellent spirits, and immediately wants to continue where he left off about the fate of Tupolev, but I shut him up and put the kettle on. There is something foreboding about the stillness in the house. Stanislav and Valentina are out, and the Rover has disappeared from the front drive. As I walk through the house clutching a cup of tea, I notice that some of the clutter in Valentina's room seems to have been cleared away, some pots and pans are missing from the kitchen, and the small portable photocopier has gone.

20

The psychologist was a fraud

Once the court has granted the injunction, I telephone my father every day to see whether Valentina and Stanislav have moved out yet, and his answer is always the same: 'Yes. No. Maybe. I don't know.'

They have removed some of their possessions, but left others. They stay away for a night or a day, then they come back. My father does not know where they go, where they stay, or when they will return. Their movements are mysterious. Valentina no longer speaks to him when she passes him on the stairs or in the kitchen – she does not even acknowledge his presence. Stanislav looks the other way and whistles tunelessly.

This war of silence is worse than the war of words. My father is beginning to crack.

'Maybe I will ask her to remain after all. She is not such a bad person, Nadia. Has some good qualities. Only has some incorrect ideas.'

'Pappa, don't be so stupid. Can't you see, you are at risk of your life? Even if she doesn't kill you, you will have a heart attack or a stroke if you go on like this.'

'Hmm. Maybe. But is it not better to die at the hands of one you love than to die alone?'

'Pappa, for goodness' sake. How could you imagine that

she ever loved you? Just remember how she used to behave towards you, the things she said, the pushing, the shouting.'

'True, this is the defect of character which is typical, by the way, of the Russian psyche, in which there is always the tendency to believe in violence as first rather than last resort.'

'Pappa we have all been running round in circles to achieve this injunction, and now you suddenly want to change your mind. What will Vera say?'

'Ah, Vera. If Valentina does not kill me, surely Vera will.'

'Nobody will kill you, Pappa. You will live to a ripe old age, and you will finish writing your book.'

'Hmm. Yes.' His voice perks up. 'You see there was one other very interesting development during the Second World War, and that was invention of the half-tractor. This was in fact a French invention which was remarkable both for its elegance and its ingenuity.'

'Pappa, please listen carefully. If you choose to stay with Valentina now, I shall wash my hands of you. There will be no calling for help to me or to Vera next time.'

I am so angry that I don't telephone him the next day, but late in the afternoon he telephones me.

'Listen to this, Nadezhda!' he shouts down the telephone, his voice fizzy with excitement. 'GCSE result of the Stanislav. Grade B in English! B in music! C in mathematics! C in science! C in technology! D in history! D in French! Grade A in religious studies only!'

I can hear Stanislav faintly protesting in the background, and my father's voice taunting, 'Grade C! Ha ha! Grade C!'

Now I hear a terrifying screech as Valentina pitches in, then a crash and the phone goes dead. I try to phone back, but get an engaged tone. Again and again. I am beginning to panic.

Then after about twenty minutes a dialling tone but no reply. I put on my coat and grab the car keys. I'd better go and rescue him. Then I dial once more and this time my father picks up the receiver.

'Hallo, Nadezhda? Yes, good job we discovered the truth. Psychologist who wrote IQ report was a fraud. Stanislav is not genius, not even very clever. Merely mediocre.'

'Oh Pappa . . .'

'There can be no excuses. In English, yes, science even maybe command of the language is a factor. But mathematics is pure test of intelligence. Grade C! Ha!'

'Pappa, are you all right? What was that crash I heard?'

'Oh, just the smallish bump. You see, she cannot stand to face the truth. Her son is not a genius, but she will not believe this.'

'Are Stanislav and Valentina still there with you?'

I want to shut him up, before she does him a serious injury.

'No is gone out. Shopping.'

'Pappa, it's more than two weeks since the court granted you the injunction. Why are they still living there? They should have moved out by now.'

It is clear to me that Valentina has another base, maybe even another home somewhere, where she and Stanislav and the small portable photocopier are installed. Why is she still hanging around my father?

'Sometimes here, sometimes not here. One day is gone, one day is back. You know, this Valentina is not a bad type, but she cannot accept that the boy is not genius.'

'So has she or has she not moved out? Where does she live?'

There is a long silence.

'Pappa?'

Then, quietly, almost with regret, he murmurs, 'Grade C!'

*   *   *

Vera has been on holiday in Tuscany, so I ring her to fill her in on what has happened in the last fortnight. I describe the scene in the courtroom, Laura Carter's speech, and my father's finger-pointing intervention.

'Bravo!' cries Vera.

I describe Valentina's impassioned but unintelligible declaration of love, and our plum wine celebration.

'We both got a bit tipsy, then he started talking about his days at the Red Plough Factory.'

'Ah yes, the Red Plough.' Vera's Big Sis voice makes me feel uneasy, as though something bad is coming next. 'You know of course that in the end they were betrayed. Somebody whose bicycle they had mended reported them to the NKVD. The director and most of the staff were carted off to Siberia.'

'Oh no!'

'Fortunately, that was after Pappa had already left. And one of the neighbours betrayed Anna and Viktor, and they ended up in Babi Yar. You know that they were Jews, of course.'

'I didn't know.'

'So you see everybody is betrayed in the end.'

I had thought there was a happy story to tell about my parents' life, a tale of triumph over tragedy, of love overcoming impossible odds, but now I see that there are only fleeting moments of happiness, to be seized and celebrated before they slip away.

'What I find hard to understand, Vera, is – why were people so quick to betray each other? You would have thought they would show solidarity in the face of oppression.'

'No no, that is the naïve view, Nadezhda. You see, this is the dark underside of human nature. When someone has power, the lesser people always try to gain favour with them.

Look at the way Father always tries to please Valentina, even when she abuses him. Look at the way your Labour politicians are creeping up to offer their homage' (she pronounces it hom-*aahj*) 'to the capitalists' (she pronounces it cap-*it*-alists) 'whom they vowed to overthrow. Of course it's not just politicians, it happens throughout the animal kingdom too.'

(Oh, Big Sis, what a nose you have for sniffing out the tainted, the soiled, the venal, the compromised. When did you learn to see so darkly?)

'They're not *my* Labour politicians, Vera.'

'Well they are certainly not mine. Nor Mother's, as you know.'

Yes, my generous dumpling-hearted stuff-'em-with-food-till-they-burst mother was a devoted supporter of Mrs Thatcher.

'Let's not talk about politics, Vera. We always seem to fall out.'

'Of course some things are so distasteful they are better not talked about.'

Instead, we make plans for the immigration tribunal hearing, which has crept up on us and is suddenly only a fortnight away. Vera and I have informally swapped roles. I am now Mrs Divorce Expert, or at least, it is my job to take care of the divorce side of things. Vera plays the part of Mrs Flog-'em-and-send-'em-home. She is superb in the role.

'The secret, Nadia, is in meticulous planning.'

*   *   *

Vera has visited the tribunal courtroom, checked out the lie of the land, and made friends with the usher. She has contacted the tribunal office, and without actually telling them that she is acting for Mrs Mayevska, has ensured that there will be an interpreter.

I travel down to London for the tribunal, because I don't want to miss the excitement. Vera and I meet in a café opposite the building in Islington where the tribunal is to be held. Although we have talked on the phone, it is the first time we have actually met since Mother's funeral. We look each other up and down. I have made a special effort, and am wearing a this-season Oxfam jacket, a white blouse and dark trousers. Vera is wearing a stylishly crumpled jacket and skirt in earth-coloured linen. Cautiously, we lean forward and each peck the air at the side of the other's cheek.

'How lovely to see you, Nadia.'

'You too, Vera.'

We are treading on eggshells.

Giving ourselves plenty of time, we take our places at the back of the courtroom, which is in a sombre oak-panelled chamber where oblique sunlight filters through windows too high to see out of. A few minutes before the hearing starts Valentina and Stanislav enter. Valentina has excelled herself: gone is the navy polyester with the pink lining. She is wearing a white dress and black-and-white hound's-tooth check jacket, cut low at the front to show her cleavage, but cleverly darted and tailored to conceal her bulk. Above her blonde bouffant perches a small white pillbox hat with cut-out flowers in black silk. Her lipstick and nails are blood-red. Stanislav is wearing the uniform and tie of his posh school, and has had a haircut.

She catches sight of us as soon as she comes in and lets out a low cry. The blond young man accompanying her, whom we take to be her counsel, follows the line of her gaze, and they confer quietly as they take their places. He is wearing a suit so sharp and a tie so bright that we are sure he is not a Peterborough lad.

Everyone has made an effort to dress up except the three members of the tribunal, who come in a few moments later, dressed in unfashionably baggy trousers and not-stylishly crumpled jackets. They introduce themselves, and at once Valentina's counsel rises to his feet and asks for an interpreter for his client. The tribunal members confer, the clerk is consulted, then a plump woman with frizzed hair enters from a side door, seats herself in front of Valentina and Stanislav and introduces herself to them. I can hear them gasp. Now the young barrister rises again, points to Vera and me sitting at the back, and objects to our presence. He is overruled. Finally he rises again, and launches into a long and eloquent account of the love-match between Valentina and my father, how love-at-first-sight swept them off their feet at a function in the Ukrainian Club in Peterborough, how he pleaded with her to marry him, bombarded her with letters and poems – the young man waves a wodge of photocopies in the air – and how happy they were before the two daughters – he points to me and Vera – started to interfere.

He has been speaking for perhaps ten minutes when there is a commotion and the usher rushes in with several sheets of paper which she places before the chairman. He skims through them and then passes them to the other two panellists.

'And he would be present in person to testify his love for my client, were it not that a chest infection, coupled with his extreme age and frailty, have prevented him from travelling here today.' The young man's voice rises to a climax. The chairman politely waits for him to finish, then he holds up the papers which the usher brought in.

'I would find your speech most convincing, Mr Ericson,' he says, 'were it not that just at this moment we have received a fax from Mrs Mayevska's husband's solicitor in Peterborough, with details of a divorce petition he has filed in respect of your client.'

Valentina jumps to her feet, and turns to where Vera and I are sitting.

'This is doing of this evil witch sister!' she cries combing the air with her scarlet nails.

'Please listen, Mr Sir,' she puts her hands together in a gesture of prayer and appeals to the chairman, 'I am love husband.'

The interpreter, miffed at being excluded from the drama, butts in:

'She says that the sisters are evil witches. She wants to say that she loves her husband.'

Vera and I keep quiet and look prim.

'Mr Ericson?' the chairman asks.

The young man has gone scarlet beneath his pale hair.

'I would like to ask for a ten-minute adjournment while I consult with my client.'

'Granted.'

As they file out of the courtroom, I can hear him hissing beneath his breath to Valentina something like, '. . . you've made a complete fool of me . . .'

Ten minutes later, Mr Ericson comes back on his own.

'My client is withdrawing her appeal,' he says.

*　　*　　*

'Did you see the way he winked at us?' says Vera.

   'Who?'

   'The chairman. He winked.'

   'No! I didn't see. Did he really?'

   'I thought he was so sexy.'

   'Sexy?'

   'Very sort of English and crumpled. I do so like English men.'

   'But not Dick.'

   'Dick was English and crumpled when we first met. I liked him then. Before he met Persephone.'

We are sitting side by side with our feet up on a wide sofa in Vera's Putney flat. In front of us on a low table are two glasses and a bottle of chilled white wine, almost empty. Dave Brubeck plays quietly in the background. After the alliance of the courtroom, it seemed the most natural thing in the world for me to come back here. It is a cool white-painted flat, with deep pale carpets and very little but very expensive furniture. I have never been here before.

'I like your flat, Vera. It's so much nicer than where you used to live with Dick.'

   'You haven't been here before? Of course not. Well, maybe you'll come again.'

   'I hope so. Or maybe you'll come up to Cambridge one weekend.'

   'Maybe.'

When Vera lived with Dick, I visited their house once or twice – it was full of polished wood and elaborate wall-paper which I found pretentious and gloomy.

'What do you suppose it means, Vera – that she's withdrawing her appeal? Will she give up altogether? Or do you think it just means she will ask for another date?'

'Perhaps she will simply melt away into the criminal under-world where she belongs. After all, they can only deport her if they can find her.'

Vera has lit a cigarette and thrown off her shoes.

'Or it could just mean she will go back and work on Pappa. Get him to back down on the divorce. I'm sure he would if she went about it the right way.'

'He's certainly stupid enough.' Vera watches a long finger of ash glow at the end of her cigarette. 'But I think she will go to ground. Hide herself in a secret lair somewhere. Live off fraudulent benefit claims and prostitution.' The ash falls silently into a glass ashtray. Vera sighs. 'Soon enough she will latch on to another victim.'

'But Pappa can divorce her in her absence.'

'Let's hope so. The question is how much he has to pay her to get rid of her.'

As we are talking, my eyes wander around the room. There is a vase of pale pink peonies on the mantelpiece, and beside them a row of photographs, mainly of Vera and Dick and the children, some in colour, some in black and white. But one photograph is in sepia, in a silver frame. I stare. Can it be? Yes it is. It is the photograph of Mother wearing the hat. She must have taken it from the box in the sitting-room. But when? And why didn't she say anything? I feel an angry colour rising in my cheeks.

'Vera, the photograph of Mother . . .'

'Oh, yes. Delightful isn't it? Such an enchanting hat.'

'But, it isn't yours.'

'Not mine? The hat?'

'The photograph, Vera. It's not yours.'

I jump to my feet, knocking over my wineglass. A pool of Sauvignon blanc forms on the table and drips on to the carpet.

'What's the matter, Nadia? It's only a photograph, for goodness' sake.'

'I must go. I don't want to miss the last train.'

'But won't you stay the night? The bed's made up in the little room.'

'I'm sorry. I can't stay.'

What does it matter? It's only a photograph. But *that* photograph! But is it worth losing a new-found sister over? These thoughts race through my mind as I sit on the last train home, watching my reflection in the window as it fleets over the darkening fields and woods. The face in the window, colours washed out in the dusky light, has the same shape and contours as the face in the sepia photograph. When she smiles, the smile is the same.

Next day I telephone Vera.

'So sorry I had to rush off. I'd forgotten I had an early morning appointment.'

21

The lady vanishes

A few days after the botched tribunal, Eric Pike calls round at my father's house in a big blue Volvo estate. He and my father sit in the back room amicably discussing aviation, while Valentina and Stanislav run up and down the stairs piling all their possessions in black bin bags into the back of the car. Mike and I arrive just as they are ready to leave. Eric Pike shakes my father's hand and takes the driver's seat, and Stanislav and Valentina squeeze into the passenger seat together. My father hovers on the doorstep. Valentina winds down the window, sticks her head out and shouts,

'You think you very clever, Mr Engineer, but you wait. Remember I always get what I want.'

She spits, 'Thphoo!' The car is already moving forward. The gob of spit lands on the car door, hangs for a moment, and slides slimily to the ground. Then they are gone.

'So are you all right, Pappa? Is everything all right?' I give him a hug. Under the cardigan, his shoulders are bony.

'All right. Yes everything all right. Good job. Maybe one day I will telephone to Valentina and seek reconciliation.'

And now for the first time I hear a new tone in my father's voice: I realise how lonely he is.

*   *   *

I telephone Vera. We must make plans for how Father is to be supported now that he is on his own. Big Sis is all for getting him certified and carted off to a residential home.

'We must face the truth, Nadezhda, unpalatable though it is. Our father is mad. It's only a matter of time before he gets into some other lunatic scheme. Better put him where he can cause no more trouble.'

'I don't think he's mad, Vera; he's just eccentric. Too eccentric to live in a home.'

Somehow, I can't see my father with his apples and his tractor talk and his strange habits fitting easily into the routine of a residential home. I suggest that sheltered housing, where he will have a greater degree of independence, might be more suitable, and Vera agrees, adding with strong emphasis that this is what should have happened in the first place. She thinks she has scored a victory. I let it pass.

*   *   *

After Valentina and Stanislav had left, I cleared out enough rubbish from their rooms to fill fourteen black plastic bin bags. Out went the soiled cotton wool, the crumpled packaging, the cosmetics bottles and jars, the holey tights, the papers and magazines, mail-order catalogues, junk mail, discarded shoes and clothes. Out went the half-eaten ham sandwich and several apple cores and a decayed pork pie which I found under the bed in the same place I had once found a used condom. In Stanislav's room I discovered a little surprise – a carrier bag full of porn magazines under the bed. Tut tut.

Then I turned my attention to the bathroom, and with the help of a wire coat-hanger pulled out a sticky clump of matted blonde hair and brown pubic hair that was clogging the bath outlet. How was it possible for one person to generate so much mess? As I cleaned I realised with a flash of insight that Valentina must have had someone to clean up after her for most of her life.

I set to work in the kitchen and pantry, clearing off the grease from the cooker and surrounding walls – it was so thick I scraped it off with a knife – throwing out scraps of food, mopping up sticky patches on floors, shelves and worktops where unidentified fluids had been spilled and never wiped up. Pots, jars, tins, packets, had been opened, started, and then the contents left to fester. A jar of jam left open in the pantry had cracked, turned rock hard, and stuck to the shelf so fast that as I tried to pull it away it shattered in my hands. The shards of glass fell to the floor among a debris of newspaper, empty boil-in bags, spilled sugar, broken pasta shells, biscuit crumbs and dried peas.

Under the sink, I found a stash of tinned mackerel – I counted forty-six tins altogether.

'What's this?' I asked my father.

He shrugged. 'Buy one get one free. She likes.'

What can you do with forty-six tins of mackerel? I couldn't throw them away. What would Mother have done? I took them and distributed them to everyone we knew in the village, and gave the rest to the vicar, for the poor. For several years afterwards, tins of mackerel turned up in little heaps before the altar at harvest festival.

In the outhouse, in a cardboard box, were several packets of biscuits. All had been opened, and crumbs and bits of wrapping were everywhere. In another corner were four mouldy loaves of white sliced bread. Again, all the packets were torn open and their contents scattered. Why would someone do that? Then I noticed something large and brown scurrying in the corner.

Ohmygod! Call the council, quick!

In the sitting-room, kitchen, and pantry, saucers of food and milk had been put down for Lady Di which had not been to his taste, and they too had been left to rot in the August heat. One was infested with brown mushroom-like growths. In another, white maggots were squirming. The milk had soured to a green cheesy slime. I put the saucers to soak in bleach.

I am not usually the sort of woman who finds cleaning therapeutic, but this had the feel of a symbolic purging, the utter eradication of an alien invader who had tried to colonise our family. It felt good.

*   *   *

I am cautious about mentioning to Vera that my father has talked about reconciliation with Valentina, for I know that if there is one thing that will surely drive him back into her arms, it is a confrontation with Big Sis. But somehow I let it out.

'Oh the fool!' I can hear her intake of breath as she chooses her words. 'Of course you social workers are familiar with this syndrome of abused women clinging to their abusers.'

'I'm not a social worker, Vera.'

'No, of course, you're a sociologist. I forgot. But if you *were* a social worker that is what you would say.'

'Maybe.'

'So I think it's so important to get him out of harm's way, for his own sake. Otherwise he will simply fall victim to the next unscrupulous person to come along. Weren't you supposed to be looking for some sheltered housing, Nadia? Really, I think it's time you started taking some responsibility, as I did for Mother.'

But my father is determined to make the most of his new freedom. When I raise the possibility of sheltered housing, he says he will stay where he is. He is far too busy to consider moving. He will get the house in order, and maybe even rent out Valentina's old room on the top floor to a suitable middle-aged lady. And then he still has his book to write.

'Did I ever finish telling you about the half-tractor?'

He reaches for the narrow-lined A4 notepad, which is now almost full with his masterwork, and reads:

The half-tractor was invented by French engineer by the name of Adolph Kegresse, who had worked in Russia as technical director to the Tsar's automobile fleet, but at the time of the 1917 revolution he made his way back to France, where he continued to perfect his designs. The half-tractor is based on the simple principle of normal tyred wheels in front of vehicle, and caterpillar tracks at back. The half-tracked tractors, cavalry cars and armoured cars were especially popular with the Polish military, where they were deemed suitable for driving on the country's poorly maintained roads. The historic union of Adolph Kegresse with André Citroën is said to have given birth to the whole phenomenon of all-terrain vehicles. In their time these seemed to promise a revolution in agriculture and heavy transport, but alas they have become one of the curses of our modern age.

*   *   *

After my big clean-up, only two things remained to remind father of Valentina, and they were not so easy to remove: Lady Di (and his girlfriend and the girlfriend's four kittens) and the Roller on the lawn.

We all agreed that Lady Di and his family should stay, as they would be company for my father, but that their eating and toilet habits should be taken in hand. I was all for getting a litter tray, but Big Sis put her foot down.

'It's utterly impractical. Who's going to empty it? There's only one thing to do – they have to be taught not to make their mess indoors.'

'But how?'

'You grab them by the scruff of the neck and rub their noses in it. It's the only way.'

'Oh Vera, I can't do that. And Pappa certainly can't.'

'Don't be such a milk-sop, Nadia. Of course you can do it. Mother did it to every cat we had. That's why they were all so clean and docile.'

'But how will we know which cat made the mess?'

'Every time there is a mess, you rub *all* their noses in it.'

'All six of them?' (It sounded like something out of Russia in the 1930s.)

'All six.'

So I did.

Their feeding was rationalised, too. They were to be fed in the back porch only, twice a day, and if they didn't eat the food, it was to be thrown away after a day.

'Can you remember that, Pappa?'

'Yes yes. One day. I leave for only one day.'

'If they're still hungry, you can give them dry cat biscuits. They won't smell.'

'Systematic approach. Advanced technological feeding. Is good.'

The council came round and put down rat poison, and soon four brown furry corpses were found lying belly-up in the outhouse. Mike buried them in the garden. The cats were banned from sleeping in the house or in the Rolls-Royce, and a box lined with an old jumper of Valentina's was provided for them in the outhouse. Lady Di protested at the new regime, and tried to scratch me once or twice during nose-rubbing sessions, but he soon learnt to obey.

Lady Di's girlfriend turned out to be a star – friendly, affection-ate, and clean in her habits. My father decided to call her Valyusia after Valentina, and she would curl up purring on his lap while he snoozed in the afternoon, as no doubt he had hoped the real Valentina would. Notices were put up in the village post office advertising delightful kittens free to good homes. An unexpected bonus was that a number of elderly ladies in the village, who had been friends of my mother, dropped by to admire the kittens and stopped to chat to my father, and after that they continued to call in from time to time, lured perhaps by the air of scandal which still surrounded the house. He commented rather ungraciously to Vera that he found their conversation tedious, but at least he was polite to them, and they kept an eye on him. The vicar called round to thank him for the tins of mackerel, which had been donated to a family of asylum seekers from Eastern Europe. Gradually he was being reintegrated into the community.

On the car front, things were not so straightforward. Crap car disappeared mysteriously one night, but the Roller remained on the front lawn. Although my father paid £500 for it, Valentina had both the keys and the documents, without which it could not be sold or even towed away. I telephoned Eric Pike again.

'Could I speak to Valentina please?'

'Who am I speaking to?' said the gritty oily voice.

'I'm Mr Mayevskyj's daughter. We spoke before.' (I should have prepared a false name and a cover story.)

'I wish you'd stop telephoning me, Mrs er . . . Miss er . . . I can't imagine why you think Valentina is here.'

'You drove away into the sunset with her. And all her possessions. Remember?'

'I was just doing her a good turn. She's not staying here.'

'Where did you take her, then?'

No reply.

'Please – how can I contact her? She's left some things behind I thought she might want. And mail keeps arriving for her.'

There was a moment's silence; then he said,

'I'll pass her a message to get in touch with you.'

A few days later my father got a letter from Valentina's solicitor, saying that all correspondence should be forwarded to his office, and all contact was to be through him only.

*   *   *

I could understand the desolation my father must feel, because, strangely, I shared it. Valentina had become such a huge figure in my life that her disappearance left a gaping void, in which questions wheeled around like startled birds. Where had she vanished to? Where was she working? What was she planning to do next? Who were her friends? What man or men was she sleeping with? Was there a succession of sleazy pick-ups, or was it a special someone – a nice innocent English bloke, who found her excitingly exotic but was too shy to make a pass at her? And Stanislav – where was he laying down his new stash of porn?

The questions consumed me. My imagination created one scene after another: Valentina and Stanislav lying low in squalor somewhere in Peterborough in a rented room with chipboard furniture; or crammed with all their bin bags into the attic of a fly-blown boarding-house; or maybe living in style in a chic love-nest paid for by a lover; the pots and pans which had been my mother's bubbling away, filling the kitchen with boil-in-bag steam, the small portable photocopier perched on the table beside them when they ate. When they have eaten, do they go out? Who with? Or if they stay in, who taps on the door in the middle of the night?

I drive past the Zadchuks' house in the village again and again, looking to see whether Crap car is parked outside. It is not. I ask the neighbours whether they have seen Stanislav or Valentina. They have not. The man in the post office and the woman at the corner shop have not seen her. Neither has the milkman on his rounds.

I have become obsessed with finding Valentina. Each time I drive into the village or through Peterborough, I seem to catch a glimpse of Crap car disappearing up every side street. I slam on the brakes or perform wild U-turns, and other drivers beep annoyance at me. I tell myself it's because I need to know what her plans are – whether she will contest the divorce, how much money she will ask for, whether she will be deported first. I convince myself that I need to find out because of the Roller and the mail that keeps pouring through the letter box for her – mostly junk mail offering dodgy get-rich-quick schemes and dubious beauty treatments. But really it's a burning curiosity that has possessed me. I want to know her life. I want to know who she is. I want to know.

One Saturday afternoon, in a frenzy of curiosity, I go and stake out Eric Pike's house. I find the address from the telephone directory and the A-to-Z. It is a modern neo-Georgian bunga-low set back behind a sloping lawn in a cul-de-sac of similar bungalows, with white columns beside the door, lions' heads on the gateposts, leaded windows, a Victorian gas-lamp in the drive (converted to electricity), plenty of hanging baskets spilling mauve petunias, and a large pond with a fountain and Koi carp. In the driveway are two cars – the big blue Volvo estate and a small white Alfa Romeo. No sign of Valentina's Rover. I park up a little distance away, turn the radio on, and wait.

Nothing happens for an hour, an hour and a half. Then a woman emerges from the house. She is an attractive woman in her mid-forties, wearing full make-up, high heels and, I notice, a little gold ankle-chain under her tights. She walks over to my car and gestures to me to wind down the window.

'Are you a private detective?'

'Oh, no, I'm just . . .' My imagination deserts me. 'I'm just waiting for a friend.'

'Because if you are, you can fuck off. I've not seen him for three weeks. It's all over.'

She turns and marches back towards the house, her heels sinking into the crunching gravel.

A few moments later, a man emerges and stands in the doorway staring in my direction. He is tall and thickset with a heavy black moustache. As he begins to walk down the drive towards me, I quickly turn the key in the ignition and drive off.

On my way back, I have another idea. I make a detour to Hall Street, to Bob Turner's house, where we once delivered the fat brown envelope. But the house is clearly empty, with a For Sale sign by the front gate. I peer in through the window; the net curtains are still up but I can see that there is no furniture inside. A neighbour sees me and sticks her head, bristling with curlers, round the door.

'They've gone away.'

'Stanislav and Valentina?'

'Oh, they went ages ago. I thought yer meant the Linakers. Left last week. Gone to Australia. Lucky sods.'

'Did you know Valentina and Stanislav?'

'Not much. Made a lot of noise, him and her romping about the house in the middle of the night. Don't know what the lad made of it.'

'You don't know where she's living now?'

'Last I heard she married some old pervert.'

'A pervert? Are you sure?'

'Well, a dirty old man. That's what Mr Turner called him – "Valentina's dirty old man". 'Appen he had a load of money – that's what they said.'

'That's what they said?'

The watery eyes below the curlers blink and continue to stare. I meet their gaze.

'She married my father.'

The eyes blink again, and look down.

'Have you tried the Ukrainian Club? 'Appen she goes in there once in a while.'

'Thank you. That's a good idea.'

I recognise the elderly lady on reception at the Ukrainian Club as a friend of my mother's, Maria Kornoukhov, whom I had last seen at the funeral. We greet each other with hugs. She has not seen Valentina for several weeks. She wants to know why I am looking for her, and why she isn't living with my father.

'Painted doll. I never liked her, you know,' she says in Ukrainian.

'Neither did I. But I thought she would care for my father.'

'Ha! She will care only for his money! Your poor mother, who saved every penny. All spent on greasepaint and see-through dresses.'

'And cars. She has three cars, you know.'

'Three cars! What folly! Who needs more than a good pair of legs? Mind you, *she* won't walk far on those stab-stab shoes she wears.'

'Now she's disappeared. We don't know how to find her.'

She drops her voice to a whisper and puts her mouth close to my cheek.

'Have you tried the Imperial Hotel?'

The Imperial Hotel isn't really a hotel, it's a pub. It isn't really Imperial, either, though the maroon dralon upholstery and mahogany panelling suggest it has pretensions. I still feel awkward going into pubs alone, but I buy a half of shandy at the bar, and take it to a corner where I can sit and observe the whole room. The clientele are mainly young, and very noisy; the men drink bottled lager, the women drink vodka chasers or white wine, and they shout across the room to each other in a relentless ear-splitting banter. They seem to be regulars, for they call to the barman by his first name and make jokes about his bald-look haircut. How do Valentina and Stanislav fit in to this place? At the far side of the lounge I notice a young man clearing glasses from the tables. He has longish curly hair and a horrible purple polyester jumper.

As he reaches my table, he looks up at me, and our eyes meet. I smile a broad friendly smile.

'Hi there, Stanislav! Great to see you! I didn't know you worked here. Where's your Mum? Does she work here too?'

Stanislav does not reply. He picks up my glass, which is still half full, and disappears into the room behind the bar. He does not re-emerge. After a while the barman comes up and asks me to leave.

'Why? I'm not doing any harm. I'm just enjoying a quiet drink.'

''Appen yer've finished yer drink.'

'I'll get another.'

'Look, just piss off, will yer?'

'Pubs are supposed to be public, you know.' I try to muster my middle-class dignity.

'I said, piss off.'

He leans over me so close I can smell his beer-breath. His bald-look haircut suddenly doesn't look very amusing.

'Fine. I'll cross this hotel off my recommended list, then.'

It is dusk when I find myself out on the pavement again, but still warm from the afternoon sun. It hasn't rained for a fortnight, and the yard at the back of the pub smells of beer and urine. I am surprised to feel that my hands are shaking as I reach for my car keys, but I am not ready to give up yet. I sneak round to the back and peep through the open scullery window. There is no sign of Stanislav or of Valentina. Inside I can hear one of the rowdy regulars calling, 'Hey, Bald Ed – what was all that about?' and Bald Ed's reply: 'Oh, some old cow that was threatening the staff.' I sit down on an empty barrel and feel the tiredness sink into my bones. All the encounters of the day bang around in my head: so much aggression. I can do without it. I climb into my car and, without going back to my father's house, drive straight home to Cambridge and to Mike.

*   *   *

Vera puts her finger on it straightaway.

'They are working illegally. That's why he doesn't want you asking questions. Of course Stanislav is probably under age to be working in a pub, too.'

(Oh, Big Sis, what a instinct you have for digging up the dodgy, the dirty, dishonest.)

'And the woman at Eric Pike's house?'

'Obviously his wife has been having an affair while he has had an affair with Valentina.'

'How do you know all these things, Vera?'

'How do you *not* know them, Nadia?'

22

Model citizens

After they came to England in 1946, my parents were model citizens. They never broke the law – not even once. They were too scared. They agonised over filling in forms that were ambiguously worded: what if they gave the wrong answer? They feared to claim benefits: what if there was an inspection? They were too frightened to apply for passports: what if they weren't allowed back in? Those who got up the nose of the authorities might be sent off on the long train journey from which there was no return.

So imagine my father's panic when he receives a summons through the post to appear in court for non-payment of Vehicle Excise Duty. Crap car has been found parked on a side street without a tax disc. He is the registered keeper of the vehicle.

'You see, through this Valentina for the first time in my life I am become a criminal.'

'It's OK, Pappa. I'm sure it's a misunderstanding.'

'No no. You know nothing. People have died from misunderstanding.'

'But not in Peterborough.'

I telephone the DVLA and explain the situation. I tell the voice on the other end of the phone that my father has never driven the car, is no longer physically able to drive. I had been braced for an encounter with a distant bureaucrat, but the voice – older, female, with a touch of Yorkshire about the vowels – is gently sympathetic. Suddenly for no reason I burst into tears and find myself pouring out the whole story: the enhanced bosom, the yellow rubber gloves, the pork-cutlet driving licence.

'Oh my! Oh, I never!' coos the gentle voice. 'The poor duck! Tell him he's not to worry. I'll just send him a little form to fill in. He only has to give the details of her name and address.'

'But that's just it. He doesn't know her address. We have to communicate through the solicitor.'

'Well, put the solicitor's address. That'll do.'

I fill the form in for my father, and he signs it.

A few days later, he rings me again. Overnight, Crap car has reappeared on the drive. It sits with two wheels on the grass, next to the rotting Roller. It has a flat rear tyre, a broken quarter light on the driver's side, and the driver's door is buckled and tied up with string to the door pillar, so that the driver has to get in on the passenger side and climb over the gear lever. There is no tax disc. Meanwhile, the Lada has disappeared from the garage.

'Something fishy has occurred,' says my father.

There are now two cars in the front garden, and they are parked in such a way that my father has to squeeze up against the prickly pyracantha hedge to get to his front door. The thorns catch at his coat, and sometimes scratch his face and hands.

'This is ridiculous,' I say to my father. 'She *must* take her cars away.'

I telephone Ms Carter, and she writes to Valentina's solicitor. Still nothing happens. I telephone a second-hand dealer, and offer them for sale at an advantageous price. He is very interested in the Roller, but backs off as soon as I tell him there are no papers. I don't even get to mention that there are also no keys.

'But couldn't you just tow them away, and use them for parts or scrap?'

'You need a registration document, even to scrap a car.'

*   *   *

Valentina's solicitor has stopped responding to our letters. How are we to persuade Valentina to move the car, when we do not even know where she lives? Vera recommends Justin, the five-o'clock-shadow man who delivered the divorce papers to Valentina. I have never hired a private detective before. The idea seems fantastic – something people in TV thrillers do.

'My dear, you will find him *quite* exciting,' says Vera.

'But won't she recognise him? Won't she spot the black BMW outside her house?'

'Oh, I'm sure he will go undercover. Probably he has an old Ford Escort he uses for such occasions.'

I contact Justin through Ms Carter and leave a long rambling message on his answering machine, for I have no idea what I really want to say. He rings me back in a few minutes. His voice is deep and confident, with traces of the Fenland accent that he has tried to iron out. He is sure he can help me. He has contacts in the police and in the council. He takes down all the details I can give him, her variously spelled names, her date of birth (unless she has made that up too), her National Insurance number (I found it on one of the papers in the car boot), Stanislav's name and age, all I know about Bob Turner and Eric Pike. But he seems more interested in negotiating the fee. Do I want to pay by results, or by the day? I choose to pay by results. So much for her address, so much for details of her work, more for the evidence of a lover that will stand up in court. After I put the phone down I am pleased and excited. If Justin can find this information, it will be cheap at the price.

*   *   *

While I am busy trying to get rid of the Rolls-Royce, my father is eulogising machinery of another kind.

The end of the war was a time of extraordinary advance and progress in the history of tractors, as swords were once more beaten into ploughshares, and a hungry world began to consider how it would feed itself. For successful agriculture, as we now know, is the only hope of the human race, and in this, tractors have a central part to play.

The Americans entered the war only after the industries and populations of Europe had already been tested almost to annihilation. American tractors, which had formerly lagged behind their European counterparts in technical excellence, now seized the centre stage. Foremost among these was the John Deere.

John Deere himself was a blacksmith from Vermont, a tall man built like an ox, who in 1837 with his own hands fashioned a steel plough which was most excellent for turning the virgin soil of the American prairies. Thus it could be said that it was the Deere tractor, more than the foolish cowboys glorified in post-war cinema, that opened up the American West.

His great genius was less as an engineer than as a businessman, for by making deals and offering finance to buyers, this former workshop operation was by the time of his death in 1886 one of the biggest companies in America.

John Deere's famous twin-cylinder model with 376-cubic-inch diesel engine was both economical to run and easy to handle. But it was the mighty Model G which up to 1953 was exported all over the world, and played its part in the American economic dominance which characterises the post-war period.

*   *   *

One afternoon in early October, my father is taking a break from his great work and snoozing in the armchair in the front room, when he becomes aware of an unusual sound that seeps into his dream. It is a soft repetitive mechanical whirr – quite a pleasant sound, which he says reminds him of his old Francis Barnett struggling to get started on a dewy morning. He lies suspended between sleep and wakefulness, listening to the sound, remembering the Francis Barnett, the winding Sussex lanes, wind in his hair, fragrant blossomy hedgerows, the scent of freedom. He listens intently, with pleasure, and then he picks up another sound, so quiet it is almost inaudible, a faint susurration – voices talking in whispers.

His senses are now fully alert. Someone is in the room. Lying perfectly still, he opens one eye. Two figures are moving about near the window. As they move into his line of vision, he recognises them: Valentina and Mrs Zadchuk. Quickly he closes the eye again. He hears their movement, their whispers, and another sound: the rustle of paper. He opens the other eye. Valentina is rifling through the dresser drawer where he keeps all his letters and documents. From time to time, she pulls out a sheet and passes it to Mrs Zadchuk. Now he recognises the other sound – the whirring mechanical sound. It is not the Francis Barnett, it is the small portable photocopier.

He stiffens. He cannot help himself. He opens both eyes, and finds himself staring straight into the Cleopatra-lined syrup-coloured eyes of Valentina.

'Ha!' she says. 'The corpse is come to life, Margaritka.'

Mrs Zadchuk grunts and feeds more paper into the copier. It whirrs again.

Valentina bends down and puts her face very close to my father's.

'You think you clever clever. Soon you will be dead, Mr Clever Engineer.'

My father lets out a shriek, and what he later describes as a 'rear end discharge'.

'Already you look like corpse – soon you will be. You carcass of dog. You walking skeleton.'

She leans over him, pinioning him to the chair with one hand on each side of his head, while Mrs Zadchuk continues to photocopy the correspondence from Ms Carter. When she has finished, she bundles together the papers, unplugs the photocopier, and stows them all in a large Tesco carrier bag.

'Come, Valenka. We have all what we need. Leave this bad-stink corpse.'

Valentina stops in the doorway and blows him a mock kiss.

'You living dead. You graveyard escapee.'

23

The graveyard escapee

Maybe Valentina knew, or maybe it was an inspired guess, but my father is indeed a graveyard escapee.

It happened in the summer of 1941 when the German troops swept into Ukraine and the Red Army fled eastwards, burning bridges and fields behind them. My father was in Kiev with his regiment. He was a reluctant soldier. They had shoved a bayonet into his hands and told him he had to fight for the motherland, but he didn't want to fight – not for the motherland, not for the Soviet state, not for anybody. He wanted to sit at his desk with his slide rule and his sheets of blank paper and puzzle over the drag–lift equation. But there was no time for that – no time for anything except stab and run, shoot and run, dive for cover and run, and run and run. Eastwards, through the harvest-yellow wheat fields of Poltava, under a blazing blue sky, the army ran, to regroup finally at Stalingrad. Only the flag they followed wasn't yellow and blue: it was scarlet with yellow.

Maybe this was why, or maybe he had just had enough, but my father didn't go with them. He slipped away from his regiment and found a place to hide. In the old Jewish cemetery in a quiet leafy quarter of the city he lowered himself into a broken tomb, replacing the heavy stones behind him, and sheltered there, cheek to cheek with the dead. Sometimes, as he crouched in the dark, he could hear the voices of bereaved Jews wailing above his head. He stayed there in the cool, damp silence for almost a month, living on the food he had brought with him, and, when that ran out, on grubs, snails and frogs. He drank from the trickle of water that made a puddle in the earth when it rained, and contemplated his closeness to death, adjusting his eyes to the darkness.

Except that it was not completely dark: there was a gap between the stones through which sunlight beamed at a certain time of day, and through which, when he pressed his eye to it, he could see the world outside. He could see the gravestones, half-overgrown with pink roses, and beyond that, a cherry tree, laden with ripening fruit. He became obsessed with the tree. All day he watched the cherries ripen while he hunted in the dark underground for grubs which he wrapped in a handful of leaves or grass to make them more palatable.

There came a day – an evening – when he could bear it no longer. As dusk fell, he crept out of his hiding-place and climbed the tree, and plucked fistfuls of cherries, cramming them into his mouth. More and more, so that the juice ran down his chin. He spat the stones in all directions, till his clothes were covered in smatterings of cherry juice, like blood. It seemed he could never get enough. And then he filled his pockets and his cap, and stole back to his underground den.

But someone had seen him. Someone reported him. At daybreak, soldiers came and dragged him out and arrested him as a spy. As they grabbed him and manhandled him into the truck, the acid mass of cherries in his belly combined with the terror of arrest caused him to soil himself shamefully.

They took him to an old mental hospital on the edge of the city which was their command headquarters, and locked him in a bare room with bars over the windows, to sit in his stench and await interrogation. My father was not a brave man, not the heroic type. He knew how brutally the Germans treated captive Ukrainians. What would you or I do in that situation? My father smashed a window with his fist, and with a shard of broken glass, he cut his throat.

The Germans did not give up on him so easily. They found a doctor, an aged Ukrainian psychiatrist who had stayed behind in the hospital to look after his patients. He had never stitched together a wound since his days as a medical student. He repaired my father's throat with rough stitches of button thread, leaving a jagged scar that caused him to cough when he ate for ever after. But he saved my father's life. And he told the Germans that the larynx was irreparably damaged, that the man would never be able to speak under interrogation, and in any case, he was no spy but a poor lunatic – a former mental patient who had tried to harm himself before. So the Germans let him go.

He stayed in the hospital, under the care of the elderly psychiatrist, with whom he played chess and discussed philosophy and science. As the summer passed, the Germans too moved on, pursuing the Red Army eastwards. When he thought it was safe, he slipped away, made his way back through the German lines, westwards, towards Dashev to join his family.

But Mother and Vera had already gone. Two weeks before my father returned, the Germans had taken over the village, put all the able-bodied young adults on to trains, and transported them to Germany to work in munitions factories. *Ostarbeiter*, they were called: workers from the East. They had wanted to leave Vera behind – she was only five – but Mother had kicked up such a fuss that she came too. Father stayed in Dashev for long enough to recover his strength, then he talked his way on to a train and followed them to the West.

*   *   *

'No, no,' says Vera. 'It didn't happen like that. They were plums, not cherries. And it was the NKVD that caught him, not the Germans. The Germans came afterwards. And when he came back to Dashev, we were still there. I remember him coming back, with this terrible scar on his throat. Baba Nadia looked after him. He couldn't eat anything except soup.'

'But he told me himself . . .'

'No, he went west first, got on a transport to Germany. When he told them he was an engineer they gave him a job. Then he sent for Mother and me.'

That is the story of how my family left Ukraine – two different stories, my mother's and my father's.

'He was an economic migrant, then, not an asylum seeker?'

'Nadia, please. Why are you raising these questions now? We should be concentrating our energies on the divorce – not on this endless carping about the past. There is nothing to say. Nothing to be learned. What's over is over.'

There is a catch in her voice, as though I have touched a nerve. Can I have hurt her?

'I'm sorry, Vera.' (I *am* sorry.)

It dawns on me: Big Sis is no more than a carapace. My real sister is somebody different, somebody I am only just beginning to know.

'Now.' Her voice steadies. She takes control. 'You say Valentina has copied all his papers. There can be only one reason for this – she wants to use them for her divorce hearing. You must let Laura Carter know at once.'

'I will.'

Ms Carter is incandescent when I tell her about the photocopying of the papers.

'Some of these solicitors are hardly better than their crooked clients. If these papers are shown in court, we shall protest. Did you get anywhere with that private detective?'

*   *   *

Justin delivers on his promise. A week or so later he telephones to say that he has tracked down Valentina: she and Stanislav are living in two rooms above the Imperial Hotel. She works behind the bar, and Stanislav washes pots. (I had guessed as much.) She is also claiming social security benefit, and housing benefit on a rented terraced house in Norwell Street, which she is subletting to a Ghanaian trainee audiologist who had somehow wandered into the Imperial Hotel for a drink. Does she have a lover? Justin is not sure. He has spotted a dark blue Volvo estate parked nearby once or twice, but not overnight. Eric Pike is a long-standing regular at the Imperial Hotel. There is no evidence that will stand up in court.

I thank Justin profusely and put a cheque in the post.

I telephone Vera, but her line is busy, and while I am waiting, I decide to make a call to Chris Tideswell at the Spalding Police Station. I tell her about the withdrawal of the appeal at the tribunal, and I tell her that Valentina is now living at the Imperial Hotel with her son, where they are both illegally employed.

'Hm,' says Chris Tideswell in her chirpy young-girl voice. 'Yer a right detective. Yer should join the force. I'll see what I can do.'

Vera is delighted with Justin's findings.

'You see, it confirms what I always believed. She is a criminal. Not satisfied with ripping off Pappa, she is also ripping off our country.' (*Our* country?) 'And what about this Ghanaian? Probably he is also some kind of asylum seeker.'

'Justin said he's a trainee audiologist at the hospital.'

'Well, he could still be an asylum seeker, couldn't he?'

'All we know is that he's renting the house from her. Probably she's ripping him off too.'

There are ten years between Vera and me – ten years that gave me the Beatles, the demonstrations against the Vietnam War, the student uprising of 1968, and the birth of feminism, which taught me to see all women as sisters – all women except my sister, that is.

'And maybe he is subletting rooms in the house to other asylum seekers.' (She won't let it go.) 'You see when you enter this shady world of criminality, you discover that there are layers upon layers of deceit, and you have to be both clever and persistent to find out the truth.'

'Vera, he's a trainee audiologist. He works with deaf people.'
'That doesn't mean anything, Nadia.'

Once, not so long ago, Big Sis's attitudes would send me into a rage of righteousness, but now I see them in their historical context, and I smile to myself in a superior way.

'When we first came here, Vera, people could have said the same things about us – that we were ripping off the country, gorging ourselves on free orange juice, growing fat on NHS cod-liver oil. But they didn't. Everyone was kind to us.'

'But that was different. *We* were different.' (We were white, of course, for one thing, I could say, but I hold my tongue.) 'We worked hard and kept our heads down. We learned the language and integrated. We never claimed benefits. We never broke the law.'

'*I* broke the law. I smoked dope. I was arrested at Greenham Common. Pappa got so upset that he tried to catch the train back to Russia.'

'But that's exactly my point, Nadia. You and your leftish friends – you never really appreciated what England had to offer – stability, order, the rule of law. If you and your kind prevailed, this country would be just like Russia – bread queues everywhere, and people getting their hands chopped off.'

'That's Afghanistan. Chopping hands off *is* the rule of law.'

Both of us have raised our voices. This is turning into an old-style argument.

'Whatever. You see my point,' she says dismissively.

'What I appreciated about growing up in England was the tolerance, liberalism, everyday kindness.' (I drive home my point by wagging my finger in the air, even though she can't see me.) 'The way the English always stick up for the underdog.'

'You are confusing the underdog with the scrounger, Nadia. We were poor, but we were never scroungers. The English people believe in fairness. Fair play. Like cricket.' (What does *she* know about cricket?) 'They play by the rules. They have a natural sense of discipline and order.'

'No no. They're quite anarchic. They like to see the little man stick two fingers up to the world. They like to see the big shot get his come-uppance.'

'On the contrary, they have a perfectly preserved class system, in which everyone knows where they belong.'

See how we grew up in the same house but lived in different countries?

'They make fun of their rulers.'
'But they like strong rulers.'

If Vera mentions Mrs Thatcher, I shall put the phone down. There is a short pause, in which we both consider our options. I try an appeal to our shared past.

'Remember the woman on the bus, Vera? The woman in the fur coat?'
'What woman? What bus? What are you talking about?'

Of course she remembers. She hasn't forgotten the smell of diesel, the swish of the windscreen wipers, the unsteady sway of the bus as it churned newly fallen snow into slush; coloured lights outside the windows; Christmas Eve 1952. Vera and I, muffled against the cold, snuggling up against Mother on the back seat. And a kind woman in a fur coat who leaned across the aisle and pressed sixpence into Mother's hand: 'For the kiddies at Christmas.'

'The woman who gave Mother sixpence.'

Mother, our mother, did not dash the coin in her face; she mumbled, 'Thank you, lady,' and slipped it into her pocket. The shame of it!

'Oh, that. I think she was a bit drunk. You mentioned it once before. I don't know why you go on about it.'

'It was that moment – more than anything that happened to me afterwards – that turned me into a lifelong socialist.'

There is silence on the other end of the telephone and for a moment I think she has hung up on me. Then: 'Maybe it was what turned me into the woman in the fur coat.'

24

Mystery man

Vera and I decide that together we will confront Valentina outside the Imperial Hotel.

'It is the only thing to do. Otherwise she will keep on evading us,' says Vera.

'But she might just turn and run away when she sees us.'

'Then we will follow her. We will track her down to her lair.'

'But what if she has Stanislav with her? Or Eric Pike?'

'Don't be such a baby, Nadia. If necessary we will call for the police.'

'Wouldn't it be better to leave it to the police in the first place? I spoke to this young woman officer in Spalding who seemed really sympathetic.'

'Do you still believe that the law will oust her? Nadia, if we don't do this, nobody will.'

'OK.' Although I make objections, I am excited by the idea. 'Maybe we should arrange for five-o'clock-shadow Justin to be there. Just as back-up.'

But before we can arrange a suitable date, my father calls in a state of great agitation. A mystery man has been seen hanging around the house.

'Mystery man. Since yesterday. Peeping in at all windows. Then disappears.'

'But Pappa, who is it? You should call the police.'

I am alarmed. It seems obvious that someone is casing the house for a break-in.

'No no! No police! Definitely no police!'

My father's experience of the police has not been positive.

'Call a neighbour, then, Pappa. And confront him together. Find out who he is. It's most likely a burglar, looking to see what you have worth stealing.'

'Does not look like burglar. Middle-aged. Short. Wears brown suit.'

I am intrigued.

'We'll come on Saturday. Lock your doors and windows until then.'

We arrive at about three o'clock on the Saturday afternoon. It is mid-October. The sun is already low in the sky, and a fenland mist shrouds the countryside in a damp haze, lingering around the low-lying fields and marshes, stealing like a wraith out of drainage culverts and watercourses. The leaves have started to turn. The garden is thick with windfalls, apples, pears and plums, over which a cloud of small flies hovers.

My father is asleep in his armchair by the window, his head thrown back, mouth open, a silver thread of saliva running from his lip to his collar. Lady Di's girlfriend is curled up on his lap, her striped belly quietly rising and falling. A miasma of somnolence hangs over the house and garden, as if a fairytale witch has cast a spell, and the sleeper is waiting to be awakened with a kiss.

'Hallo, Pappa.' I kiss his scrawny stubbly cheek. He wakes

with a start, and the cat jumps on to the floor, purring in greeting, rubbing herself against our legs.

'Hallo, Nadia, Michael! Good you can come!' He stretches out his arms in welcome.

How thin he has become! I had hoped that after Valentina left things would suddenly change; he would start to put on weight, and clean up the house, and everything would get back to normal. But nothing has changed, except that a bulky Valentina-shaped emptiness now sits in his heart.

'How are you, Pappa? Where's this mystery man?'

'Mystery man has disappeared. Not seen since yesterday.'

I must confess to a pang of disappointment – my curiosity had been aroused. But I put the kettle on, and while it is boiling I wander outside and start to gather up the windfalls. I am concerned that my father has not pursued his annual ritual of gathering, storing, peeling and Toshiba-ing. Self-neglect is a sign of depression.

Mike settles himself in the other comfortable chair in listening mode.

'So, Nikolai, how's the book coming along? Have you got any more of that excellent plum wine?' (He's been showing too much interest in that plum wine for my liking. Doesn't he realise it is dangerous stuff?)

'Aha!' exclaims my father, handing Mike a glass. 'Now is coming a very interesting time in the history of tractors. As Lenin said of the capitalist time, the whole world is unified into one market, with concentrations of capital increasing markedly. Now in relation to engineering of tractors, my thoughts on this are as follows . . .'

I never found out what his thoughts were, because by this point, Mike has surrendered to the plum wine, and I have ranged out of earshot. I am paying tribute to Mother's garden. It makes me sad to see the havoc four years of neglect have wreaked; yet it is the havoc of superabundance. In such a rich soil, everything that takes root thrives: weeds proliferate, creepers run amok, the grass is grown so tall it is almost like a meadow, fallen fruit rots, yielding curious spotted fungi; flies, gnats, wasps, worms and slugs feast on the fruit, birds feast on the worms and flies.

Underneath the washing-line, half hidden in the long grass, a piece of shiny cloth catches my eye. I bend down closer to look. It is the green satin bra, the colour now almost faded out. A startled earwig scurries out of one of the enormous cups. On impulse I pick it up and try to read the size on the label. But that too has faded away, washed out by soap powder, sun and rain. Holding this tattered relic in my hands gives me a strange sense of loss. *Sic transit gloria mundi.*

I don't know what makes me look up from my contemplation, but at that moment my eye catches a movement, a fleeting figure perhaps, at the side of the house. Then it is gone; maybe it was just a brownish shadow, or maybe a glimpse of someone in brown. The mystery man!

'Mike! Pappa! Come quick!'

I run into the front garden which is still dominated by the two rusting cars. At first it seems there is no one there. Then I see someone standing very still in the shadow of the lilac tree. He is quite short and squat, with curly brown hair. He is wearing a brown suit. There is something strangely familiar about him.

'Who are you? What are you doing here?'

He doesn't say anything, nor move towards me. His stillness is uncanny. Yet he is not frightening. His face is open, attentive. I come a couple of steps closer.

'What do you want? Why do you keep coming here?'

Still he says nothing. Then I remember where I have seen him before: he is the man in the photographs I found in Valentina's room – the man with his arm around her strapless shoulders. He is a little older than the man in the photos, but it is definitely him.

'Please, say something. Tell me who you are.'

Silence. Then Mike and Pappa appear at the front door. Mike is rubbing his eyes sleepily. Now the man steps forward, and stretching out his hand says one word.

'Dubov.'

'Ah! Dubov!' My father rushes forward, seizes both his hands, and lets flow a stream of rapturous welcome in Ukrainian. 'Highly esteemed Director of Polytechnic in Ternopil! Renowned leading Ukrainian scholar! You are most welcome in my modest house.'

Yes, it is Valentina's intelligent-type husband. As soon as I realise this, I recognise also the resemblance to Stanislav: the brown curls, short build, and now, as he steps out of the shadows, the dimpled smile.

'Mayevskyj! Acclaimed engineer of first order! I have been honoured to read your fascinating thesis on tractor history which you sent to me,' he says in Ukrainian, pumping my father's hands up and down. Now I understand why he did not respond to my questions. He does not speak English. My father introduces us.

'Mikhail Lewis, my son-in-law. Distinguished trade unionist

and computer expert. My daughter Nadezhda. She is a social worker.' (Pappa! How could you!)

Over tea and a packet of past-sell-by-date biscuits I have found in the larder, we gradually discover the reason for the mystery man's visit. It is simple enough: he has come to find his wife and son, and to take them home to Ukraina. He has grown increasingly concerned about the letters he has been receiving from England. Stanislav is not happy at his school, where he says the other boys are lazy, obsessed with sex, they boast endlessly of their material possessions, and the academic standard is low. Valentina is also unhappy. She has described her new husband as a violent and paranoid man, from whom she is seeking a divorce. Though now that he has met the respected gentleman-engineer (with whom he has already enjoyed a stimulating correspondence on the subject of tractors) he is inclined to believe that she may have exaggerated a little, as she has sometimes been known to do in the past.

'One may forgive a beautiful woman a little exaggeration,' he says. 'The important thing is that all is forgiven, and now it is time for her to come home.'

He has come over to England on an exchange programme with Leicester University to extend his knowledge of superconductivity, and he has been allowed to take some weeks' leave in addition. His mission is to find his wife (although he granted her a divorce, he has never for one moment ceased to consider her as such) and woo her, and win back her heart.

'She loved me once – surely she can love me again.'

On his free days, he has caught the train from Leicester and lain in wait outside the house, hoping to catch her by surprise. He has scoured the town, and enlisted the help of the President of the Ukrainian Club, but as the days have gone by and she has not appeared, he fears he may have lost her for ever. But now – now he has met the eminent Mayevskyj and his charming daughter and distinguished son-in-law – now maybe they will help him in his endeavours.

I can see my father stiffen, as he realises that this renowned leading Ukrainian scholar is also a rival in love. It is one thing for him to divorce Valentina himself, quite another to have her snatched away from under his nose.

'This you must discuss with Valentina. My impression is she is absolutely determined she must stay in England.'

'Yes, for such a beautiful flower, the wind in Ukraina blows very hard and cold at this moment. But it will not always be so. And where there is love, there is always enough warmth for the human soul to thrive,' says the intelligent-type husband.

'Tosh!' I snort into my teacup, but manage to disguise it as a sneeze.

'One snag remains,' says my father. 'Both have disappeared. Valentina and Stanislav. No one knows where they are. She has even left two cars here.'

'I know where they are!' I cry. Everyone turns to stare at me, even Mike, who cannot understand a word of what is going on. My father catches my eye and glowers, as if to say, Don't you dare tell him.

'The Imperial Hotel! They're living at the Imperial Hotel!'

⋆   ⋆   ⋆

The pubs in Peterborough are all busy on Saturday afternoon, with shoppers, market folk and tourists. The Imperial Hotel is heaving. Some regulars have taken their drinks outside on to the pavement and are clustered around the doorway, talking about the football. I park the Ford Escort a few yards away. We decide Mike should be sent in to reconnoitre – he will merge with the crowd. He is to look out for Valentina or Stanislav, and if he sees them he is to slip out discreetly and alert Dubov, who will then move in for his charm offensive. He and my father are sitting in the back of the car, with excited looks on their faces. For some reason everyone is talking in whispers.

After a few moments Mike emerges, pint in hand, to report that there is no sign of Valentina or Stanislav. Nor is there anyone who matches my description of Bald Ed. There is a double sigh of disappointment from the back of the car.

'Let me look!' says Pappa, his arthritic fingers struggling with the catch of the car door.

'No no!' cries Dubov. 'You will frighten her away. Let *me* look!'

I am worried that my father seems to be on another emotional rollercoaster. I fear that Dubov's competitor presence has pricked his male pride, and rekindled his interest in Valentina. He knows she is no good for him, but he cannot resist the magnetism that draws him despite himself. Foolish old man. It can only end in tears. Yet beneath the contrariness of his behaviour, I sense that he is driven by a deeper logic, for Dubov has the same magnetism, the same seductive energy as Valentina. Father is in love with both of them: he is in love with the life-beat of love itself. I can understand the fascination, because I share it too.

'Shut up, both of you, and stay where you are,' I say. 'I'll go and look.'

The back doors of the car are fitted with childproof locks

that cannot be opened from the inside, so they have no choice in the matter.

Mike has found a seat near the door. A crowd of young men is clustered around the TV screen, and every few minutes they let out a chorus of roars. Peterborough are playing at home. Mike has his eyes fixed on the screen as well – his pint is now drunk half-way down. I go up to the bar and look around. Mike was right – there is no sign of Valentina, Stanislav or Bald Ed. Suddenly there is a surge of cheering. Someone has scored. The man pulling pints at the other end of the bar had his head lowered, but now as he turns towards the TV our eyes meet, and at once we recognise each other. It *is* Bald Ed – but he isn't bald any more. Some scraps of shaggy grey fluff cover his pate. His belly has grown, and started to sag down over his belt. In the weeks since I last saw him, he has really let himself go.

'You again. What do you want?'

'I'm looking for Valentina and Stanislav. I'm a friend, that's all. I'm not from the police, if that's what you're worried about.'

'They're gone. Done a runner. Moonlight.'

'Oh no!'

''Appen yer scared them off last time.'

'But surely . . .'

'Her and t' lad. Both gone. Last weekend.'

'But have you any idea . . . ?'

''Appen she reckoned she were too good for me.' He looks at me with sad eyes.

'You mean . . . ?'

'I don't mean nothing. Now, fuck off, will yer? I've got a pub to run, and I'm on me own.'

He turns his back once more and starts to gather glasses.

*   *   *

'Oh no! Gone!' There are gasps of dismay from the rival lovers in the back seat, then a glum silence settles over the car which, after a few moments, is broken by a long trembling sigh.

'Come, come, Volodya Simeonovich,' murmurs my father in Ukrainian, reaching his arm around Dubov's shoulder. 'Be a man!'

I have never heard him use the patronymic before. Now he and Dubov are starting to sound like something out of *War and Peace*.

'Alas, Nikolai Alexeevich, to be a man is to be a weak and fallible creature.'

'I think we all need cheering up,' suggests Mike. 'Why don't we go in for a drink?'

The crowd has dispersed at the end of the match and we manage to find enough stools to squeeze around the table; even a chair with a back for Pappa. The noise in the pub is too much for him, and he withdraws into a wide-eyed blankness. Dubov perches his broad buttocks on the small round stool spreading his knees for balance, chin up, alert, drinking in the atmosphere. I notice his eyes scanning the crowd, keeping a hopeful watch on all the entrances.

'What would everyone like to drink?' asks Mike.

Father asks for a glass of apple juice. Dubov asks for a large whiskey. Mike orders another pint. I would really like a cup of tea, but I settle for a glass of white wine. We are served by Bald Ed, who for some reason brings the drinks over to our table on a tray.

'Cheers!' Mike lifts his glass. 'To . . .' He hesitates. What is the appropriate toast for such a diverse group of people with such conflicting desires and needs?

'To the triumph of the human spirit!'

We all raise our glasses.

25

The triumph of the human spirit

'The triumph of the human spirit?' Vera snorts. 'My dear, that is charming but quite naïve! Let me tell you, the human spirit is mean and selfish; the only impulse is to preserve itself. Everything else is pure sentimentality.'

'That's what you always say, Vera. But what if the human spirit is noble and generous – and creative, empathic, imaginative, spiritual – all those things we try to be – and sometimes it's just not strong enough to withstand all the meanness and selfishness in the world?'

'Spiritual! Really, Nadia! Where do you think the meanness and selfishness come from, if not from the human spirit? Do you really believe there is an evil force stalking the world? No, the evil comes from the human heart. You see, I *know* what people are like deep down.'

'And I don't know?'

'You are fortunate that you have always lived in the world of illusion and sentiment. Some things it is better not to know.'

'We'll just have to agree to disagree.' I feel my energy draining away. 'Anyway, she's disappeared again. That was what I was ringing to tell you.'

'But did you try the other house – the house in Norwell Street with the deaf asylum seeker?'

'We called in there on the way home, but there was no one. It was all dark.'

Tiredness settles over me like a damp blanket. We have been talking for almost an hour, and I haven't the energy to argue any more. 'Vera, I'd better go to bed now. Good-night.'

'Good-night, Nadia. Don't worry too much about what I said.'

'I won't.'

And yet this dark knowledge of Vera's troubles me. What if she is right?

*   *   *

Despite being rivals in love, Pappa and Dubov get on like a house on fire, and under strong invitation from my father Dubov moves out of his cell in the hall of residence at Leicester University and makes himself at home in what was formerly my parents' bedroom, then Valentina's room. His belongings are carried in a small green rucksack, which he stows at the foot of the bed.

Three days a week, he catches the train to Leicester and comes back late in the evening. He explains to my father the latest developments in superconductivity, drawing neat diagrams in pencil, which are labelled with mysterious symbols. My father waves his hands in the air and declares that it is all as he predicted back in 1938.

Dubov is a practical man. He wakes early, and makes tea for my father. He cleans the kitchen and puts things away after every meal. He gathers up the apples in the garden, and my father teaches him the Toshiba method. Dubov declares that he has never tasted anything so delicious in all his life. They spend the evenings talking about Ukraine, philosophy, poetry and engineering. At weekends they play chess. Dubov listens raptly as my father reads him long chapters from the *Short History of Tractors in Ukrainian*. He even asks intelligent questions. In fact, he could be the perfect wife.

Like my father, Dubov is an engineer, though he is an electrical engineer. While he has been hanging around the garden looking out for Valentina, he has had plenty of opportunity to study the two derelict cars, and he is smitten with the Rolls-Royce. Unlike my father, however, he can actually get down under the chassis. His diagnosis is that her sickness is not too serious: she is leaking oil from the sump because the plug is loose. As for the suspension sag, the most likely problem, he believes, is a broken spring bracket. The reason she does not run is probably an electrical fault, maybe the generator or the alternator. This he will look at. Of course if Valentina and the key cannot be found, she will also need new ignition.

Over the next week my father and Dubov decide to strip down the engine, clean all the parts, and spread them out on the ground on old blankets. Mike's help is enlisted. He spends two evenings on the internet and on the telephone trying to track down scrap dealers who might have a similar Rolls-Royce in their yard, and finally locates one near Leeds, two hours' drive away.

'Really, Mike, you don't have to drive all the way up there, you know. The car's probably a write-off anyway.'

He says nothing, and looks at me with a dreamy stubborn expression I have sometimes seen on my father's face. I can see he has been smitten too.

Eric Pike volunteers to mend the spring bracket. He arrives on Sunday in his blue Volvo with a welding torch and a mask.

How dashing he looks with his sweeping moustache and big leather gauntlets, bravely gripping the red-hot metal in a pair of huge pincers and bashing it with a hammer! The others stand in a semicircle a good distance away, and gasp in admiration. When he has finished, he flourishes the glowing bracket in the air to allow it to cool, and accidentally leaves the torch propped up against the toolbox still turned on, laying waste to the pyracantha hedge in the process. Then, fortunately, it rains, and all four of them huddle in the kitchen poring over technical manuals that Mike has downloaded from the internet. It's all much too masculine for my liking.

'I'm off to Peterborough,' I say. 'I'll get something for supper. What would anybody like?'

'Get some beer in,' says Mike.

Of course the shopping is just a front. I am really going to look for Valentina. I am certain Bald Ed was not lying when he said she was gone; but where could she go? For a while I drive around aimlessly, peering between the swishing windscreen wipers, up and down the empty Sunday streets still littered with Saturday-night debris. I have worked out a circuit: Eric Pike's house, Ukrainian Club, Imperial Hotel, Norwell Street. On the way I call at the supermarket and load up a trolley with the sorts of things I think that my father and Dubov might like: lots of sweet and fatty cakes, meat pies that can be reheated in the oven, frozen vegetables that are already prepared, bread, cheese, fruit, salad that can be shaken out of bags, soup in tins, even a frozen pizza – I draw the line at boil-in-the-bag – plus a few six-packs of beer. I load the shopping into the boot and drive round the circuit once more. As I am heading up past the Imperial Hotel on my second loop, a green car parked half on the pavement catches my eye. It is a Lada – in fact it looks like Valentina's Lada.

It can't be.

It is.

*   *   *

Valentina and Bald Ed are sitting opposite each other at a round table in one corner of the lounge. The door is of panelled glass, and I can see her quite plainly. She is fatter than ever. Her hair is a mess. Her eye make-up is smudged. Then I see that it is more than smudged, it is running down her cheeks: she is crying. As Bald Ed raises his head, I see that he is crying too.

'Oh, for goodness' sake,' I want to yell, but I stand back and say nothing, watching them holding hands across the table and snivelling shamelessly. Their tears make me suddenly unaccountably incensed: what do *they* have to weep about?

Then someone pushes past me into the lounge, and they both look up and see me standing there. Valentina jumps to her feet with a cry, and as she does so, her coat slips off her shoulders, and I clearly see what I should have seen before – what I *did* see before but did not recognise: Valentina is pregnant.

We stand facing each other for a few moments. Both of us are speechless. Then Bald Ed lumbers to his feet.

'Can't you see we're talking? Can't you leave us alone?'

I ignore him.

'Valentina, I have some important news for you. Your

husband has arrived from Ukraina. He is staying with my father. He would like to see you. And Stanislav. He has something he wants to tell you in person.'

Then I turn on my heel and leave.

*   *   *

The light is already fading when I get back to my father's house and the rain has stopped, leaving the air moist and smelling of mysterious autumn fungi. Perhaps it is a trick of the twilight, but the house seems larger than before, the garden more spacious, set back from the road behind its row of lilacs. It takes me a few seconds to realise that the Rolls-Royce has gone. So have the four men.

I suppose I should be pleased, but I am just irritated. There they are, enjoying their laddish fun, while I have been doing the unacknowledged but important chores – replenishing food and drink supplies. Typical. And there is no one to congratulate me on my masterly piece of detective work. Well, there is one person who will appreciate my efforts. I put on the kettle, slip my shoes off, and telephone my sister.

'Pregnant!' cries Vera. 'The slut! The hussy! But listen, Nadia, maybe this is just another ploy. I bet it's not a baby at all, just a pillow pushed up inside her jumper.'

My sister's capacity for cynicism never ceases to amaze me. And yet . . .

'It looks very real, Vera. Not just the bulge, but the way she stands, the puffiness around her ankles. And besides, she's been piling the weight on for quite some time. We just didn't put two and two together.'

'But how incredible! Well done, Nadia, for tracking her

down!' (Coming from Big Sister, that is praise indeed.) 'Maybe I'd better come up and see for myself.'

'Suit yourself. We'll find out soon enough.'

I finish my tea, and start to unload the shopping from the boot, when I hear a car pulling up behind me. I turn, fully expecting to see four grinning men climbing out of a white Rolls-Royce. But it is the green Lada, with Valentina at the wheel.

She pulls up on the brown oil-scarred lawn and eases herself out of the driving seat. Her belly is vast, her splendid bosom engorged with milk. She has tidied up her hair and put on some fresh make-up and perfume. There is a whiff of the old glamour, and despite myself, I am pleased to see her.

'Hi Valentina. Glad you could make it.'

She says nothing, pushes past me to the back of the house, where the kitchen door is open.

''Ello! 'Ello, Volodya!' she calls.

I have followed her into the house, and now she turns on me, her mouth curled dangerously.

'Is nobody here. You tell me lying.'

'He is here, but he has gone out. Look in the bedroom if you don't believe me. His bag is there.'

She marches up the stairs and throws opens the door so forcefully that it slams against the wall with a thud. Then everything goes quiet. After a while I go upstairs to look for her. I find her sitting on the bed which used to be hers, cradling the small green rucksack in her arms as though it was a baby. She looks up at me blankly.

'Valentina.' I sit down beside her and lay a hand on the rucksack which is resting against her belly. 'It's wonderful news about the baby.'

She says nothing, gives me the same blank look.

'Is the father Ed? Ed at the Imperial Hotel?' I am pushing my luck, and she knows it.

'Why you go pocking nose in every place? Eh?'

'He seems like a very nice man.'

'Is nice man. Is no bebby father.'

'Oh. I see. What a pity.'

We sit side by side on the bed. I am turned towards her, but she stares straight ahead, frowning with concentration, showing me only her handsome barbarous profile, her cheeks flushed, her mouth impassive, her skin radiant with pregnancy. Variable lights seem to flicker in the depths of her syrup-coloured eyes. I cannot read her thoughts.

I don't know how long we have been sitting like this, before the sound of a car pulling up outside the house startles us. The white Rolls-Royce is parked on the road, for there is no room in the garden beside the Lada and Crap car. Four men climb out, with grins as big as water-melons on their faces, jabbering in a mixture of languages. Through the window I watch my father throw up his hands when he sees the Lada on the lawn. He summons Dubov, excitedly pointing out its engineering idiosyncrasies, while Dubov seems eager to establish the whereabouts of its owner. Eric Pike is gripping Mike by the elbow and making zooming gestures with the other hand. They disappear from view, and I hear their noise echoing up the stairs from the hallway and sitting-room.

Then there is silence downstairs – as sudden and total as if a switch has been turned off. Then just one voice – Valentina's.

'Is bebby father my husband Nikolai.'

They are all gathered in the sitting-room by the time I come down. Valentina is sitting upright in the beige moquette armchair like a queen on a throne, facing the room. Dubov and Pappa are sitting side by side on the two-seater settee. My father has a radiant smile on his face. Dubov has sunk his head in his hands. Eric Pike is hunched up on the footstool by the window, scowling at everybody. Mike is in the corner behind the settee. He puts an arm round my shoulder as I slip in beside him.

'Hang on a minute, Valentina,' I butt in. 'You can't get pregnant from oral sex, you know.'

She throws me a withering look.

'Why you know oralsex?'

'Well, I know . . .'

'Nadia, please!' my father interrupts in Ukrainian.

'Valenka, darling,' says Dubov, his voice creamy with love, 'maybe when you were in Ukraina last time . . . ? I know it is a long time, but when there is love, all miracles are possible. Maybe this baby has been waiting for our reunion to bless us . . .'

Valentina shakes her head. 'Not possible.' There is a quiver in her voice.

Eric Pike says nothing, but I see him counting surreptitiously on his fingers.

Valentina, too, is calculating. Her eyes move from Dubov to my father, and back to Dubov, but her face shows no expression.

At that moment, there are footsteps outside and a loud ringing on the doorbell. The door is not locked, and suddenly Bald Ed bursts in, followed closely by Stanislav. He barges his way through the sitting-room to where Valentina is sitting. Stanislav lurks in the doorway, his eyes fixed on Dubov, smiling and blinking away tears. Dubov beckons him over, and, squeezing up closer to my father, makes a space for Stanislav beside him on the settee and folds an arm around him.

'Now then, now then,' he murmurs, ruffling the boy's dark curls.

Stanislav's cheeks burn pink and a tear slips from his eye, as though he is melting under the warmth of his father's touch, but he doesn't say a word.

Bald Ed has stationed himself proprietorially at the side of Valentina's chair. 'Now, Val, come on!' (He calls her Val!) 'I think it's time you told that ex-hubby of yours the truth. He's bound to find out sooner or later.'

Valentina ignores him. Holding my father's eyes, she slides her hands around her breasts and down over her belly. Pappa quivers. His knees start to tremble. Dubov reaches across and places a large meaty hand on his thin bony one.

'Kolya, don't be a fool.'

'No, I'm not the fool, you're the fool. Whoever heard of a baby carried for eighteen months! Eighteen months! Ha ha ha!'

'It matters not who fathered the child, but who will be the father to it,' says Dubov quietly.

'What did he say?' asks Bald Ed.

I translate.

'Yes it does bloody matter! I've got rights. A father has rights, you know. Tell them, Val.'

'You no bebby father,' says Valentina.

'You no bebby father!' chimes Pappa, a mad look in his eyes. 'I bebby father!'

'There is only one answer. The baby must have a paternity test!' says a cold voice from the doorway. Vera has slipped in so quietly that no one heard her arrive. Now she steps forward into the room, and moves towards Valentina. 'If there is a baby at all!'

She lunges forward to feel Valentina's belly. Valentina jumps to her feet with a shriek. 'No! No! You cholera-sick eat-bebby witch! You put no hand on me!'

'Who the hell is she?' Bald Ed turns on Vera and grabs her by the arm.

Dubov steps forward and folds his arms around Valentina's shoulders, but she brushes him off and makes for the door.

In the doorway she pauses, reaches deep into her handbag, and takes out a small key on a fob. She flings it on the floor, and spits on it. Then she disappears.

26

All will be corrected

'So who do you think is the father? Eric Pike or Bald Ed?'

I am in the top bunk, Vera is in the bottom bunk, in the room that was formerly Stanislav's room, before that, the room where Anna, Alice and Alexandra stayed when they visited, before that the room that Vera and I shared as girls. It seems in a way amazing for us both to be here, yet in another way the most natural thing in the world. Except that Vera used to have the top bunk and I used to sleep down below.

Through the thin plasterboard wall we can hear the low murmur of male voices in the next room as Stanislav and Dubov catch up on eighteen months of separation. It is a gentle, companionable rumble, punctuated by loud bursts of laughter. From the room below comes the intermittent sound of Father's long rasping snores. Mike is in the front room, uncomfortably curled up on the two-seater sofa. Fortunately he had quite a lot of plum wine before he went to bed.

'There's someone else,' says Vera. 'You've forgotten about that man she stayed with right at the beginning.'

'Bob Turner?' The idea had not crossed my mind, and yet now that Vera says it, I remember the fat brown envelope, the head leaning out of the window, the way Father crumpled. 'That was more than two years ago. It couldn't be him.'

'Couldn't it?' says Vera sharply.

'You mean she kept on seeing him after they were married?'

'Would that be so surprising?'

'I suppose not.'

'One would have thought she could have done better. None of them seems very appealing. Really,' Vera muses, 'she is quite attractive, in a sluttish way. Then again, it is one thing to sleep with that kind of woman, quite another to marry her.'

'But Dubov married her. And he seems a decent sort of guy. Dubov still loves her. And I think she really loves him – the way she came rushing over as soon as she knew he was here.'

'And yet she abandoned him for Pappa.'

'The lure of life in the West.'

'Now she thinks with this baby nonsense she can weasel her way back in with Pappa – he's so obsessed with the idea of having a son.'

'But imagine, abandoning the love of your life for Pappa, and then finding out he isn't even rich. All he has to offer is a British passport – and that paid for by Bob Turner. Don't you feel even just a little bit sorry for her?'

Vera is silent for a moment.

'I can't say I do. Not after the incident with the Dictaphone. Why, do you?'

'Sometimes I do.'

'But she pities us, too, Nadia. She thinks we're stupid and ugly – and flat-chested.'

'The thing I can't understand is what Dubov sees in her.

He seems so ... perspicacious. You'd think he could see through her.'

'It's her boobs. All men are the same.' Vera sighs. 'Did you see the way Bald Ed ran after her? Pitiful!'

'But did you see Bald Ed's car? Did you see the way Pappa and Dubov were gazing at it?'

'And Mike.'

After Valentina left, Bald Ed rushed out into the garden calling 'Val! Val!' in a pathetic whine, but she didn't even look round. She slammed the door and drove off in the Lada leaving a cloud of acrid blue engine smoke swirling in the garden. Bald Ed waved his arms and ran down the road after her. Then he jumped into his car that was parked out on the road – it was an American 1950s-style Cadillac convertible, pale green, with fins, and lots of chrome – and chased her through the village. Father, Mike, Dubov and Eric Pike all stood at the window and stared as he drove away. Then they all got stuck into the beer I had brought back. After an hour or so, Eric Pike left, too. Then they got out the plum wine.

'Vera, you don't think Pappa *could* be the father? Men of his age have been known to father children. He did talk about it himself at the beginning.'

'Don't be silly, Nadia. Just look at him. Besides, he was the one who raised the issue of non-consummation. I think Bald Ed is the most likely candidate. Just imagine being related to a man called Bald Ed!'

'I expect he has another name. Anyway, if Pappa divorces her, we won't be related.'

'If!'

'You think he could still change his mind?'

'I'm sure of it. Especially if he convinces himself the baby is a boy. Conceived by oral sex. Or through some kind of Platonic exchange of minds.'

'Surely he couldn't be *so* stupid.'

'Of course he could,' says Vera. 'Look at his track record so far.'

We chuckle smugly. I feel close to her and far at the same time, stacked up above her in the dark. When we were children we used to share jokes about our parents.

It must be at least three o'clock in the morning. The rumbles from next door have stopped. I am almost drifting off to sleep. The darkness is comfortable, enfolding. We are so close that we can hear each other's breath, yet the shadows cloak our faces, as in a confessional, so no expression or judgement or shame is revealed. I know there may never be a chance like this again.

'Pappa said something happened to you in the camp at Drachensee. Something about cigarettes. Can you remember?'

'Of course I can remember.' I wait for her to continue, and after a while she says, 'There are some things it's better not to know, Nadia.'

'I know. But tell me anyway.'

*   *   *

The labour camp at Drachensee was a huge, ugly, chaotic and cruel place. Forced labourers from Poland, Ukraine, Belarus, conscripted to boost the German war effort, communists and trade unionists sent from the Low Countries for re-education, Gypsies, homosexuals, criminals, Jews in transit to their deaths, inmates of lunatic asylums and captured resistance fighters, all lived cheek by jowl in low concrete lice-infested barracks. In such a place, the only order was terror. And the rule of terror was reinforced at every level; each community and subcommunity had its own hierarchy of terror.

So it was that among the children of the forced labourers, the head of the hierarchy was a skinny sly-faced youth called Kishka. He must have been some sixteen years old, but he was slight for his age, maybe from a childhood of hunger, and maybe also because he had a habit to support. Kishka was a forty-a-day smoker.

Although he was small, Kishka had around him a coterie of bigger kids who would do his bidding; among these were his sidekick, a brute called Vanenko, two big, not-very-bright Moldavian lads, and a mad-eyed dangerous girl called Lena who always seemed to have plenty of cigarettes – it was said she slept with the guards. To keep Kishka and his gang in cigarettes, the other children were 'taxed' – that is to say, they had to steal cigarettes from their parents and hand them over to Kishka, who would distribute them among his gang. Those who didn't got their punishment.

Of all the children in the camp, only the shy mousy little Vera never paid her cigarette tax. How could this be allowed? Vera protested that her parents didn't smoke, that they traded their cigarettes for food and other things.

'Then you must steal them from someone else,' said Kishka.

Vanenko and the Moldavian lads smiled. Lena winked.

Vera was distraught. Where would she find cigarettes? She sneaked into the barracks when no one was there, and rummaged through the pitiful belongings stowed under the beds. But someone caught her and sent her packing with a thick ear. Numb with despair as she waited for her beating, she stood in a corner of the yard, looking for a place where she could hide, though of course she knew that wherever she hid they would find her. Then she noticed a jacket hanging on a nail by the door. It was the jacket of one of the guards – and the guard himself was over by the perimeter fence, looking out the other way, smoking a cigarette. Quick as a cat, she slid her hand in the pocket, and found the nearly full packet of cigarettes. She hid it inside the sleeve of her dress.

Later, when Kishka came looking for her, she handed over the cigarettes. He was delighted. Army cigarettes had a much higher tobacco content than the rubbish doled out to the labourers.

If Vera had taken only one or two cigarettes, perhaps the whole story would have been different. But the guard, of course, noticed that the packet was missing. He stalked through the yard with his cat-whip, picking on the kids one at a time. Lack of a smoke was making him irritable. Who had seen the thief? Someone must know. If they didn't own up, the whole block would be punished. Parents too. No one would be spared. He muttered about the existence of a correction block, from which few emerged alive. The children had heard the rumours too, and they were terrified.

It was Kishka himself who fingered Vera.

'Please sir,' he grovelled, cringing as the guard pinched his ear, 'it was her – that skinny one over there – she nicked them and gave them out to all the kids.'

He pointed out little Vera, who was sitting silently near the door of one of the huts.

'You, was it?'

The guard grabbed little Vera by the collar of her dress. She didn't have the presence of mind to deny it. She started to cry. He hauled her inside to the guardroom, and locked the door.

Mother went in search of Vera as soon as she got back from the factory and found she was missing. Someone told her where to look.

'Your daughter is a thieving little rat,' said the guard. 'She must be taught a lesson.'

'No,' Mother implored in her broken German, 'she didn't know what she was doing. The big ones put her up to it. What does she want with cigarettes? Can't you see what a stupid little thing she is?'

'Stupid, yes, but I need my cigarettes,' said the guard. He was a big man, slow in his speech, younger than Mother. 'You'll have to give me yours.'

'I'm sorry, I have none. I traded them. You see, I don't smoke. Next week, when we are paid, you can have them all.'

'What use is next week? Next week you will have another story.' The guard started to flick his whip around their legs. His face and ears had gone bright red. 'You Ukrainians are ungrateful swine. We save you from the communists. We bring you to our country, we feed you, we give you work. And all you can think of is to thieve from us. Well, you have to be taught a lesson, don't you? We have a correction block for vermin like you. You have heard about F Block? You have heard how nicely we look after you there? Soon you will know.'

Everyone had heard rumours about the Correction Block, a row of forty-eight cramped windowless concrete cells half buried underground, like upright coffins, which stood on its own at one side of the Labour Re-education Camp. In winter, cold and rain added to the torment; in summer, dehydration. Some had seen people dragged out crazed and skeletal after ten or twenty or thirty days. Longer than that, it was said, no one was dragged out alive.

'No,' pleaded Mother. 'Have pity!'

She seized Vera and pulled her into her skirt. They cowered against the wall. The guard drew closer, closer, pushing his face up to theirs. His chin gleamed with thin downy blond stubble. He must have been in his early twenties.

'You seem such a nice young man,' Mother begged, choking on the unfamiliar German words. Tears were in her eyes. 'Please, show us some pity, young man.'

'Yes, we will show pity. We will not separate you from your child.' They could feel the spray from his crooked-tooth mouth as he gabbled, excited by his power. 'You will go with her, vermin mother.'

'Why must you do this? Don't you have a sister? Don't you have a mother?'

'Why are you talking about my mother? My mother is a good German woman.' He paused for a moment, blinked, but the momentum of his excitement was too strong, or his imagination failed him.

'We will teach you to raise children not to steal. You will be re-educated. And your vermin husband, if you have one. You *all* will be corrected.'

* * *

The darkness breathes all around us. Then I hear a muffled mousy sniffy sort of sound from the bunk below. I lie quite still trying to fathom what it is, for it is a sound I have never heard before, a sound I have refused to hear, a sound I never imagined was possible. It is the sound of Big Sis crying.

One day I will ask Vera about the Correction Block, but now is not the time. Or maybe my sister is right: maybe there are some things that are better not known, for the knowledge of them can never be un-known. Mother and Father never told me about the Correction Block, and I grew up with no knowledge of the darkness that lurks at the bottom of the human soul.

How did they live the rest of their lives with that terrible secret locked away in their hearts? How did they grow vegetables, and mend motor-bikes, and send us to school and worry about our exam results?

But they did.

27

A source of cheap labour

'Pappa, please try to be sensible,' says Big Sis, slamming the milk-jug down on the table. 'You cannot be the father of the baby. Why do you think she ran off when I suggested a paternity test?'

'Vera, you have always been a nose-poking autocrat,' says Father, drenching his Shredded Wheat with the creamy top of the milk and burying it under a heap of sugar. 'Leave me alone. Now go back to London. Please go!' His hands are shaking, but he still tries to stuff his mouth, then he starts to cough and projectiles of Shredded Wheat fly across the table.

'Please try to act like an adult for once in your life. What has happened to your brains? You're not the father of the baby, you're a baby yourself. Look at the way you behave – you've become completely infantile!'

'An Infantile Disorder! Ha ha ha!' He bangs his spoon on the table. 'Vera, you become more like Lenin every day.'

'A paternity test is a good idea,' I intervene slyly, 'because then you will know not only whether you are the father of the baby, but whether it is a boy or a girl.'

'Aha.' He stops in mid-cough. 'Good idea. Boy or girl. Good idea.'

Vera throws me an appreciative glance.

Stanislav and Dubov are in the front garden, engaging in father–son bonding under the open bonnet of the Rolls-Royce. Mike is still asleep in the front room, but he has fallen off the settee on to the floor. Vera, Father and I are having breakfast in the back room, which is now both the dining-room and his bedroom. Slanted sunlight is streaming in through the dusty windows. Father is still wearing his night-shirt, a strange self-made garment constructed out of an old check Viyella shirt which he has extended in length with some pieces of a paisley winceyette fabric, stitched on to the flaps in large loops of black button-thread, and held together in front with brown shoelaces. It is opened at the neck, and his long-since-healed wound, bristling with silver hairs, winks at us as he talks.

'But . . .' he looks warily from me to Vera to me again, '. . . paternity test is only possible after birth of baby. Then it is plain whether is boy or girl without any test.'

'No, no. It is possible to have a paternity test before the baby is born. *In utero.*' Vera catches my eye. 'Nadia and I will pay.'

'Hmm.' He still looks suspicious, as though he thinks we are trying to trick him. (As if we would!)

At that moment, the letter-box rattles. The morning post has arrived. Among the pile of invitations to open credit card accounts, amazing offers on health and beauty products, and promises of fabulous prizes to be won or already won and waiting to be claimed (Pappa: 'How lucky she is to win such prizes!'), all addressed to Valentina, is a letter to my father from Ms Carter. She reminds him that the divorce hearing is to be in two weeks' time, and puts forward an offer from

Valentina's solicitor not to contest the divorce, nor to make any further claim upon my father's property, were a payment of £20,000 to be offered in full and final settlement.

'Twenty thousand pounds!' cries Vera. 'It's an outrage!'

'Anyway, you haven't got £20,000, Pappa. So that's that.'

'Hmm,' says Pappa. 'Maybe if I sell house and go into old person's home . . .'

'No!' Vera and I call out in unison.

'Or maybe you two, Nadia, Vera, maybe to help one foolish old man . . .'

He is clearly troubled by the demand.

'No! No!'

'But if the matter goes to court . . .' I am thinking aloud, 'what would the court award?'

'Well, of course they could award half the property,' says Mrs Divorce Expert, 'if he is the father of the child. If he is not, then I expect they would award little if anything.'

'Don't you see, Pappa? That is why she is asking for the settlement now. Because she *knows* the child is not yours, and the court would award her nothing.'

'Hmm.'

'It's a crafty trick,' says Mrs Divorce Expert.

'Hmm.'

'I've got a good idea, Pappa,' I say, emolliently topping up his teacup, 'why don't we telephone Laura Carter and say you are happy to offer £20,000 in full and final settlement, provided she is willing to undergo a paternity test, at our expense of course, and provided the child is found to be yours.'

'What could be fairer than that?' says Mrs Divorce Expert.

'What could be fairer than that, Nikolai?' says Mike. He has woken up and is standing in the doorway massaging his temples with both hands. 'Is there any tea left in the pot? I feel a bit rough.'

Father looks at Mike, who winks at him encouragingly and nods his head.

'Hmm. OK.' Father gives a little shrug of surrender.

'What could be fairer than that?' says Ms Carter over the phone. 'But . . . are you sure . . . ?'

I look over at my father, frowning with concentration as he sips his tea, the paisley flaps of his nightshirt extension only partly concealing swollen arthritic knees, scrawny thighs, and above . . . I refuse to imagine.

'Yes, pretty sure.'

* * *

Stanislav led Dubov to Valentina. They disappeared together in the Rolls-Royce some time in the morning.

It is past midday by the time Dubov comes back, on his own. He has a sombre look on his face.

'So tell us, where is she living?' I ask in Ukrainian.

He spreads his hands, palms up.

'I'm sorry, I cannot say. I have it in confidence.'

'But . . . we need to know. Pappa needs to know.'

'She is very afraid of you, Nadia and Vera.'

'Afraid of us?' I laugh. 'Are we so frightening?'

Dubov smiles diplomatically. 'She is afraid of being sent back to Ukraina.'

'But is Ukraina so frightening?'

Dubov considers for a moment. His dark eyebrows draw together in a frown. 'At this time, yes she is. At this time, our beloved mother-country is in the grip of criminals and gangsters.'

'Yes, yes,' chips in Father, who has been quietly sitting in the corner peeling apples, 'this is exactly what Valenka says. But tell me, Volodya Simeonovich, with such an intelligent type of people, how has this been allowed to happen?'

'Ah, this is the Wild West nature of the capitalism we are subjected to, Nikolai Alexeevich,' says Dubov in his calm, intelligent-type voice. 'Those advisers who came from the West to show us how to build a capitalist economy, their model was the rapacious type of early American capitalism.'

Mike catches the words 'Americansky capitaleesm' and now he wants to get stuck in.

'You're right, Dubov. It's all that neo-liberal garbage. The crooks grab all the wealth, consolidate it into so-called legitimate businesses. Then, if we're lucky, some of it can trickle down to the rest of us. Rockefeller, Carnegie, Morgan. They all started out as robber barons. Now the sun shines out of their million-dollar foundations.' (There's nothing he enjoys more than a good political barney.) 'Can you translate that, Nadia?'

'Not really. I'll do my best.' I do my best.

'And there are those who argue that this gangster stage is necessary in the development of capitalism,' adds Dubov.

'This is fascinating!' cries Vera. 'Do you mean to say the gangsters were brought there deliberately?' (Either her Ukrainian is rusty, or my translation is worse than I thought.)

'Not exactly,' Dubov explains patiently. 'But those gangster types who are already there, whose predatory instincts are held in check by the fabric of civil society, once that fabric is torn asunder, why, they flourish like weeds in a newly ploughed field.'

There is something irritatingly pedantic about the way he talks, a bit like Father. Normally it would drive me up the wall, but I find his earnestness is engaging.

'But do you see a way out of this, Dubov?' Mike asks. I interpret.

'In the short term not. In the long term I would say yes. Personally, I would favour the Scandinavian model. Take the best from both capitalism and socialism.' Dubov rubs his hands together. 'Only the best, Mikhail Gordonovich. Don't you agree?'

(Mike's father was called Gordon. If there is a Russian equivalent, no one knows what it is.)

'Yes, of course, you can do that in a developed industrial country with a strong trade union movement, like Sweden.' (This is Mike's home turf.) 'But could it work in a country like Ukraine?'

He asks me to translate. I'm wishing I had not got involved in interpreting. We have both already taken the morning off work, and we need to get going. If we carry on like this, we'll be getting out the plum wine next.

'Ah, there we have the big dilemma,' sighs Dubov with deep Slavic emotion, his black-pebble eyes fixed on his audience. 'But Ukraina must find her own way. At present, alas, we accept unquestioningly everything from the West. Some of course is good; some is rubbish.' (Despite myself, I carry on

279

interpreting. Mike nods his head. Vera moves over to the window and lights a cigarette. Father keeps peeling). 'When we can put behind us the terrible memories of the gulag, then we will begin to rediscover those things which were good in our former socialist society. Then these advisers will be seen for what they are – truly robber-barons who plunder our national assets and install American-owned factories where our people will work for miserable wages. Russians, Germans, Americans – all of them – when they look at Ukraina, what do they see? Nothing but a source of cheap labour.'

As he warms to his theme, he talks faster and faster, gesticulating with his large hands. I am having trouble keeping up with him.

'Once we were a nation of farmers and engineers. We were not rich, but we had enough.' (Father is nodding enthusiastically in his corner, the apple-peeling knife suspended in mid-air.) 'Now racketeers prey on our industries, while our educated youth fly westwards in search of wealth. Our national export is the sale of our beautiful young women into prostitution to feed the monstrous appetites of the Western male. It is a tragedy.'

He pauses, looks around, but no one speaks.

'It *is* a tragedy,' says Mike in the end. 'And there've been plenty in that region.'

'They laugh at us. They suppose such corruption is in our nature.' Dubov's voice has become quieter again. 'But I would argue that it is merely characteristic of the type of economy which has been thrust upon us.'

Vera has been standing by the window, looking increasingly impatient with the conversation.

'But then Valentina will feel quite at home,' she declares. I throw her a 'shut up' look.

'But tell me, Dubov,' I ask, and I can't help it if even now a note of bitchiness creeps into my voice, 'how will you ever persuade someone as . . . as *sensitive* as Valentina to return to such a place?'

He shrugs, palms upwards, but a little smile plays about his lips.

'There are some possibilities.'

*   *   *

'Fascinating man,' says Mike.

'Mmm.'

'Impressive grasp of economics, for an engineer.'

'Mmm.'

We are only half-way home, and I have a three o'clock lecture. I should be thinking about Women and Globalisation, but I too am thinking about what Dubov said. Mother and Vera in the barbed-wire camp; Valentina slaving long low-wage shifts in the nursing home, behind the bar at the Imperial Hotel, toiling in my father's bedroom. Yes, she is greedy, predatory, outrageous, but she is a victim too. A source of cheap labour.

'I wonder how it will all end.'

'Mmm.'

I was the lucky generation.

*   *   *

I do not know how Dubov pursued his courtship during the next fortnight, but Father told me that he went out in the Rolls-Royce every day, sometimes in the morning, sometimes in the evening. When he came back he was invariably pleasant and cheerful, though sometimes his mood seemed more subdued.

It was Dubov, too, who sustained my father's resolve in relation to the divorce, whenever he started to have second thoughts, which at first was almost daily.

'Nikolai Alexeevich,' he would say, 'Vera and Nadia had the benefit of your parental wisdom when they were growing. Stanislav also needs to be with his father. As for the baby – a young child needs a young father. Be content with those children you already have.'

'You're not so young yourself, hey, Volodya Simeonovich,' Father would retort. But Dubov was always calm.

'Indeed not. But I am much younger than you.'

A letter came back to Ms Carter from Valentina's solicitor refusing absolutely to consider a paternity test, but agreeing to accept the much lower sum of £5,000 in full and final settlement.

'What should I say?' asks Father.

'What should we say?' I ask Vera.

'What do you suggest?' Vera asks Ms Carter.

'Offer £2,000,' says Ms Carter. 'That is probably what a court would award. Especially as there is prima facie evidence of adultery.'

'Quite,' says Vera.

'I'll put it to Pappa,' I say.

'OK. If that's what you want,' my father concedes. 'I can see everyone is against me.'

'Don't be so stupid, Pappa,' I snap. 'The only one who is against you is your own folly. Be grateful that there are those around you to save you from yourself.'

'OK. OK. I agree to everything.'

'And when you go to court, let's have none of this nonsense about "I am bebby father". No paternity test, no "bebby father". OK?'

'OK,' he grumbles. 'Nadia, you are turning into a monster like Vera.'

'Oh, shut up, Pappa.' I slam the phone down.

It's only a week to the court hearing, and everyone is getting a bit tense.

28

Gold-rimmed aviator-style glasses

Only a day to go before the court hearing, and still there has been no reply from Valentina's solicitor regarding the £2,000 offer.

'I suppose we'll just have to go through with it, and see what the court awards.'

Is there a nervous wobble in Ms Carter's refined English-rose voice, or are my own nerves playing tricks on me?

'But what do you think, Laura?'

'It's impossible to say. Anything could happen.'

*   *   *

It is unseasonably mild for November. The courtroom, a low, modern building with tall windows and mahogany panelling, is bathed in a wintry light, which has a hard-edged crystalline quality, making everything seem at the same time both sharp and surreal, as in a film. Thick blue carpets muffle the sound of footsteps and voices. The air is conditioned, slightly too warm, and there is a smell of wax polish. Even the pot plants in the tubs are too luxuriantly green to seem real.

Vera, Pappa, Ms Carter and I are sitting in a small waiting area outside the courtroom which has been assigned to us. Vera is wearing a pale peach two-piece in fine wool crepe with tortoiseshell buttons, which sounds awful but looks stunning.

I am wearing the same jacket and trousers I wore to the tribunal. Ms Carter is wearing a black suit and white blouse. Father is wearing his wedding suit and the same white shirt, with the second-to-top button sewn on with black twine. The top button is missing, and his collar is held together by a strange mustard-coloured tie.

We are all terribly nervous.

Now a young man arrives wearing a wig and a gown. This is to be Father's barrister. Ms Carter introduces us. We all shake hands, and I forget his name instantly. What is he like, I wonder, this young man, who will play such an important part in our lives? He looks anonymous in his court uniform. His manner is brisk. He tells us that he has looked up the judge's name, and that his reputation is 'robust'. He and Ms Carter disappear into a side room. Vera, Pappa and I are on our own. Vera and I keep looking at the door, wondering when Valentina will arrive. Dubov did not come back to the house last night, and there was an awkward moment this morning when Father almost refused to come into Peterborough at all. We are worried about the effect the sight of her will have on his resolve. Vera can't stand the tension and nips outside for a cigarette. I am left sitting next to Father, holding his hand. Father is studying a small brown insect which is making its way unsteadily up the stem of one of the pot plants.

'I think it is some type of coccinella,' he says.

Then Ms Carter and the barrister come back, and the usher takes us into the courtroom, and at the same moment a tall thin man with silver-grey hair and gold-rimmed aviator-style glasses takes his place at the judge's bench. Still there is no sign of Valentina or her solicitor.

The barrister rises to his feet, and explains the grounds for the divorce, which is not, as far as he knows, to be contested. He takes the judge through the circumstances of the marriage, dwelling on the disparate ages of the parties, and my father's distressed state after his bereavement. He mentions a series of liaisons. The judge, inscrutable behind his aviator-style glasses, takes notes. The barrister now goes into some detail about the injunction, and the subsequent non-compliance therewith. My father nods vigorously, and when he gets to the bit about the two cars in the front garden, he calls out, 'Yes! Yes! I stuck in hedge!' The barrister has the pleasing knack of retelling father's story, casting him in the heroic role, much better than he could tell it himself.

He has been speaking for almost an hour when there is a commotion outside the door of the courtroom. The door opens an inch, and the usher puts her head in and says something to the judge and the judge nods his head. And then the door bursts fully open and into the courtroom comes – Stanislav!

He has spruced himself up a bit. He is wearing his school uniform and his hair is slicked down with water. He is carrying a folder of papers which flies open as he bursts in through the door. As he scrabbles to pick them up I catch sight of the photocopies of my father's poems and the childish translations. My father springs to his feet and points at Stanislav.

'It was for him! All was for him! Because she says he is genius and must have OxfordCambridge education!'

'Please sit down, Mr Mayevskyj,' says the judge.

Ms Carter throws him a beseeching look.

The judge waits until Stanislav has composed himself, and then invites him to come up to the bench.

'I am here to speak on behalf of my mother.'

Father's barrister jumps to his feet, but the judge gestures for him to sit down.

'Let the young man have his say. Now, young man, can you tell us why your mother is not represented in court?'

'My mother is in the hospital,' says Stanislav. 'She is going there to have a baby. It is Mr Mayevskyj's baby.' He smiles his dimpled chipped-toothed smile.

'No! No!' Vera jumps to her feet. 'It is not my father's baby! It is the fruit of adultery!' Her eyes are blazing.

'Please sit down, Miss ... er ... Mrs ... er ...' says the judge. His eyes meet Vera's and hold them for a moment. Is it the heat of excitement, or do I see her blush? Then without another word she sits down. Ms Carter scribbles frantically on a piece of paper and passes it across to the barrister, who steps forward at once.

'There was an offer,' he says, 'of £20,000 upon evidence from a paternity test that the child was his. But the offer was refused. A lower sum, not conditional upon a paternity test, was proposed. That was refused by Mr Mayevskyj.'

'Thank you,' says the judge. He writes some notes. 'Now,' he turns to Stanislav, 'you have explained why your mother is not in court, but not why she is not represented in court. Does she not have a counsel, or a solicitor?' Stanislav hesitates, mumbles something. The judge orders him to speak up. 'There was a disagreement,' says Stanislav, 'with the solicitor.' He has gone scarlet.

There is a loud coughing sound on my left. Ms Carter has buried her face in her hankie.

'Please go on,' says the judge. 'What was the disagreement about?'

'About the money,' whispers Stanislav. 'She said it is not enough. She said he is not a very intelligent solicitor. She said I must come to you and ask for some more.' His voice is breaking up and there is a glint of tears in his eyes, 'We need the money, you see, sir, for the baby. For Mr Mayevskyj's baby. And we have nowhere to live. We need to return to the house.'

Aah! A silence of held-in breath possesses the courtroom. Ms Carter's eyes are closed as if in prayer. Vera is tugging nervously at a tortoiseshell button. Even Pappa is transfixed. In the end, it is the judge who speaks.

'Thank you, young man. You have done what your mother asked. It isn't easy for a young person to speak up in court. Well done. Now, go and sit down.' He turns to the rest of us. 'Shall we adjourn for an hour? There's a coffee machine, I believe, in the entrance hall.'

Vera nips out the back for another cigarette. The court is a non-smoking building, and like most such buildings it has a stub-strewn area outside where smokers have unofficial licence to congregate. Father refuses coffee, and asks for apple juice. There is none in the court building, so I step outside to see whether I can find a carton in a local shop.

There is a newsagent further along the road, and I am making my way towards it when I catch sight of Stanislav disappearing round the corner. He seems to be in a hurry. Without quite knowing why, I slip past the newsagent and up to the corner, watching where he goes. Stanislav is almost at the top of the road. He crosses, and turns left, up past the Cathedral grounds. I follow. Now I have to run to catch up, as he disappears from view. When I get to the spot, I see that there is a narrow snicket that leads round the back of some shops and into a maze of shabby terraced houses. It is a part of town I do not know. Stanislav is nowhere to be seen. I stand and look around me, feeling rather foolish. Did he know I was following him?

And now I realise that my hour is almost up. I hurry back, stopping in the newsagent's I passed on the way to pick up a carton of apple juice with a straw. I cut through the car park and approach the court from the rear. Here there is a bay where bins are kept and a metal fire escape clinging to the back wall. At first-floor level on the left, I can make out Vera in her stylish peach two-piece, leaning on the railings and puffing away. There is someone else there beside her, a tall man in a suit, surreptitiously stubbing out a cigarette with his foot. As I come closer, I see that it is the judge.

Ms Carter is waiting inside with Father. He has spent most of the hour in the lavatory, and now he is in an excited mood, swinging between hope ('The judge will give her two thousand pound, and I shall be left in peace, with only memories for comfort') and despair ('I will sell all and enter old person's home'). Ms Carter does her best to calm him down. She is relieved when I hand over the apple juice carton. He pierces the foil with the pointed end of the straw and sucks greedily. Then Vera returns, and sits beside Father on the other side. 'Sssh!' she says, trying to quieten Pappa's noisy slurping. He ignores her. Suddenly, at the last minute, Stanislav comes running in, all out of breath and covered in sweat. Where has he been?

The usher opens the doors, and we are all summoned into the courtroom. A few moments later the judge comes back. The tension is unbearable. The judge takes his place, clears his throat, welcomes us back. Then he delivers his judgment. He speaks for about ten minutes, enunciating carefully, pausing over the words 'petitioner', 'decree', 'application' and 'relief'. The barrister's eyebrows rise a fraction. I think I notice a movement at the corner of Ms Carter's lips. The rest of us watch blankly – even Mrs Divorce Expert. We cannot understand a word he is saying.

He finishes speaking, and there is silence in the court. We sit as if enchanted, as if the long incantation of incomprehensible words has cast a magic spell over the courtroom. The low sun throws a slanting beam of light through the tall window which catches the gold frames of the judge's aviator-style glasses and the silver of his hair, making him blaze like an angel. Then the charm of silence is broken by a loud gurgling sound. It is Father, sucking up the last dregs of his apple juice with the straw.

Am I imagining it, or does the judge's inscrutable face register a brief smile? Then he rises (we all rise) and he walks silently across the blue carpet in his shiny black cigarette-stubbing shoes and out through the door.

*   *   *

'So what did he say?'

We are all gathered around Ms Carter in the lobby, drinking coffee out of polystyrene cups from the machine, though caffeine is the last thing we need.

'Well, he granted Mr Mayevskyj a divorce, which is what

we applied for,' says Ms Carter, with a huge smile on her face. She has taken off her black jacket and there are circles of sweat under her English-rose armpits.

'And the money?' asks Vera.

'He made no award, since none was applied for.'

'You mean . . . ?'

'Normally, an agreement about finances would happen at the same time as a divorce, but since she was not represented, no claim was made on her behalf.' She is struggling to keep a straight face.

'But what about Stanislav?' I am still uneasy.

'A good try. But it needs to be done formally, with proper representation. I think that's what Paul is explaining to Stanislav.'

The young barrister has taken his wig and gown off, and is sitting in the corner next to Stanislav with his arm around his shoulder. Stanislav is crying his eyes out.

Father has been following the discussion eagerly, and now he claps his hands with glee.

'Got nothing! Ha ha ha! Too greedy! Got nothing! English justice best in world!'

'But . . . !' Ms Carter raises a warning finger. 'But she could still make an application to the court for maintenance. Though in these circumstances it might be more usual to apply to the child's father. If she knows who it is. And if . . . and if . . .' She can no longer control her giggles. We wait. She pulls herself together. 'If she can find a solicitor to represent her!'

'What do you mean?' asks Mrs Divorce Expert. 'Surely she has a solicitor.'

'You know,' says Ms Carter, 'I'm not supposed to tell you this, but in a town the size of Peterborough, everybody on the legal scene knows each other.' She pauses, grins. 'And, by now, everybody knows Valentina. She's been through virtually every practice in town. They all got fed up of her, marching in with her ridiculous demands. She wouldn't take advice from anyone. She had got it into her head that she was entitled to half the house, and she wouldn't listen to anyone that told her otherwise. Then she insisted that she should get Legal Aid to fight for it in court – so arrogant, swanning in with her fur coat and fish-wife manners, demanding this and that. And all on Legal Aid. The rules are quite strict, you know. Some firms went along with it for a bit, while they were getting the fees. But if they didn't do what she wanted she just stormed out. That must have been what happened when we offered £2,000. I bet her solicitor advised her to accept it.' She catches my eye. 'I would have done in her position.'

'But the judge can't have known that.'

'I think he worked it out,' chuckles Ms Carter. 'He's not stupid.'

'Robust! . . .' murmurs Vera, a faraway look in her eyes.

*   *   *

After the excitement of the courtroom, the house seems cold and gloomy when we get back. There is no food in the fridge, and the central heating has gone off. Dirty pans, plates and cups are piled up in the sink, and on the table are more plates and cups which haven't even made it as far as the sink. There is still no sign of Dubov.

Father's spirits fall as soon as he walks through the door.

'We can't leave him here alone,' I whisper to Vera. 'Can you stay with him tonight? I can't take another day off work.'

'I suppose so,' she sighs.

'Thanks, Sis.'
'It's OK.'

Father protests briefly when he hears of this arrangement, but
it seems as if he too realises that things must change. While
Vera goes to get some shopping, I sit with him in the front
room.

'Pappa, I'm going to find out about some sheltered housing.
You can't live here on your own.'

'No no. Absolutely not. No shelter housing. No old person's
home.'

'Pappa, this house is too big for you. You can't keep it clean.
You can't afford to heat it. In sheltered housing you will have
a nice little flat of your own. With a warden to look after you.'

'Warden! Pah!' He throws his hands up in a dramatic
gesture. 'Nadia, today in court the English judge says I can
live in my house. Now you say I cannot live here. Must I go
to court again?'

'Don't be silly, Pappa. Listen,' I lay my hand on his, 'better
to move now, while you can still manage in your own flat,
with your own door that you can lock with your own key, so
you can do what you like inside. And your own kitchen where
you can cook what you like. And your own bedroom where
no one can come in. And your own private bathroom and
lavatory, right next to the bedroom.'

'Hmm.'

'We will sell this house to a nice family, and we will put
the money in the bank, and the interest will be enough to pay
the rent.'

'Hmm.'

I can see his face change as I talk.

'Where would you rather be? Would you like to stay here

near Peterborough, so you can be close to your friends and the Ukrainian Club?'

He looks blank. It was Mother who had friends. He had Big Ideas.

'Or would you like to move to Cambridge, so you can be near to me and Mike?'

Silence.

'OK, well, I'll look in Cambridge, so you can be near to me and Mike. We'll be able to visit more often.'

'Hmm. OK'

He settles into the armchair that faces the window, leaning his head back against a cushion, and sits there quietly watching the shadows fall over the darkening fields. The sun has already set, but I do not draw the curtains. Twilight seeps into the room.

29

Last supper

Mike is out when I get home, but Anna is in. I hear her bright voice chatting on the phone in the hall, lilting high on eddies of laughter, and my heart tightens with love. I have been careful not to tell her too much about Father and Valentina and Vera, and when I have talked about them, I have made light of our disharmonies. I want to protect her, as my parents protected me. Why burden her with all that old unhappy stuff?

I kick my shoes off, make myself a cup of tea, put some music on, and stretch out on the sofa with a pile of papers. Time to catch up on a bit of reading. Then there is a tap on the door and Anna puts her head round.

'Mum, have you got a minute?'

'Of course. What is it?'

She is wearing skin-tight jeans and a top that barely covers her midriff. (Why does she dress like this? Doesn't she know what men are like?)

'Mum, I want to talk to you.' Her voice is serious.

My heart has started to thump. Have I become so engrossed in my father's drama that I have failed my own daughter?

'OK. I'm all ears.'

'Mum,' she settles herself on the end of the sofa by my feet, 'I've been talking to Alice and Alexandra. We went out for lunch last week. That was Alice on the phone just now.'

Alice, Vera's younger daughter, is a few years older than Anna. They have never been close. This is something new. I feel a prick of disquiet.

'Oh, that's nice, dear. What did you talk about?'

'We've been talking about you – and Aunty Vera.' She pauses, watches me widen my eyes in feigned surprise. 'Mum, we think it's stupid, this feud you have with Aunty Vera.'

'What feud is that, love?'

'*You* know. About the money. About Grandma's will.'

'Oh,' I laugh, 'why have you been talking about that?' (How dare they? Who told them? Trust Vera to go blabbing.)

'We think it's really stupid. We don't care about the money. We don't care who gets it. We want us all to get on together like a normal family – *we* get on together, Alice, Lexy and me.'

'Darling, it's not as easy as that . . .' (Doesn't she realise that money is all that stands between us and starvation?) 'And it's not just about money . . .' (Doesn't she realise how time and memory fix everything? Doesn't she realise that once a story has been told one way, it cannot be retold another way? Doesn't she realise that some things must be covered up and buried, so the shame of them doesn't taint the next generation? No; she's young, and everything is possible.) '. . . But I suppose it's worth a try. What about Vera? Hadn't someone better tell Vera?'

'Alice is going to talk to her tomorrow. So, Mum, what do you think?'

'OK.' I reach forward to hug her. (How skinny she is!) 'I'll do my best. You should eat more.'

She's right. It *is* stupid.

*   *   *

There are waiting lists at all the sheltered housing developments within reach of Cambridge, but before I can go out and
visit them, I get another phone call.

'Dubov is back. Valentina is back with baby. Stanislav is
back.'

His voice is excited, or maybe agitated. I can't tell.

'Pappa, they can't all stay there. It's ridiculous. Anyway, I
thought you'd agreed to think about sheltered housing.'

'Is all right. Is temporary arrangement only.'

'Temporary for how long?'

'Few days. Few weeks.' He coughs and splutters. 'Until is
time to go.'

'Go where? When?'

'Please, Nadia, why you asking so many question? I tell you,
everything is OK.'

After he rings off, I realise I forgot to ask whether the baby is
a boy or a girl, or whether he knows who the father is. I could
ring him back, but I already know that I must go there, see
for myself, breathe the same air, in order to satisfy my . . .
what? Curiosity? No, this is a hunger, an obsession. Next
Saturday I set out in the morning, full of anticipation.

*   *   *

The Lada is parked out on the road when I arrive. Crap car
and the Rolls-Royce are in the front garden, and Dubov is
there, fiddling around with some bars of metal.

'Ah, Nadia Nikolaieva!' He grabs me in a bear hug.
'Have you come to see the baby? Valya! Valya! Look who
is here!'

Valentina appears at the door, still wearing her dressing-gown and a pair of fluffy high-heeled slippers. I can't say that she looks pleased to see me, but she beckons me inside.

In the front room is a white-painted wooden cot, and in it a tiny baby, fast asleep. Its eyes are closed, so I cannot tell what colour they are. Its arms reach up above the coverlet, the hands clenched in little fists beside its cheeks, thumbs out, the nails gleaming like minute pink shells. Its mouth, open and gummy, breathes and sighs and makes a little sucking sound in its sleep, and the downy skin of the fontanel rises and falls in time with the breathing.

'Oh, Valentina, it's beautiful! He . . . she . . . is it a boy or a girl?'

'Is a girl.'

And now I notice that the baby's coverlet is embroidered with small pink roses, and the sleeves of her little jacket are powder-pink.

'She's beautiful!'

'I think so.' Valentina beams proudly, as though the baby's beauty is her personal achievement.

'Have you got a name for her yet?'

'Name is Margaritka. Is name of my friend Margaritka Zadchuk.'

'Oh, lovely.' (Poor child!)

She points to a pile of lacy pink baby clothes on a chair at the side of the cot, knitted with great skill out of soft polyester yarn.

'She make it.'

'Gorgeous!'

'And is name of most famous English President.'

'I'm sorry?'
'Mrs Tatsher.'
'Ah.'

The baby stirs, opens her eyes, sees us standing looking down into her cot, and her face puckers, poised between crying and smiling. 'Guh guh,' she says, and a trickle of whitish fluid runs from the corner of her mouth. 'Guh guh.' Then little dimples appear in her cheeks.

'Ah!'

She is beautiful. She will make her own life. Nothing that has happened before is her fault.

Father must have heard me arrive, for now he comes in beaming.

'Good you can come, Nadia.'

We hug.

'You're looking good, Pappa.' It's true. He's put a bit of weight on, and he is wearing a clean shirt. 'Mike sends his love. He's sorry he couldn't come.'

Valentina ignored him when he came in, and now she leaves the room, turning on her high-heeled slippers without a word. I pull the door closed, and whisper to Pappa.

'What do you think of the baby then?'

'Is girl,' he whispers back.

'I know. Isn't she lovely? Have you found out who the father is?'

Pappa winks and pulls a mischievous face.

'Not me. Ha ha ha.'

From one of the upstairs rooms comes the rhythmic thud-kerboom-thud of heavy metal music. Stanislav's musical tastes have obviously matured from Boyzone. Father catches my eye and puts his hands over his ears with a grimace.

'Degenerate music.'

'Do you remember, Pappa, how you wouldn't let me listen to jazz when I was a teenager? You said it was degenerate.'

I have a sudden recollection of him storming down into the cellar and turning the electricity off at the mains. How my cool adolescent friends sniggered!

'Aha,' he nods. 'Probably it was so.'

No jazz. No make-up. No boyfriends. No wonder I started to rebel as soon as I could.

'You were a terrible father, Pappa. A tyrant.'

He clears his throat. 'Sometimes tyranny is preferable to anarchy.'

'Why have either? Why not have negotiation and democracy?' Suddenly this conversation has become too serious. 'Shall I ask Stanislav to turn it down?'

'No no. Never mind. Tomorrow they going.'

'Really? Going tomorrow? Where are they going?'

'Back to Ukraina. Dubov is building roof-rack.'

In the front garden, there is a sudden roar of a car engine. It is the Rolls-Royce springing into life. We go over to the window to watch. There is the Rolls-Royce, throbbing away, and it has indeed been fitted with a sturdy home-made roof-rack across its whole length. Dubov has the bonnet up and is doing something to the engine to make it run alternately fast and slow.

'Fine tuning,' Father explains.

'But will the Rolls-Royce make it to Ukraina?'

'Of course. Why not?'

Dubov looks up, sees us at the window, and waves. We wave back.

*   *   *

That evening six of us sit down to dinner around the table in the bedroom-dining-room: Father, Dubov, Valentina, Stanislav, Margaritka, and I.

Valentina has rustled up five portions of boil-in-the-bag beef slices with onion gravy, which she serves with frozen peas and oven chips. She has changed out of her dressing-gown, but is wearing the same high-heeled fluffy slippers, with elasticated trousers that have loops under the heels to stretch them tight over her bottom (wait till I tell Vera!), and a tight-fitting, pastel-blue polo-neck. She is in high spirits, and smiles at all of us except Father, whose beef slices are slapped down in front of him with a little more force than is strictly necessary.

Father sits in the corner, fussily cutting everything up into little pieces and examining it closely before putting it in his mouth. The skins of the peas irritate his throat, and he starts to cough. Stanislav is next to him, eating silently with his head bowed low over the plate. I feel sorry for him after his humiliation in court, and try to open up a conversation, but he gives one-syllable answers and avoids my eyes. Lady Di and his girlfriend have, in the short space of their former mistress's visit, unlearned all their careful training, and are prowling around the table yowling for tit-bits. Everyone obliges, especially Father, who gives them most of his dinner.

Dubov is sitting at the other end of the table, carefully cradling the tiny baby in his arms, feeding her milk from a bottle. Valentina's superior breasts are evidently for display purposes only.

*   *   *

After supper I wash up, while Valentina and Stanislav go upstairs to continue with their packing. Father and Dubov retire into the front room, and after a few minutes I join them. I find them poring over some papers on which they are drawing something technical – a car beside a vertical post and some straight lines connecting them. They put aside the papers and Father takes out the manuscript of his master work, and settles himself into the armchair with his parcel-taped reading glasses on his nose. Dubov sits opposite him on the settee, still cradling the sleeping baby in his arms. He makes way for me to sit next to him.

> *Every technology which is of benefit to the human race must be used appropriately and with respect. In no instance is this more true than in the case of the tractor.*

He is reading easily, in Ukrainian, pausing from time to time for dramatic effect, his left hand poised in the air like a conductor's baton.

> *For the tractor, despite its early promise to free mankind from grinding toil, has also brought us to the brink of ruin, through carelessness and over-use. This has happened throughout its history, but the most striking example is in America in the 1920s.*
>
> *I have said that it was the tractor which opened up the great prairies of the West. But those who followed the early pioneers were not satisfied with this. They believed that if use of tractors*

*made the land productive, greater use of tractors would make the
land more productive. Tragically it was not so.*

*The tractor must always be used as an aid to nature, not as a
driver of nature. The tractor must work in harmony with the
climate, and the fertility of the land, and the humble spirit of the
farmers. Otherwise it will bring disaster, and this is what happened
in the Midwest.*

*The new farmers of the West, they did not study the climate.
True, they complained of the lack of rain, and the strong winds,
but they did not heed the warning. They ploughed and they
ploughed, for more ploughing, they believed, would bring more
profit. Then winds came and blew away all the earth that had
been ploughed.*

*The Dust Bowl of the 1920s, and the extreme hardship which
stemmed from it, led ultimately to the economic chaos which culmi-
nated in the collapse of the American Stock Exchange in 1929.*

*But it could be added, further, that the instability and impoverish-
ment which spread throughout the world were also factors behind
the rise of Fascism in Germany and Communism in Russia, the clash
of which two ideologies almost brought the human race to its doom.*

*And so I leave you with this thought, dear reader. Use the
technology which the engineer has developed, but use it with a
humble and questioning spirit. Never allow technology to be your
master, and never use it to gain mastery over others.*

He stops with a flourish, and looks to his audience for
approval.

'Bravo, Nikolai Alexeevich!' cries Dubov clapping his hands.
  'Bravo, Pappa!' I cry.
  'Guh guh!' cries baby Margaritka.

Then Father gathers together all the sheets of his manuscript, which are scattered over the floor, and wraps them together in a piece of brown paper which he secures with string. He hands the parcel to Dubov.

'Please, Volodya Simeonovich. Take it with you to Ukraina. Maybe someone will publish it there.'

'No, no,' says Dubov. 'I cannot take it, Nikolai Alexeevich. It is your life's work.'

'Pah!' says Father with a modest shrug. 'It is finished now. Take it please. I have another book to write.'

30

Two journeys

I wake up early, with a stiff neck. The choice last night was between sharing the bunk-bed with Stanislav, or sleeping on the two-seater settee, and I chose the latter. It is still not fully light outside, the sky slate-coloured and overcast.

But the house is already full of sound and movement. Father is singing in the bathroom. Valentina, Stanislav and Dubov are rushing around loading up the car. I make a cup of tea, and stand at the window to watch.

The capacity of the Rolls-Royce is amazing.

In go two enormous bin bags of indeterminate contents, which Valentina stows in the boot with a shove. In go Stanislav's CD collection in two cardboard boxes, and his CD player, wedged in place between two huge bales of disposable nappies beneath the back seat. In go two suitcases, and Dubov's small green rucksack. In go a television (where did that come from?) and a deep-fat-fryer (ditto). In go a cardboard box of assorted boil-in-bags, and another of tinned mackerel. In goes the small portable photocopier. In goes the blue civilised-person's Hoover (which, Pappa later tells me, he and Dubov have adapted to take ordinary bags), and my mother's pressure cooker. (How dare she!)

Now the boot is full (slam!) and they start loading up the roof-rack. Out comes the baby's painted wooden cot, which has been disassembled and tied together with string. One, two, three – up! – goes an enormous fibreglass suitcase, as big as a small wardrobe. Out comes – surely not – Stanislav and Dubov struggle under its weight as they lug it across the garden – bend your knees, Stanislav! bend your knees! – the brown not-peasant-cooking not-electric cooker. But how will they lift it on to the roof-rack?

Dubov has constructed a sort of hoist out of thick rope and some stout canvas sheeting. He has slung the rope over a strong branch of the ash tree by the road in front of the house, and pulled it so that it rests securely in a fork. He and Stanislav lower the cooker, on its side, on to the canvas cradle. Then Valentina jumps into the Lada, and Dubov directs her into position in front of the cooker, and the other end of the rope is attached to the bumper. As she inches forward – 'Slowly, Valenka, slowly!' – the cooker rises into the air, swings, and hangs suspended, steadied by Dubov until he motions to her to stop. The Lada is smoking a bit, the engine running rough, but the handbrake holds. Now the Rolls-Royce is brought round – Stanislav is at the wheel! – and positioned directly underneath the cooker swinging in its cradle. Father has come out into the front garden, and is helping Dubov to give directions, waving his arms wildly – forward a bit – back a bit – stop!

Dubov motions to Valentina.

'Back now, Valenka. Gently! Gently! STOP!'

Valentina's clutch control is not brilliant, and the cooker lands with a bit of a bump, but the Rolls-Royce, and Dubov's roof-rack, can take it.

Everybody cheers, including the neighbours who have come out into the street to watch. Valentina gets out of the Lada, minces over to Dubov in her high-heeled slippers (no wonder her clutch control is wanting) and gives him a peck on the cheek – '*Holubchik!*' Stanislav beeps the horn of the Rolls-Royce – it makes a deep sophisticated sound – and everybody cheers again.

Then the canvas is wrapped around everything on the roof-rack and secured with the rope, and that's it. They are ready to go. Valentina's fur coat is spread across the back seat, and on it, wrapped in layers of blankets, is placed baby Margaritka. Everybody exchanges hugs and kisses, apart from Father and Valentina, who manage to avoid each other without causing a scene. Dubov takes the driver's seat. Stanislav sits in front, next to him. Valentina sits in the back beside the baby. The engine of the Rolls-Royce purrs as contentedly as a big cat. Dubov engages gear. And they're off. Father and I come out on to the road to wave to them, as they disappear round the corner and out of view.

*   *   *

Can this really be the end?

There are still some loose ends to be tied up. Fortunately Valentina left the keys to the Lada in the car, so I bring it in and put it in the garage. In the glove-compartment are the papers, and also – surprise – the papers and key for Crap car. They will not be much use to Father as his licence expired years ago, and Doctor Figges refused to sign a form authorising its renewal.

In the kitchen, Mother's old electric cooker has been reinstalled in place of the gas one, and seems to be working, even the ring that was broken before. There is a bit of clearing up to be done, but not on the same scale as last time. In Stanislav's room I find a very smelly pair of trainers under the bed, and nothing else. In the front bedroom there are some discarded clothes, quite a lot of wrapping paper, empty carrier bags, and make-up-smudged balls of cotton wool. One of the carrier bags is full of papers. I leaf through – they are the same papers I had once stowed in the freezer. In among them I notice the marriage certificate and wedding pictures. She won't be needing those where she's going. Should I throw them away? No, not yet.

'Do you feel sad, Pappa?'

'First time when Valentina left was sad. This time, not so sad. She is beautiful woman, but maybe I did not make her happy. Maybe with Dubov she will be happier. Dubov is good type. In Ukraina maybe he will now become rich.'

'Really? Why?'

'Aha! I have given him my seventeenth patent!'

He leads me into the sitting-room, and pulls out a box-file of papers. They are technical drawings, fine and precisely detailed, annotated with mathematical hieroglyphs in my father's hand.

'Sixteen patents I have filed in my life. All useful. None made money. Last was seventeenth – no time to register.'

'What is it for?'

'Tool bar for tractor. So that one tractor may be used with different tools – plough, harrow, crop spray – everything easily interchangeable. Of course something like this was already in existence, but this design is superior. I have shown it to Dubov. He understands how it can be used. Maybe this will be rebirth of Ukrainian tractor industry.'

Genius or bonkers? I have no idea.

'Let's have some tea.'

*   *   *

That evening, after supper, my father spreads a map out on the table in the dining-bedroom, and pores over it, pointing with his finger.

'Look. Here,' he points, 'they are already crossing from Felix-stowe to Hamburg. Next Hamburg to Berlin. Cross into Poland at Guben. Then Wroclav, Krakow, cross border at Przemysl. Ukraina. Home.'

He has gone very quiet.

I stare at the map. Criss-crossing the route he has traced with his finger, another route is marked in pencil. Hamburg to Kiel. Then from Kiel the line dips south into Bavaria. Then up again into Czechoslovakia. Brno. Ostrava. Across into Poland. Krakow. Przemysl. Ukraina.

'Pappa, what is this?'
   'This is our journey. Ukraina to England.' He traces the line backwards. 'Same journey, other direction.' His voice is laboured, croaky. 'Look, here in south near Stuttgart

is Zindelfingen. Ludmilla was working in Daimler-Benz assembly. Ludmilla and Vera stayed here nearly for one year. Nineteen forty-three.'

'What did they do there?'

'Milla's job was to fit fuel pipe to aircraft engine. First-class engine but somewhat heavy in the air. Poor lift–drag ratio. Poor manoeuvrability, though some interesting new developments in wing design were just . . .'

'Yes yes,' I interrupt. 'Never mind about the aircraft. Tell me what happened in the war.'

'What happened in war? People died – that is what happened.' He fixes me with that stubborn clenched-jaw look. 'Those who were bravest perished first. Those who believed in something died for belief. Those who survived . . .' He starts to cough. 'You know that more than twenty million Soviet citizens perished in this war.'

'I know.' And yet the number is so vast it is unknowable. In that measureless ocean of tears and blood, where are the landmarks, the familiar bearings? 'But I don't know the twenty million, Pappa. Tell me about you and Mother and Vera. What happened to you after that?'

His finger moves along the pencilled line.

'Here, near Kiel, this is Drachensee. I was some time in this camp. Building boilers of ships. Ludmilla and Vera came near end of war.'

Drachensee: there it sits on the map, shameless, a black dot with red lines of roads leading from it, as though it were any other place.

'Vera said something about a correction block?'

'Aha, this was an unfortunate episode. Caused entirely by cigarettes. I have told you, I think, that I owe my life to cigarettes. Yes? But I have not told you also that I almost lost

310

my life through cigarettes. Through Vera's adventure with cigarettes. Lucky that war ended then. British came just in time – rescued us from Correction Block. Otherwise we surely would not have survived.'

'Why? What . . . ? How long . . . ?'

He coughs for a moment, avoiding my eyes.

'Lucky also that at liberation we were in British zone. Another piece of luck was Ludmilla's birthplace, Novaya Aleksandria.'

'Why was that lucky?'

'Lucky because Galicia was formerly part of Poland, and Poles were allowed to stay in West. Under Churchill–Stalin agreement, Poles could stay in England, Ukrainians sent back. Most sent to Siberia – most perished. Lucky that Millochka still had birth certificate, showed she was born in former Poland. Lucky I had some German work papers. Said I came from Dashev. Germans changed Cyrillic to Roman script. Dashev Daszewo. Word sounds like same, but Daszewo is in Poland, Dashev is in Ukraina. Ha ha. Lucky immigration officer believed. So much luck in such a short time – enough to last a lifetime.'

In the dusky light of the forty-watt bulb, the lines and shadows of his wrinkled cheeks are as deep as scars. How old he looks. When I was young, I wanted my father to be a hero. I was ashamed of his graveyard desertion, his flight to Germany. I wanted my mother to be a romantic heroine. I wanted their story to be one of bravery and love. Now as an adult I see that they were not heroic. They survived, that's all.

'You see, Nadezhda, to survive is to win.'

He winks, and the scar-wrinkles at the corners of his mouth and eyes crease with merriment.

*   *   *

After Father has gone to bed, I telephone Vera. It is late, and she is tired, but I need to talk. I start with the easy stuff.

'The baby is beautiful. It's a girl. They called her Margaritka after Mrs Thatcher.'

'But did you find out who the father is?'

'Dubov's the father.'

'But he can't be . . .'

'No, not the biological father. But he's the father in every way that matters.'

'But didn't you find out who the real father is?'

'Dubov *is* the real father.'

'Really, Nadia. You *are* hopeless.'

I know what she means, but after I saw the way Dubov wielded that baby-bottle, I lost interest in the biological paternity. Instead I tell her about the pink lacy baby clothes, the elasticated loop-under-heel slacks, the last boil-in-bag supper. I describe the way they hoisted the non-electric cooker on to the roof-rack, and how everybody cheered. I reveal the secret of the seventeenth patent.

'Really!' she exclaims from time to time as I talk, and I keep wondering whether I will dare to ask her about the Correction Block.

'I can't get over how lovely the baby is. I thought I would hate her.' (I had imagined that when I looked into the cot, I would know who the father was – that her corrupt progeniture would shine in her face.) 'I thought she would be like a miniature version of Valentina, a thugette in nappies. But she's just herself.'

'Babies change everything, Nadia.' There is a scuffling sound on the other end of the phone, and a slow intake of breath. Vera is lighting a cigarette. 'I remember when you were born.'

I don't know what to say, so I wait for her to follow up the remark with some reminiscences, but there is a long sigh as she exhales, then silence.

'Vera, tell me . . .'

'There's nothing to tell. You were a beautiful baby. Let's go to bed now. It's late.'

She doesn't tell me, but I have already worked it out.

*   *   *

Once, there was a War Baby and a Peacetime Baby. War Baby was born on the eve of the greatest conflict the world has known, into a country already ravaged by famine and choked in the mad grip of a paranoid dictator. She cried a lot, because her mother had little milk to give her. Her father did not know what to say to her, and didn't say much. After a while he left. Then her mother left too. She was brought up by an elderly aunt who doted on her, and whom she grew to love. But when the war broke out, the industrial town where her aunt lived was too dangerous, so her mother came to fetch her, and took her to a village to stay with her father's parents, where she would be safe. She never saw her aunt again.

War Baby's paternal grandparents were an eccentric elderly couple, with strict ideas of how children should be raised.

They also had care of their daughter's child, a chubby rollick-some little girl called Nadezhda, a couple of years older than her cousin, whose parents lived in Moscow. She had been named after her grandmother, and was the apple of her eye. War Baby was a thin, spiritless child, quiet as a mouse. She stood for hours at the gate, waiting for her mother to come back.

War Baby's mother divided her time between War Baby and War Baby's father, who lived in a big city to the south, and seldom came to visit, for he was engaged in Important Work. Her mother's visits often ended in a row with Baba Nadia, and when her mother had gone, her grandmother would tell War Baby terrifying stories about witches and trolls that gobbled up naughty children.

War Baby was never naughty; in fact she hardly said anything at all. Nevertheless, from time to time she would manage to spill some milk or to drop an egg, and then she would be punished. The punishments were not cruel, but they were unusual. She would be made to stand for an hour in the corner, holding the shell of the broken egg, or holding a handwritten sign that said 'Today I spilled some milk.' Cousin Nadia would pull faces at her. War Baby said nothing. She stood silently in the corner holding her icons of breakage. She stood in the corner and watched.

The worst thing of all was to be sent into the hen-house to collect eggs, for they were guarded by a fearsome cockerel with blazing eyes and a fiery crown. When he stretched up and flapped his wings and crowed, he was almost as tall as

War Baby. He would dart forward and peck at her legs. No wonder she so often dropped the eggs.

One day, the winds of war blew War Baby's mother back to the village: she came back and she didn't leave. At night, War Baby and her mother snuggled up in bed together and her mother told her stories about Great-Grandpa Ocheretko and his amazing black horse called Thunder, about Baba Sonia's wedding in the Cathedral of the Golden Domes, and about brave children who slew witches and demons.

Mother and Baba Nadia still argued, but they didn't argue as much as before, for Mother went out to work every day in the local *kolkhoz*, where her veterinary skills were very much in demand, even though she had only completed three years of training. Sometimes she was given money, but more often the farm manager paid her in eggs, wheat, or vegetables. Once she stitched up the belly of a pig that had been gored by a cow, using black button thread, for surgical suture was nowhere to be found. The sow lived, and when it produced eleven piglets, Mother was given one to bring home.

Then soldiers came to the village – German soldiers, then Russian soldiers, then German soldiers again. The village watch-mender and his family were taken away one afternoon in a tall windowless van, and were never seen again. Their oldest daughter, a pretty quiet girl aged fourteen or so, had managed to run away when the soldiers came, and Baba Nadia took her in and hid her in the hen-house (the fearsome cockerel had long since been stewed and his spurred feet turned into the most delicious chicken soup). For although Baba Nadia was a strict woman, she knew what was right and what was wrong, and taking people away in the tall windowless van was wrong. Then one night, someone set fire to the hen-house. No one knows who it was. The watch-mender's daughter and the two remaining chickens perished in the blaze.

Eventually, the winds of war blew War Baby's father home, too. Very early one morning, while it was still dark, an emaciated man with a terrible suppurating wound on his throat arrived at the door. Baba Nadia let out a scream, and prayed for mercy. Grandfather Mayevskyj went into the village and bribed someone to let him have some medicines that were supposed to be for the soldiers. Mother boiled rags and cleaned the wound. She stayed at his bedside day and night, and sent War Baby out to play with cousin Nadia. From time to time, War Baby crept into his room and was allowed to sit on the bed. He squeezed her hand, but he didn't say anything. After a few weeks, he was well enough to get up and wander about the house. Then just as mysteriously as he had arrived, he disappeared.

Soon after, it was time for War Baby and her mother to leave too. German soldiers came into the village and took all the healthy people of working age, and put them on a train. They took War Baby's mother. They would have left War Baby behind, but Mother screamed so much, they let her come too. It was a goods wagon with no seats: everyone sat crammed together on bales of straw, or on the floor. The train journey lasted for nine days, with only sour bread to eat, and very little water, and just a bucket in the corner of the wagon for the toilet. But there was an air of excitement.

'We are going to a camp,' said War Baby's mother, 'where

we will be safe. We will work, and we will get good food to eat. And maybe Father will be there.'

To War Baby's dismay, the camp was not a circle of tents and tethered horses, as her mother had described the Cossack encampments, but a maze of concrete buildings and high barbed-wire fences. Still, War Baby and her mother had a bed to share and food to eat. Every day, Mother and the other women were taken in a truck to a factory where they assembled aeroplane engines for twelve hours. War Baby was left behind in the camp with the children, who were all much older, and a guard who spoke a language she didn't understand. She spent hours looking through the wire fence watching for the truck that would bring her mother home. At night, her mother was too tired to tell her stories. Pressed up close in the dark, War Baby listened to her breathing, until they both fell asleep. Sometimes, in the night, she was woken by the sound of her mother crying, but in the morning her mother got up and washed her face and went to work as if nothing had happened.

Then one day, the winds of war blew Mother and War Baby to another camp, and Father was there. It was like the first camp but bigger and more frightening, for there were many other people there apart from the Ukrainians, and the guards carried whips. Something terrible happened in that camp that it would be better to forget – better not to know that it had happened at all.

Then suddenly, it was no longer wartime, it was peacetime. The family boarded a huge ship and sailed away across the sea to another country where the people talked in a funny language, and though they were still in a camp, there was more to eat, and everybody was kind to them. And as if to celebrate the coming of peace to the world, another baby was born into the family. Her parents called her Nadezhda, after those Nadezhdas they had left behind, for the name means 'hope'.

Peacetime Baby was born in a country that had just been victorious in war. Although times were hard, the mood of the country was hopeful. Those able to work would work for the benefit of all; those in need would be provided for; and children would be given milk, orange juice and cod-liver oil, so they would grow strong.

Peacetime Baby lapped up all three fluids greedily and grew up stubborn and rebellious.

War Baby grew up into Big Sis.

I salute the sun

The Sunny Bank sheltered housing complex lies in a quiet cul-de-sac on the southern outskirts of Cambridge. It is a low-rise modern purpose-built development of forty-six flats and bungalows set in a large well-maintained garden, with lawns, mature trees, rose beds, and even a resident owl. There is a communal lounge where residents can watch television (Father grimaces), attend coffee mornings ('But I prefer apple juice!') and take part in other activities from ballroom dancing ('Ah, but you should see how Millochka could dance!') to yoga ('Aha!'). It is owned by a charitable trust, and let out at non-profit rents to those lucky enough to make it to the top of the waiting-list. The warden, Beverley, a middle-aged widow with a bouffant of bleached hair, a throaty laugh, and an enormous bosom, seems in many ways like an older and more benign version of Valentina. Maybe this is why Sunny Bank is Father's first choice of sheltered housing.

'I will go here,' he insists. 'Nowhere else.'

There is of course a waiting-list, and Beverley, who has taken quite a shine to Father, tells me that the best way is to get a doctor's letter – or better still more than one. Doctor Figges is pleased to write. Sheltered housing is just what he needs, she says. She describes my father's frailty, the distance he has to walk into the village to get his shopping, the problems he has in maintaining the house and garden, his arthritis and dizzy spells. The letter is sympathetic, personal, moving. But is it enough? Who else can I approach? On impulse, I write to the psychiatrist at the Peterborough District Hospital. A week or so later comes a letter in reply, to whom it may concern. In the psychiatrist's opinion Mr Mayevskyj is of sound mind, with no evidence of dementia, and is well able to look after himself, but the doctor is concerned that 'living in isolation without regular social contact may cause his mental condition to deteriorate'. In his opinion, 'a structured social environment with non-intrusive supervision would allow Mr Mayevskyj to live independently for many more years'.

The letter does the trick for the sheltered housing waiting-list, but it leaves me disappointed. Where is the talkative Nietzsche-admiring non-paranoid philosopher and his mouthy many-years-junior wife? Does the psychiatrist remember the consultation that my father described to me in such detail, or was his letter simply a formulaic response to a routine question, compiled from a brief glance through the notes by his secretary? Maybe he is keeping to strict guidelines about patient confidentiality, or he is so busy that all his patients become just one blur. Maybe he sees so many crazy people that Father doesn't even register on the scale. Maybe he knows, but doesn't want to say. I want to ring him up and ask him – I want to ask him the question that has smouldered unformulated in the pit of my mind for as long as I can remember: is my father . . . *normal*?

No. Leave it alone. What good will it do?

*   *   *

A short time before Christmas, Vera and I spend a few days up at the house together, clearing it out, preparing it to be put on the market in spring. There is so much to look through, clean up, throw out, that we don't have much time to talk in the intimate way I had hoped for. At night, I sleep in the top bunk, while Vera sleeps in Valentina's old room.

Vera is skilled at dealing with solicitors, estate agents, builders. I let her get on with it. She leaves me to dispose of the cars, find new homes for the cats and sort out the things Father says he will need in his new life (all his tools, for a start, not forgetting the clamps, a good steel tape measure, and some kitchen utensils, sharp knives, and of course he must keep his books, and the photographs, for now he has finished the tractor book he is thinking of writing his memoirs, and his record player, and the records, yes, and the leather flying helmet, and Mother's sewing machine for he has plans to convert it to run on electricity using the motor from the electrical can-opener left behind by Valentina, which was never much good by the way, and the gearbox of the Francis Barnett, which is wrapped in an oiled cloth in a toolbox at the back of the garage, and maybe a few clothes) and what will fit into his tiny flat (not a lot).

Working together like this, I realise that Vera and I have developed a different kind of intimacy, based not on talking but on practicalities – we have learned to be partners. Everything that needed to be said has been said, and now we can just get on with our lives. Well, not quite everything.

One afternoon, when the sun is low but bright, we take time off to walk to the cemetery to visit Mother's grave. We have cut the last of the roses from her garden – the amazing white Icebergs, that bloom right into the winter – and some evergreen foliage, and arranged them in an earthenware vase by the headstone. We sit on the bench under the bare cherry tree and look out over the wide hedgeless fields to the horizon.

'Vera, there's one more thing we need to sort out. It's about the money.' My palms are sweating, but I keep my voice steady.

'Oh, don't worry, I've found a high-interest bank account, and we can set up a direct debit to go straight to the housing association to cover the rent and other expenses. We can both be signatories.'

'No, not that. Mother's money. The money she left in her will.'

'Well, why don't we just add it to that account?'

'OK.'

And that is that.

'And the locket – I don't mind if you keep the locket, Vera. Mother gave it to you.'

*   *   *

Before Father takes up residence at Sunny Bank, I give him a little pep talk.

'Now, Pappa, you must try to fit in with the other residents. Do you understand? In your own flat you can do what you like, but when you are with the others, you must try to behave in a normal way. You don't want them to think you're crazy, do you?'

'*Tak tak*,' mutters Pappa crossly.

Mike thinks I am fussing too much, but he doesn't know what I know – he doesn't know what it is to be the one that's different, the one that stands out, the one that everyone else sniggers about behind their back. For good measure, I take away Father's home-made paisley-extended nightshirt and buy him a normal pair of pyjamas.

On Christmas Eve, in the morning, Mike and I go to visit Father at Sunny Bank. We knock on the door, but he doesn't answer, so we go in anyway.

'Hallo, Pappa!'

We find him crouching down on all fours, completely naked, on a mat which he has placed in the centre of the floor in front of the window. Fortunately his flat is not overlooked. All the furniture has been pushed up against the walls.

'Pappa, what . . . ?'

'Sshh!' He holds a finger up to his lips.

Next, still crouching, he stretches out one skinny leg towards the back of the mat, then the other, and lowers himself down until he is lying on his stomach on the mat. He rests there for a moment, panting a little. The skin of his shrunken buttocks hangs loose, pearly white, almost translucent. Now he pushes himself up off the floor with his forearms, staggers to his feet and folds his hands palms together, eyes closed, as if in prayer. Then he pulls himself up to his full crooked height and stretches both arms out, reaching as high as he can into the air, breathes deeply, and turns towards us in all his shrivelled, aged, joyful nakedness.

'You see what I have learned yesterday?'
     He raises his arms once more, draws a deep breath.
   'I salute the sun!'

Website acknowledgements

http://www.battlefield.ru/library/lend/valentine.html

Neil M. Clark (1937), John Deere: He Gave To The World The Steel Plow on http://members.tripod.com/~Rainbeau/deere.html

http://www.deere.com/en_US/compinfo/history

Unnamed author, Harry Ferguson: The Man and The Machine Yesterdays Tractors Magazine http://www.ytmag.com/articles/artint262.htm

Phillip Gooch, A very brief history Charles Burrell & Sons Ltd. Thetford England on www.gooch.org.uk/steam/history

http://www.jacksac.freeserve.co.uk/valentine_tanks.htm

Leonid Lvovich Kerber, *Stalin's Aviation Gulag: A Memoir of Andrei Tupolev and the Purge Era*, ed. Von Hardesty, Smithsonian Institution Press reviewed by Major David R. Johnson, USAF on http://www.airpower.maxwell.af.mil/airchronicles/apj/apj00/win00/kerber.htm and by Dr Paul Josephson on http://muse.jhu.edu/demo/tech/40.1br kerber.html

Michael Lane on http://www.steamploughclub.org.uk/history.htm

Website acknowledgements

http://www.morozov.com.ua

The PIBWL military site *http://derela.republika.pl/index.htm*
Sources: 1. Jan Tarczyński, K. Barbarski, A. Jońca, 'Pojazdy w
Wojsku Polskim – Polish Army Vehicles – 1918–1939'; Ajaks;
Pruszków 1995.
2. A. Jońca, R. Szubański, J. Tarczyński, 'Wrzesień 1939 –
Pojazdy Wojska Polskiego – Barwa i broń'; WKŁ; Warsaw
1990.

http://www.russianspaceweb.com/people.html

http://www.vintagetractors.freeserve.co.uk.

www.wwiivehicles.com Source: The Encyclopedia of Tanks and
Armored Fighting Vehicles ed. Christopher F. Foss, 2002

Martin Wilson, Alexander Velovich, Carl Bobrow, Russian
Aviation Heritage on *http://aeroweb.lucia.it/~agretch/RAP.
html*

Eugene E. Wilson on *http://www.sikorskyarchives.com/characl.
html*